Exhausted. So
his forehead, blind
gravel and dragged himself further from the drop-off,
then rolled onto his back and closed his eyes. He would
definitely lecture Candace. Just let him catch his breath
first.

"Logan, are you all right?" Candace wasn't content
to wait for him to recover his strength. She crawled
onto his chest and put her ice-cold hands on either side
of his face, pushing his hair out of his eyes. "Logan,
answer me."

He cracked his eyes open. Her fair hair was
soaking wet and plastered to her skin. Water droplets
slid down her cheeks, and off her nose.

"You told me you were safe, you silly man," she
half-yelled, half-sobbed. "You're lucky your car
stopped where it did instead of crashing into the gorge."
She gestured wildly behind her.

Shivers wracked her slight frame. Was she
frightened? Cold? He lifted one exhausted arm and
swiped her hair back from her cheeks. "Let's get you
home," he said.

For a moment she stared at him with the blankest
expression—then laughter burst from her lips. "You're
crazy."

"*I'm* crazy? You just took a joy ride in the middle
of a tropical storm."

She sat back on his stomach and smiled at him. A
big beautiful smile that lit her whole face. Something
warm and wonderful filled Logan's chest and he did the
only thing he *could* do at that moment. Grasping her
nape with one hand, and her shoulder with the other, he
dragged her down and kissed her.

Kudos to Kimberly Keyes

Finalist in STAR's (SpacecoasT Authors of Romance)
Launching a Star contest
~*~
Finalist in RWI's (Romance Writer's Ink)
Where the Magic Begins contest
~*~
Finalist in COFW's (Central Ohio Fiction Writers)
Ignite the Flame contest

Lover's Leap

by

Kimberly Keyes

Lover's Leap

Cover Art by *Kim Mendoza*

The Wild Rose Press, Inc.
PO Box 708
Adams Basin, NY 14410-0708
Visit us at www.thewildrosepress.com

Publishing History
First Champagne Rose Edition, 2015
Print ISBN 978-1-5092-0380-2
Digital ISBN 978-1-5092-0381-9

Published in the United States of America

Dedication

To Frank and Pappi,
my faithful fur children.

Chapter One

Logan trotted down the spiral stone staircase, running a hastily grabbed hand towel over his damp hair. He'd come inside from the rooftop terrace after having seen the town car cruising up the gravel drive. He wondered if the passenger had seen him standing like a fool out in the open, getting soaked by the rain-turned-drizzle while listening to the fading thunder booms and looking out over Lake Tahoe.

On the other hand, did he care if she spotted him? The sight of the water after a big storm was really something. Almost enough to tempt a man to pull out his dusty camera. Almost.

It had to be Eric's friend, Candace Riley, arriving. Logan was curious about the woman he'd been warned off of. Curious and still a little annoyed. First, because he'd come here to be alone, and now he was being asked to share.

Though to be fair—it was Eric's vacation home, and Logan had invited himself to stay.

But mainly he was pissed off that his old friend had felt the need to lecture him on the ground rules concerning Miss Riley.

Logan reached the first floor, and glanced from the foyer to the living area. Strange, no one had come in yet. Matter of fact, he didn't hear any sounds of life coming from the forecourt. No car doors slamming, no murmurings between driver and drivee, no nothing.

Maybe it hadn't been her arriving after all? But what other town car would be rolling up the private road leading nowhere but here? No one coming for him, that's for sure. He hadn't told anyone where he'd escaped to lick his wounds.

He glanced out the front window.

Huh. The shiny black car was parked out front, motor off. No one had gotten out, and they'd been sitting there long enough the windows were fogged. Were they afraid they'd made a wrong turn?

All at once, the rear passenger door flew open, and a pair of sandals attached to shapely, tanned legs emerged, followed by the rest of a well-put-together blonde in a sundress. Candace? Assuming so, she was moving like she was on fire, literally running to the back of the car before the driver had even dragged himself out of the vehicle.

Logan huffed out a laugh. What in the world?

She had the trunk open, and appeared to be grabbing all her bags at once—and there were more than a few.

The driver, to his credit, seemed intent on helping, but she was having none of it.

Had the driver done something to scare her? Maybe locked her in the car? Something was off. Morbid curiosity propelled Logan to the front door. He swung it open and found himself staring into a set of wide blue eyes, channeling the proverbial deer in the headlight look to a tee.

"Uh…Candace?" Logan asked the frazzled, albeit pretty twenty-something woman before him. She had her hands full with a tote lodged under one arm, a black roller board gripped in her hand, and another bag and largish purse hanging from the crook of her other arm.

She smiled broadly and nodded. "That's me. Excuse me a moment?" She blew a falling lock of golden hair that had escaped her loose ponytail out of her eyes and shifted on the stoop to call over her shoulder to the driver. "Thank you, Bobby, now get out of this weather. I've got this. Bye."

Logan glanced up at the overcast skies. He'd hardly call this weather. *Weather* had been here an hour ago. Flashing lightning, winds, torrential rain. This was nothing.

For a little thing, she practically bulldozed Logan out of the way into the foyer, where she dumped the bags, and let out a hearty sigh.

Logan frowned at her backside, hands on his hips, then glanced outside to see the car gliding away. The driver gave the horn a friendly double tap before speeding off.

Candace turned to face him. "And you must be Logan, Eric's *friend*." She waggled her brows meaningfully. "I'm so glad to meet you."

Chapter Two

Jeez-Louise, Eric's new boyfriend was a hot-tee, and he wore the California cool look like he'd invented it. Candace hadn't known what to expect when her friend, who'd pushed his lake house on her in the heat of her distress had suddenly remembered his other house guest—his "special friend, Logan"—but it certainly wasn't this. Longish hair, bronzed skin, shoulder-hugging faded tee, jeans worn out in all the right places, and tanned feet in flip flops to boot. Eric's last partner, Tony, had been so much more like Eric himself who, even when he wasn't doing his agenting thing, always dressed in suits.

But maybe this wasn't Logan. Whoever he was, he was studying her with an odd expression. She groaned inwardly. Was it because she'd brought up his and Eric's new relationship? Normally she wouldn't have gone there with a total stranger, but she was beyond flustered by her grand entrance

With any luck, this was a lost neighbor or something.

He reached out a hand. "I'm Logan Shaw, all right."

She allowed her hand to be enveloped by his in a warm, firm shake, and resisted an urge to giggle. Tilting her head to look up, she noted he was frowning a little—which did absolutely nothing to detract from his eyes. They were the color of the Mediterranean.

Logan cleared his throat. "What…ah…happened just now?" He jerked a thumb over his shoulder toward the driveway.

Oh crap. Which part had he noticed? The part where she wouldn't let the driver out of the car, the part where she'd grabbed all her own bags, or the part where she'd run to the door? "What do you mean?"

"Between you and the driver. I got the impression something was wrong."

"No, no, no. Nothing wrong. Bobby was a perfect gentleman, right on time to pick me up, too. And he drove very well. I hardly even noticed the monsoon we just made it through. Do those happen often? Not that I care…much." Great. Now she was babbling. She was definitely making a stellar impression on her friend's new man.

Spinning on her heel, she moved further into the house where the travertine foyer opened into a huge sunken living area made even more spacious by beamed cathedral ceilings. The grandeur didn't detract from the inviting, welcoming feel of the place, from the rich looking carpets, to the overstuffed taupe suede furniture, to the milk-chocolate colored walls. The two-sided massive stone grate would've been the room's focus if not for the bank of floor to ceiling, single-paned glass partitions making up the entire back wall.

"Ah. There's that magnificent view Eric told me about." Candace drank in the unfettered, breathtaking vista spread out below. Lush greens and exotic blooms of magenta, fuchsia, and gold, tumbled downhill in riotous chaos as if announcing the pièce de résistance.

"Lake Tahoe, in all its glory," Logan said, reading

her mind.

"It looks so…I don't know. Spectacular. Turbulent or something. Like the ocean…"

"After a storm," he added.

She heard the smile in his voice, and felt herself begin to relax. This was why she'd come here. To get away from the madness that was her life in Florida.

So he'd noticed something of her odd arrival. So what? Evidently he was gentlemanly enough to let the subject drop.

"I'll take your things to your room for you," he said in a rich baritone, already grabbing her bags.

He made it look so easy—nothing like her graceless flight into the house. She suppressed a snort.

Murmuring thanks, she followed Logan to a spiral staircase tucked between the living area and what looked to be a formal dining room. Behind him on the stairs, she inhaled the subtle scent of shampoo, aftershave, and something she couldn't place, something intrinsically male. He smelled delicious. She took a slow, deep breath and her stomach did a funny little flip.

Alarm sparked through her. A flip? As in butterflies? Just a remnant of her overreaction to the lightning outside. Nothing to do with any sort of inappropriate response to *Eric's boyfriend*. Even if he did resemble a cover model for GQ. Hell, he probably *was* a cover model. Maybe that's how he and Eric had met. Eric was a literary agent, *her* literary agent, but his agency covered a variety of talents.

"Have you been here long, Logan? Eric didn't tell me much other than you'll be leaving at the end of the week. I was hoping you could fill me in on a few things like where the grocery is, and where to find a good meal, and did Eric tell me there was a scooter around here somewhere?"

"Ready to get rid of me already, are you?" He glanced over his shoulder.

Those *eyes*. She grinned like a schoolgirl and a bloom of heat spread over her face. "I think I can put up with you a few days, at least."

"In that case, I'll be happy to show you around." Logan punctuated his offer with a friendly wink.

From the second floor landing the stairwell narrowed a bit but continued upward. Logan stepped into the dark hall and turned left.

"Where does the staircase lead?" she asked.

"Up one more flight is a rooftop patio with a panoramic view of the lake. That's where I was when you got here."

"Out in that lightning?" she squeaked. "I figured you were wet from a shower."

He slowed and shifted his gaze over his shoulder, fixing her with a steady eye. "I didn't notice any lightning. Just a bit of thunder moving a ways off. But to put your mind at ease, I did shower today." He gave a soft laugh as he continued down the hall.

An answering smile curved her lips.

"Your room is on this end. I've got the other master."

Candace flicked a glance behind her, toward the opposite end of the hallway where Logan slept, before following him into hers.

The warm color scheme of coral, gold, and rust made her feel immediately at home. She moved to the room's center and ran a hand over the smooth, curved footboard of the king-sized sleigh bed. An elegant mahogany dresser lined one wall. A matching armoire and two nightstands, completed the set.

To the right, Candace stepped one foot into a large, floor to ceiling travertine-tiled bathroom, then opened the door to a walk-in closet. She moved toward an archway to peek at…an adjoining sitting area? She could definitely see herself getting a lot of work done here.

"Yep. Heaven," she said.

"You ain't seen nothin' yet." Logan strode toward the back wall.

With a few twists of his long tanned fingers, he parted the gauze-covered verticals, revealing a wall of sliders, and an incredible view of a small private stretch of white sandy beach. Blue water glistened in the burgeoning sunlight as far as the eye could see.

"Nothing like bedding down in paradise to take your mind off things," he added, almost as if speaking to himself.

He slid open one door and stepped out, beckoning to Candace. Balmy air carried on the breeze filled the room with the scent of honeysuckle and wild rose.

"Adjoining balconies, so no naked sunbathing," he said in mock seriousness, pointing to an identical set of sliding glass doors opening into his suite. "The pool's just down there." Logan inclined his head.

Candace's gaze swept over a paved deck and designer swimming pool. One side of it fed into a man-made stone waterfall. The far corner opened into what looked like a hot tub.

The perfect scene for a honeymoon. She found the thought mildly depressing.

Several lawn chairs bordered the pool, each precisely lined with the next. Except for one. The one Logan used, she presumed.

"Remind me to give Eric a huge hug next time I see him. He's so sweet to let me stay here."

"Yeah, the use of this place is definitely a perk of knowing him."

She shot Logan a look out of the corner of her eye. That was a weird thing to say about your boyfriend to his good friend whom you'd never met. Unromantic, to say the least.

Logan didn't look the least repentant. "I'll leave you to get settled, then." He headed for the hallway. Turning just outside the door, a hand lightly gripping the jamb, he added, "I've got to go out to take care of some errands, but how about joining me for dinner on the upper deck later? It's supposed to be a perfect night."

She didn't even consider turning him down. Logan would only be here till the end of the week, and this might be her only opportunity to get to know the man, and didn't she owe it to Eric to make a full report? "Love to. What can I do to help?"

"Leave it to me. Consider it a Welcome to Tahoe dinner. Say, seven?"

Chapter Three

Logan drove past the house to park inside the adjacent garage. As he turned off the ignition, he wondered briefly what Candace had been up to during his trip to the market and umpteenth fruitless visit to the post office. Had she explored the huge house—or was she more of a napper type after a long flight? Or maybe she'd gotten right on the phone to report to Eric on whether or not Logan had hit on her.

He got out of the car, and retrieved the groceries from his trunk.

Except...for a minute there this afternoon, it had seemed like Candace thought Logan and Eric were lovers, which would be wrong on so many levels, the primary issue being Luke. *Luke.*

An image of his twin brother, smiling, paintbrush in hand, flashed before his eyes.

Frowning, Logan hit the remote lock on his key fob and started for the house.

He hadn't thought about his brother in a long time, but ever since he'd arrived in Tahoe several weeks ago, Luke seemed to be in the forefront of his mind. It was only natural, he supposed, Luke being the tie that bound he and the house's owner together forever more.

He stepped out of the sunshine and into the cool foyer and headed for the kitchen.

What he didn't know was why his thoughts kept

straying to Candace, as in how did she fit in the picture? Was she one of the authors Eric represented, a family friend, or what?

And there he went wondering about her again. It had nothing to do with those ice-blue eyes of hers, or that warm smile that actually met those eyes.

Probably it had to do with Eric's stern warning to stay far, far away from his 'special' friend. He'd stressed that she was in a fragile place in her life and didn't need any Loganesque complications, whatever that meant.

Logan wasn't a skirt chaser. Never had been. Just because women had a habit of coming after him… He pushed the notion aside, not wanting the reminder of his most recent screw-up.

After putting away the groceries for tonight's dinner, he headed upstairs. He found himself straining his ears for telltale sounds from Candace's room. Nothing. Maybe she'd gone for a walk?

Or maybe she'd headed out to the pool.

He slipped on sunglasses and stepped onto the balcony from his bedroom. Leaning over the rail, he saw Candace stretched out on a recliner near the one he usually used, nose-deep in a thick book. Several more tomes were piled on an adjoining lounger.

Her long blonde hair had gone from a low ponytail to a loose knot, hanging slightly askew at her nape. She wore large black sunglasses and a white one-piece swimsuit. Hard to tell her figure from here. *Just idle curiosity*, his inner voice defended when Eric's warning sounded in his head.

He studied her a moment longer, wondering what she was reading so intently. Abruptly she closed the book and stood, leaning over the pile of tomes to shuffle through the stack.

Finally she straightened, book in-hand. As she scanned the back cover, Logan resisted the urge to emit a slow whistle. Miss fragile Candace had a very nice physique. Toned, yet curvy in all the right places.

She sat and resumed reading.

He glanced up at the afternoon sun. It had come back with a vengeance after the late morning storms, and now blazed in a cloudless sky. What time was it—four-thirty? He could do with a dip about now. Besides, what else did he have to do?

****

Candace set the book on poisons she'd been studying on the lounger beside her and stretched, arching her back against the incessant hunch that was a side effect of her work. She sat back and a droplet of sweat trickled between her breasts. It was downright hot. How long had she been out here, reading and soaking up the sun? At least an hour.

She snorted and wriggled her toes, alternately pointing and flexing her feet. She'd meant to come out here and think, and not about work. She was all but finished with the manuscript she owed the publisher, and had a pretty decent idea where she was going with her next project, yet she'd spent the last hour deep in the trenches of period clothing and methods of murder.

She needed to get her head on straight, and that meant focusing on her defunct relationship with her cheating ex, Roger. But as usual, the higher the stress level, the more she could concentrate on work.

She smiled to herself. One noted exception to the rule had materialized today. Her mind kept straying to

Logan Shaw. He was nothing like she'd expected. He was so...so...sexy. And so unlike Eric. Not type A at all from what she'd seen. He wore *laid back* in that way only a rare few could. As if she could announce the roof was on fire and he'd nod and look at her with those half-mast eyes and say, "Really?"

And she was doing it again.

She put fingertips to her temples. *Focus.* Roger. He'd cheated. She'd caught him. He'd blamed her for keeping him at arm's length. For not moving forward with their wedding plans. And he'd sort of been right.

Now he wanted her back. And while a reconciliation wasn't in the future—she couldn't stomach cheaters—she felt sad. Like she'd failed. *Again.*

God, what was wrong with her? By almost twenty-nine, she should be better at this relationship thing. Why hadn't she given her all to Roger? Or any of her boyfriends, for that matter?

Eric said she hadn't tried with Roger because she suspected all along he had a less than savory character. Was that it? Or was it simply that she was missing the 'in-love' gene? Sure, she knew what love felt like, but she'd experienced it only vicariously through the characters of her romance novels. Why?

She closed her eyes. Waited for insight to dawn.

Nothing.

Shoving off the lounger, Candace flung her sunglasses onto the towel, then marched to the deep end of the pool. Maybe shock therapy would work. She dove in to the chilly water and swam the length of the pool to the shallow end. She came up with a gasp. "Cold...cold," she squeaked as she sprang from foot to foot to reach the steps.

On the sunbaked deck she turned toward her chair, intent on getting to her towel, and let out a chirp of alarm as she nearly collided with a tall, dark, shirtless man dressed in swim baggies.

He grasped her shoulders with two warm hands. "Whoa. Didn't anyone ever tell you not to run on the pool deck, little girl?" Logan's white teeth flashed with amusement. He gave her arms a small squeeze and dropped his hands.

"I was cold," she said, for lack of a better answer. "And you scared the bejesus out of me." She wrapped her arms around herself, not that she was cold any longer. He was standing so close, heat radiated off him.

He laughed. "Sorry. I waved to get your attention." He backed up a step, clearing the path for her toward her lounger. "I can see you're knee deep in reading material. Should I make myself scarce, or may I join you?"

And take away her excuse to think about something, anything, other than her screwed up life? "I'm done with work for the moment. Please join me."

Chapter Four

Logan lowered himself onto the lounger *not* covered with books. "Work, you said?" He gestured toward the mound.

She smiled. "Yes. Research for a new project."

He eyed a few of the titles. *Poison: Silent and Deadly Potions through the Ages. Unsolved Murders of the Mid-Twentieth Century. Fashion Plates of the Twentieth Century.*

"What line of work are you in?" Logan asked, extremely curious.

She looked up at him in unmistakable surprise. "I'm a writer. Eric's not only my friend, he's my agent. It's how we met." A frown puckered her brows. "He never mentioned me?"

For some reason, he didn't want to admit how little the two of them stayed in touch. "The details must've slipped my mind. What have you written? Anything I'd know?" Logan twisted to face her, leaning on his elbow and propping his head in his hand.

"Let's see." The corners of her mouth curved up in a slow, sensual smile that captured Logan's complete attention. Smooth, plump rose-colored lips. "I doubt it."

Huh? He tried to remember what they'd been talking about.

"Unless you read romance."

Aha. He'd asked what she wrote.

"Normally I consider the genre to be written for women, but some men do enjoy romances. Like Eric. Do you, Logan?" She turned her face so her gaze rested on him, though he couldn't read her expression through the dark glasses.

He smiled. When she didn't smile back, he decided she'd actually meant that as a serious question. "Uh…no. I also don't think I've ever met a romance writer. Are you fairly successful?"

She lifted one slim but well-toned shoulder in a half-shrug. "I'm no Nora Roberts, but I'm lucky enough to get paid to do what I love. And I get to make people happy."

He grinned. "Romance novels make people happy?"

A jaunty smile curved her lips. "Of course. People love to fall in love." Abruptly her smile sagged. She let out a sigh and flopped back on her chair. "What about you—what do you do?"

"I'm in photography."

"Oh?"

She'd left the door open for him to elaborate, but he wasn't in the mood. He needed a break. From everything. It's why he'd come here, and why he wasn't looking forward to a return to reality in less than a week. "Are you wearing sunscreen? Your shoulders are looking pink."

She grimaced. "No. In my packing frenzy I forgot to bring any."

"I have some here. You're welcome to use it. Don't be fooled, the afternoon sun's a killer."

"Thanks."

She swung smooth skinned legs over the side of the

16

chair toward him and took the bottle.

He made a valiant effort to not watch her smear a generous amount of the white liquid over her thighs. Then her arms. Her chest. When her manicured fingertips smoothed across the pale skin peeking out above the edge of her bathing suit top, lust shot through Logan, as unexpected as it was unwelcome. By force of will he concentrated on remembering the titles of her research books till his potential erection problem went away.

What the hell was that? He'd only been secluded here for a couple weeks. Maybe Eric was right. Maybe he was a lecher.

"Logan?" She said, drawing his attention back to her. She smiled at him hopefully and held out the sunscreen. "Would you mind doing my back?"

He was a grown man. He could handle it. He took the bottle and worked some of the lotion into his palms to warm it.

She twisted in the lounger and held her hair out of the way.

He rubbed lotion over her nape, shoulders, upper back. Her skin was warm and as silky smooth as it looked. Leaning this close he smelled a subtle, utterly feminine fragrance—perfume, lotion, shampoo, he couldn't tell. But it smelled good. It smelled like he wanted to grab her hair, loosen the knot and press his face into it.

And he was getting hard again. "All set. Think I'll swim a few laps." With that, he turned and dove into the water.

Chapter Five

A little after five, Candace left Logan at the pool to shower and make a few phone calls. She'd delayed as long as her conscience would allow.

First she called her mother to let her know she arrived safe and sound in Tahoe.

"I really don't see why you had to go all that way to finish a book you're already nearly done with," her mother said with a sniff. "And to not even tell your fiancé where you are."

They'd been over this, but Candace wasn't surprised her mother opted not to let the subject lie.

Her bias toward Candace's ex was natural. He was a son of one of her mother's Bunko friends who'd wowed her with his salesman charm over the years. When he broke up with his last girlfriend, Candace's mother had been thrilled to say the least. She'd practically driven Candace and Roger on their first date. Since their break-up was only a week old, her mother evidently still held out hope they would sort things out, regardless of the fact Candace told her she wouldn't even consider it.

"He's my ex-fiancé, Mom. As for why I left, and the reason my agent was kind enough to offer the use of his house, I needed to get away to focus." *On my screwed-up love life.*

Candace had already made the mistake of voicing

her worries about her commitment problems to her mom, specifically her disinclination to set a wedding date with Rog. Her mother latched on to that as the root of all their problems, and hadn't changed her tune yet. She really did want to help, of that Candace was sure, but her mother was the last person Candace would go to for romantic advice.

"I'll be home soon enough. Remember, please, I don't want any distractions—like a surprise visit from Roger. So do not, under any circumstances, tell him where I am."

"All so dramatic," her mother teased, though Candace knew she meant the sentiment. "If you'd listened to me, and set that date, none of this would have happened. He said as much himself when he came to see me."

"He came there?" Candace asked, exasperated.

"Well, yes, after the whole messy ordeal. He said he's sorry, and I believe him. He just wants a chance to make it up to you, and to move *forward* with your lives."

Candace sighed. She'd heard it all before.

"I can see I'm talking to a wall." Her mother paused. "At least you checked in with me. You know how I worry when you travel, especially with no one there to look after you."

"I know you do, Mom. If it helps, there is—" She broke off, rethinking her response. She didn't need anyone to take care of her.

"Yes?"

She sighed inwardly. "There is a man here with me."

"Oh my God. Don't tell me you've jumped into

another relationship. That's no better than what you've accused Roger of doing—"

"Of course I haven't. He's Eric's friend."

"Oooh," her mother intoned knowingly. "Well, I suppose having a man there is something. Even if he is a little light in the loafers."

Candace rolled her eyes, not bothering to correct her mother's lack of PC.

Her mother sighed, and reverted to her favorite topic. "You know, Candace, I just want you to be happy. I want to see you settled with a nice man, and not to end up alone like me."

"You're not alone, Mom. You have me, and Aunt Lindsey, and Uncle Joe."

"It's not the same. You have your life to live, and I'm a third wheel with them. I've felt alone ever since your father left us."

Which Candace knew very well. Her father's infidelity had done a number on her mother.

"I won't keep you, dear. Promise to check in regularly?"

"I will."

"You have your cell phone in case I need to reach you?"

"I do."

By the time Candace hung up, she felt emotionally drained. She loved her mother, but her mom needed some serious counseling. Even knowing that, after being on the receiving end of one of her lectures on relationships, Candace always ended up feeling confused and guilty.

Was she purposefully sabotaging her own relationships? Was that the real reason she'd hit the age of twenty-eight without having been truly *sure enough* about any man to embrace marriage?

Slumping on the edge of the bed, she glanced at the time on her cell and decided her one obligatory call to Roger would have to wait. She had just enough time to clean up for dinner with Logan. She smiled. She was still having a hard time envisioning him with Eric. They didn't seem to go together. Eric was Mr. Clean-cut, while Logan looked like… She pictured his sleepy sea-blue eyes, and sensual mouth.

He looked like sex personified.

Maybe he was Eric's type. Maybe he was one of those *everybody's type* types. She wished she could talk to Eric about him. Then she could hear it straight from the horse's mouth about how they were a couple, so she could picture the two of them together and quit thinking of Logan…well, like sex personified. Unfortunately, Eric was attending a writers' conference in Europe and was unavailable.

She hopped off the bed and made a beeline for the shower.

One thing was sure, she would grill Eric on why he'd kept Logan a secret. My gosh, she'd never have known he existed if Eric hadn't belatedly realized his friend was already staying there after he offered the use of this house.

****

Showered and freshened with a touch of makeup and a casual dress, Candace stepped onto the rooftop patio.

Logan was leaning against the black iron railing, gazing out at the lake. He turned to greet her, a welcoming smile on his face. A pair of well-worn jeans, faded and fitted in all the right places, and a snug black t-shirt showed off his muscular build to perfection.

Up closer, she noticed the writing on his shirt. *It's a camera, not a video recorder. No, you won't be on the six o'clock news.*

She raised her brows.

"A gift from my editor. I guess she thinks I'm a little jaded."

"I see. Your editor from an undisclosed company," she teased. His obvious reluctance to discuss his work had her curiosity in overdrive. But the man was entitled to his privacy.

He smiled and dipped his head in a wry acknowledgement, but still didn't elaborate. "Let me pour you some wine, then I'll grab the salads."

"A glass of wine sounds great."

To Candace's delight, the Adonis could really cook. After a delicious salad of greens and goat cheese, he'd pulled swordfish and asparagus off the grill, then produced a homemade béarnaise sauce to top off the vegetables. When she complimented him on his culinary skills, he accepted her praise with charming humility.

"I think the wine's coloring your acuity. Speaking of which, I need a refill. And so do you."

Candace wasn't so sure about that. She was already feeling the first glass—which she'd drained. But between her pleasantly full belly and the balmy night air, not to mention the magnificent view, she didn't have the will to refuse. Another glass? Why not?

Logan retrieved the bottle from the dripping ice bucket and the hilarity of her situation struck her full on. This was the best date she'd had in months. Dining under the stars with a beautiful—albeit gay—male. Had she dined al fresco with Roger in the two years they'd dated? No, never. Pathetic.

Not a week ago they'd been engaged to be married, and yet neither of them had ever thought to suggest a candlelight dinner for two on the deck of her—*their*—backyard.

Her mental slip had her replaying one of Roger's complaints in her head. "*We're engaged to be married and you still think of this place as* yours."

Which, by the way, she did.

Showing up is ninety percent of the job, her father had said a thousand times. Well, she'd shown up. Then she sat on her hands. Deep inside, hadn't she felt like something was missing? Wasn't that the reason she avoided setting a wedding date?

The question was, had she been honoring her inner knowledge that Roger wasn't the one for her? Or had she merely been playing it safe by trying to wield all the power in the relationship? If so, her strategy hadn't worked out too well since she'd ended up walking in on her so-called loving fiancé in bed with his client. *In her, yes* her, *TempurPedic bed.*

Which now led to the ugliest truth of all. She didn't much care.

Well, damn. She'd come all this way to get her head on straight after Roger blew up their life. So how was it she was the one who felt guilty?

Logan had filled their glasses without her even noticing, and now he raised his in a silent toast. "You're concentrating hard on something. The plot for your next book?"

Candace picked up her glass and took a healthy

swallow. "Nope. I'm thinking about men. Me and men."

"This sounds interesting." He flashed a wicked grin.

Just like that, heat swirled in her lower abdomen, and her pulse kicked up a notch.

What was wrong with her? Her body was reacting. Sexually. To Eric's boyfriend.

Eric's hot, masculine, testosterone oozing boyfriend who seems to own the space around him, said a naughty inner voice. Okay, maybe the wine refill had been a mistake. Abruptly she shoved her glass away.

"Did a bug land in your chardonnay?"

"No." She laughed softly. "I just think I've had enough."

"You seem very sure of that." A glint of amusement flickered in his eyes.

If you only knew. "Trust me on this."

He gave a querulous glance, but thankfully opted not to press. "Tell me about your relationship with Eric. He seems to really care for you."

"The feeling's mutual. Let's see… We met a few years ago at a writer's conference in New York."

"Is that where you're from?"

"No. Florida. You?"

"A Florida girl, huh?" Another one of those easy, glamorous smiles spread over his GQ face. "I'm from San Francisco."

Candace stared into his dreamy eyes and felt herself blush down to her toes. Forgetting her vow not to, she reached for the wine. "Are you?" she heard herself squeak. She cleared her throat, and tried again. "That's where you met Eric, then? He's from San

Francisco, too, isn't he?"

"Yes, we met there. But go on with your story."

She gave a one-shoulder shrug. "There's not much to tell. We met, I pitched him, he liked my pitch."

"Pitch?" Logan gave her a blank look.

Evidently they rarely talked about Eric's business. "Authors often go to conferences to meet with prospective agents in the hopes of luring them to take them on as clients. Agents go to pick up the next best-selling author. As for me, I went to that conference specifically to meet with *The Palmer Agency*, aka Eric."

"So your pitch worked?"

She smiled, remembering. "Enough to get my work in front of him, and then, lucky me, he got excited about my story and I signed with him. Not long after, he got me my first contract—a two-book deal. I was so thrilled I flew up to New York to take him to dinner. I remember that night we talked and talked like a couple of old friends. Not about anything in particular at first. Just about traveling, the City—he told me how odd it was adjusting to New York after growing up in San Fran."

The corners of Logan's mouth tightened, and his fingers squeezed the stem of his wine glass till his fingertips turned white.

"What is it? You're not a fan of the City?"

He looked taken aback. "Why do you ask?"

"You...got a look." Which she noticed since she couldn't take her eyes off him.

He gave a closed mouth grin and lowered his lashes. "I've got nothing against the Big Apple. It's just—something you said reminded me of another time in my life. Totally unrelated to our conversation." He shook his head as if sloughing off the memory. "You were saying?" He lifted his gaze, and raised his wine to take a long, slow sip.

"I was saying…" She angled her head and gazed into the darkening night sky. "Oh, yes. The night Eric and I bonded. Our conversation moved into—what else—our love lives." Her mouth twisted into a grin, and she lounged back, draping one arm along the edge of her chair. "Correction. Eric introduced the topic. Relentlessly."

Logan gave her a knowing look. "He started digging. That sounds familiar."

"To be fair, he told me about Tony first…" God, had she just brought up Eric's ex? She took a deep breath, and barreled full steam ahead, hoping the stream of words would divert Logan's attention. "…and at the time I'd just broken up with my boyfriend, who'd been pressuring me for a deeper commitment, and Eric called me a…" Candace scrunched her brows together as his words came back—and struck a chord that had nothing to do with the distant past.

Eric had used the term serial dater, if memory served. How was it he knew her better than she knew herself?

She put a hand to her temple as if to rub some sense into her head. "Why am I telling you all this? I'm sure you're not interested in hearing me blather on about…" She waved her hand in the air and laughed at herself. "…me and men."

He put an elbow on the glass top table and dropped his chin in his palm. "I thought we'd already established my interest."

She shook her head, chagrined. "I don't know

what's gotten into me tonight. The wine, too much sun, the recent upheaval in my life."

"What sort of upheaval?" he asked in a velvet soft voice.

She hesitated. "Eric didn't mention anything about my…situation? Why I'm here?"

"No."

"Oh."

"Candace, you can't say something like that and leave me hanging."

"Hmm," she hedged.

"Come on." He gave a crooked smile and angled his head so that an inky lock of hair fell over his thick brow. "Please?"

What the heck? She talked to Eric about practically everything, and he always gave the best advice. Probably Logan as his counterpart would offer good insight as well.

"I might need another glass of wine for this."

Logan stood, dumped her now-warm wine over the railing, and refilled her glass.

She took one long drink of the crisp, cool chardonnay, and set the glass down with a decisive clink. Her words came tumbling out. "I went to a writer's convention last week with one of the girls from my local chapter. Roger—that's my fiancé…ex-fiancé."

"Ex," Logan said with calm assurance, and pushed the wineglass toward her.

She smiled gratefully and took another sip. "Roger was going out of town that same weekend. On business. He's in real estate," she said.

He nodded.

"He suggested I stay in Houston—that's where the

conference was—one more night, rather than rush home to an empty house, and said he'd pick me up from the airport on his way back into town the following morning."

"Sounds like a good plan."

"Yes, it did, and I booked my flights accordingly. Then, the day before I left, we had a minor argument about…" She hesitated, biting her lower lip.

He leaned back in the chair, lacing his fingers behind his neck and smiled, letting her know he had all the time in the world.

"He said he felt like I was keeping him at arm's length."

"Do you?" Logan asked.

"Let's just say in retrospect, I decided he may have had a point."

Logan frowned slightly. "Give me an example."

She thought a moment. "Roger said he felt like our relationship wasn't moving in the right direction." She spread her arms. "Here, I thought everything was going fine. I let him move in with me a little less than a year ago, after we got engaged. We rarely fought—before now. He's neat, takes care of his own laundry, pays the bills on time. Plus, we like a lot of the same food. See, I like to eat healthy—"

"He sounds more like a roommate than a lover."

"We made love often enough," she said defensively, sending him a sidelong glance and a petulant one-shoulder shrug.

He threw his head back and laughed. "A stellar endorsement if ever I heard one. Candace, tell me why you moved in together."

She blinked. "He wanted to."

"That's it?"

"He'd been pressuring me to set a date for the wedding."

"Oh." Logan's voice resonated with dawning understanding. "This is the guy you'd broken up with when you first met Eric? The one who'd been pressuring you for a commitment?"

She shifted in her seat. "No. That was someone else."

"Huh."

Silence hung in the air.

"So, last week you fought with your roommate." the corners of his eyes crinkled with undisguised amusement, "then you went away for your conference and he went out of town on business."

"Except his trip got cancelled. So, wanting to show him I'd listened to his complaints, I changed my flight to arrive home a day early. To surprise him. I was going to slip into a sexy nightie, get into bed..."

"I get the picture," he said.

Her face grew hot. "Sorry. That was probably TMI."

He lowered his eyes and laughed softly, shaking his head. "What happened next?"

She gave him a morose look. "First of all, I had to go through a monsoon to get to the front door."

"A monsoon?"

"Thunder, lightning, wind, rain. By the time I got from the car to the house I was soaked to the bone, and my nerves were stretched tighter than a drum. Getting amorous with Roger was the furthest thing from my mind." She shuddered. "But I forged on. Long story short, I walked in on him in bed with another woman."

Logan went still, his sea-blue eyes wide as he stared at her. "And he had the nerve to complain about *your* commitment issues? Is he dead now? Are you hiding out here because you're on the lam from the law?"

She laughed. "Not quite. Eric offered the use of this place when I told him Roger suggested we work things out and—"

Logan interrupted, sounding seriously appalled. "You're not going to give that—" He broke off to clear his throat, and when he spoke again, his voice was level. "—jerk another chance?"

She spread her arms wide. "I'm only considering his position."

Logan narrowed his eyes at her, as if he was trying to understand. "What exactly is Randy's 'position'?"

"Roger's," she corrected.

"I know," he said.

She giggled and waggled her finger at him. "*Roger* says…" As she contemplated how to explain her inner dilemma, her smile faded. She didn't want to unearth all her deep, dark, personal baggage, did she? About her apparent inability to either choose the right guy, or fall in love? No, she wouldn't open that can of worms. Not here. Not tonight. Eric's Logan notwithstanding.

Squaring her shoulders, she opted for the Reader's Digest version instead. "He says I drove him into the other woman's arms. Now, stop," she said through her laughter as Logan began playing an imaginary violin.

When he dropped his air instrument, she wrapped up the story. "I can't say he's wrong. Not entirely. I also can't say I can be any different." *With him, or anyone else.* "That's what I need to figure out, and that's why I'm here. That and work."

Logan cocked his head to study her. "What do you mean, what you need to figure out?"

She met his gaze. "I think that's a question for another night, Mr. Shaw."

He nodded. "Fair enough. So. You're here until…"

"Until I finish the book I owe my editor. Roughly a month and a half."

"Sounds like a well thought out plan, Candace Riley." Logan's voice came out all velvet and smoke. His fingertips played up and down the stem of his wineglass. Slow. Almost caressing. Definitely not with the intention of causing her mind to wander to how those fingers might feel against her skin.

She swallowed hard. Was he aware he reeked of sex appeal? She'd never in her twenty-eight plus years met a man so…yummy.

It must be the wine. Couldn't someone just shoot her and put her out of her misery? She was seriously screwed up. "Your turn." She dragged her eyes from his fingers, hoping her attraction wasn't written all over her face.

He shrugged. "What would you like to know?" Picking up the glass, he took a small sip and eyed her over the rim.

"I'm curious about you and Eric. Besides Tony, which was a long time ago," she hastened to add, "he's never introduced me to anyone he was dating."

Chapter Six

Dating?

Logan sucked in a sharp breath, inhaling some wine in the process. It practically came out his nose as his lungs struggled to recover and his mind reeled.

"Are you all right?" Candace asked, her eyes wide with alarm, her hand poised mid-air.

"Wine down...wrong pipe," he wheezed. He hadn't misconstrued her inference this morning. She thought he and Eric were lovers. Which meant Eric had fed her a line of bull. "What did Eric tell you?" he asked hoarsely.

Her lips twisted in a wry grin, and she lowered her hand to her lap. "Not much. Only that he considers you a quote-unquote special friend."

"I see." Logan studied Candace through hooded lids. She looked deadly serious. He was going to kill Eric.

On the other hand. Eric had an agenda. He'd known Logan would be attracted to Candace, with her sky blue eyes, glowing skin, and easy smile. What straight man wouldn't be? So, besides getting Logan's hands-off promise, he'd formulated a back-up plan to protect her.

Logan would be furious over the lie, if Eric's prediction hadn't proved dead-on.

"Logan? I didn't mean to intrude."

"No, no, it's not that. It's just, Eric and I have a…complicated past." Understatement of the decade.

She looked bemused. "How long have you known each other?"

"We've been friends about…" he blew air out of his cheeks as he mentally calculated the time, "…eight years."

She blinked. "That long? That's longer than I've known him."

He nodded slowly as he gazed into his glass—and saw a dark haired man that resembled himself. Enough so that a stranger would know they were relatives, but not so much anyone would know they were twins. "Another lifetime ago. My brother, Luke, introduced us. Eric and Luke were very close."

Her brows furrowed. "What do you mean were? Was there a falling out between the three of you due to," she hesitated as if carefully choosing her words, "your relationship with Eric?"

She'd noted Logan's use of the past tense. "I said they were close because my brother died a little over six years ago in a car accident. We were twins," he heard himself say, as if it wasn't him speaking.

"Oh my goodness," she gasped. "I'm so very sorry. Twins." Candace shook her head in obvious dismay and placed one of her hands on his forearm. "Identical?"

The cool, silky feel of her skin sent a shockwave up his arm that shot straight down his torso to his groin. Logan froze and concentrated on schooling his breathing, which had gone suddenly erratic and shallow. Did she have any inkling of the cataclysmic effect her touch was having on him?

He raised his eyes to meet her gentle gaze and

decided she hadn't a clue.

"Fraternal. I was the elder by twenty-eight seconds."

"You must miss him terribly. I can't say I've known any twins personally, but I hear the bond between you is immense."

"It was a long time ago," Logan said, gruffly. He wanted to groan. Her light touch, and her magnetic pull on his emotions had his head spinning.

She gave his arm a little squeeze, then caressed his skin in an attempt to soothe him, he guessed. It made his flesh prickle with intense awareness.

"But you still miss Luke," she stated with soft certainty.

Luke. It had been so long since anyone had spoken his twin's name. His fault, of course. Everyone feared his reaction. Everyone, it seemed, except Candace Riley.

He took a deep breath and gave into the craving he'd been denying all night, to eye her head to toe, and drink in every physical nuance of her. He started with the tips of her bent knees peeking from beneath the pale blue sundress, and slowly worked up her torso. He took in the swell of her breasts, the elegant curve of her neck, the soft, moist lips. An almost overwhelming desire to pull her into his arms and kiss her senseless gripped him. Then she licked her lips and he turned rock hard.

Abruptly he leaned back, away from her gentle touch. It was either that or embarrass both of them totally. He was breaking out in a cold sweat, for Christ's sake.

Get a grip, Logan. Focus. Where were we? Eric.

She'd asked about Eric. "Eric and I don't see each other much these days. But we stay in touch. And there's the occasional visit."

Logan read Candace's internal struggle all over her beautiful, expressive face. Part of her wanted to ask more questions, another part hesitated to pry into a subject he clearly didn't wish to discuss. Finally, she gave a resigned sigh.

Good. He didn't mind—make that didn't mind much—allowing her misconception about his and Eric's relationship to continue. But he was damned if he'd outright lie about it.

Candace shifted, folded her napkin, placed it over the dinner plate. Next she would get up and go inside. But Logan was no more ready for her to leave than he was ready to examine his desire for her to stay.

"About your boyfriend. Can I give you some advice?" he asked.

"If you can do it without being bossy." Even though one corner of her mouth hitched upward playfully, Logan got the distinct impression she wasn't kidding.

"I promise to try." He smiled, intentionally aiming to disarm her. Just a test. Any number of women had told him his smile melted their knees.

Her reaction? Nothing. Nada.

"I say move on. Once a guy cheats, he'll do it again."

She cocked her head, and her flaxen hair tumbled over her shoulders like silk. "Are you by any chance speaking from first hand knowledge?"

His lips twitched. "You mean...what's my cheat factor?"

35

She nodded.

He shook his head, locking eyes with her. "I don't cheat."

She didn't so much as blink. "But, you do something. What is it?"

A slow smile spread over his face. She missed nothing and didn't mind saying so. "I don't exactly commit."

"I see." She fingered the stem of her wineglass. "Does Eric know?"

Protective. Nice. "I expect he does." In this, at least, he could be completely honest.

"Mmm," she murmured, sounding sage and all-knowing.

"Mmm?" Logan drummed his fingers on the table.

Candace graced him with an angel's smile—all the more disarming because it lacked the coyness women usually aimed at him. "I was just wondering...why don't you 'exactly commit'?"

His fingers stilled.

She leaned forward to rest on her forearms, folding her arms beneath her breasts. "Haven't you ever been tempted?"

You're tempting me right now. "Never really thought about it."

She regarded him with clear blue eyes that threatened to see right through him. "Yes, and I'm sure you've never been pressed on the issue by any of your boyfriends?"

He snorted softly. Now, had she said *girlfriends*... He opted not to answer.

Candace's smug grin told him she registered his silence as an admission.

"It's largely the nature of my work. As an on-site photographer, I'm rarely in one place for longer than a month. Hardly enough time to develop a lasting relationship."

"Surely you don't always travel."

For some reason, her assertion irked Logan, leaving him more than a little defensive. "I'm honest from the beginning. I let…the person know they can't expect anything from me, and if they're looking for something long-term, they need to look elsewhere."

"Sounds kind of lonely." Candace dropped her chin into her palm.

Logan resisted the urge to scowl. "It's not. I'm not."

She nodded, but Logan could see she didn't believe him.

"You think I'm a jerk, don't you?"

"Not at all," she said, her face showing genuine surprise. "And anyway, I'm in no position to judge. I barely know you. I was only thinking how different we are. I never dabble in relationships. None of this playing the field. I wouldn't know how."

He felt his lips curve upward. "But that's not really true, is it?"

She blinked. "What do you mean?"

"Let me see…what do I mean? Believe it or not, I don't usually psychoanalyze people."

Her eyes twinkled with intrigue, which for some reason pleased him inordinately.

"But in my case, you'll make an exception?" she said.

He licked his lips and narrowed his eyes in concentration. "Take your relationship with Rodney."

37

He bit back a grin as her shoulders trembled with silent giggles. "I submit to you, even though you're monogamous—you are monogamous?"

She smiled sardonically. "One of us is."

"Even though you're monogamous, you're not committed."

"We live together," she objected. "We're engaged."

"Set a date yet?"

She developed a sudden fascination for her shiny red fingernails.

"You're outwardly committed, but inwardly, you're completely disengaged. Maybe you're afraid to commit for personal reasons. Or maybe you aren't really into this guy. Either way, you should leave him in your dust." He sat back and waited to see how she'd take the advice.

"I appreciate your input, Logan. I'll think about what you said." She looked up with soft, trusting eyes.

His heartbeat did a funny little skip.

He'd said enough on the subject of Candace's love life. Whether or not she chose to work things out with her cheating ex was none of his business. But somehow he heard himself add, "You're too beautiful to settle for second best, Candace."

Chapter Seven

He'd read her like a cheap novel—seeing into her soul after knowing her for what—five minutes?

And then he called her beautiful. In his sexy, smoky voice. Had she said thank you? She couldn't remember. Couldn't think. Not while gazing into his island-blue eyes, and certainly not with the sound of alarm bells clanging in her head.

"You're welcome," Logan said.

Okay, so she had thanked him.

Beside her, Logan dropped his napkin onto his dinner plate and leaned back in the chair, arms linked behind his neck and spread wide in a thoroughly masculine stance. She tried to imagine Eric in such a posture and nearly laughed aloud. Logan was as different from Eric as day was from night, by her estimation.

Seemingly lost in his thoughts, Logan stared out over the expansive sparkling water. The moon glowed bright in the clear night-sky, washing his broad, high cheekbones and square jaw in its silvery light emphasizing his wide, sensuous mouth.

She shouldn't be looking at the man's mouth.

Abruptly she pushed back from the table and stood.

Logan followed her lead, rising with languid grace.

"I just remembered I need to make a few phone calls before it gets too late on the east coast. Do you mind terribly if I dash down to do the dishes and then call it a night?" She picked up her plate and laid her silverware across the top.

"Don't worry about the cleanup, Candace," Logan said.

"It's only fair. You cooked, I'll clean. It's the least I can do to thank you. I can't remember the last time someone cooked for me, let alone served me a gourmet meal. Lucky Eric," she muttered, mainly as a reminder to herself.

"Believe it or not I love to cook, but I rarely take the time to do it when it's just for me."

Candace nodded, and reached for his plate.

He pulled his dish out of her reach. "I thought you had calls to make."

"They can wait." She reached for his plate again, then laughed as he again thwarted her efforts.

Setting his plate back on the table, Logan gave a lazy grin and shook his head. A lock of glossy black hair fell over his brow. He ignored it, circling the round glass-top table until he stood directly beside her.

He took the plate she held, and set it beside his. Then he placed one hand on her lower back, and gave a gentle nudge toward the house. The warmth of his palm penetrated the thin material of her sundress. Awareness of him, his touch, his nearness, rippled through her, causing an involuntary shiver to course down her spine. She hoped like hell he didn't notice.

"You should've told me you were cold," he said in a low voice.

"I…ah…hadn't realized until just this moment."

With his palm still at her back, he leaned across to open the door, and the subtle notes of his aftershave invaded her senses. Something wicked stirred in the pit of her stomach. The urge to turn into his solid chest, to nuzzle that bronzed neck and feel the scrape of his early evening stubble against her cheek swamped her. Candace had never had this kind of reaction to a man. Not one she'd barely met, and definitely not one who was so totally out of reach.

She hurried inside, tossing a quick, "Thanks again. Good night," over her shoulder.

Tonight was a mirage. By the next time she saw him, this silly fantasy crush she'd nurtured all night would be history. *Logan is Eric's boyfriend. Logan is Eric's boyfriend*, she told herself silently, all the way down the stairs and back to her room.

Once there, thoughts of Logan fled, replaced by the dread she'd managed to forget all night. She smiled inwardly. Turning to mush in his company had had some merit after all.

She stared at the phone, sitting innocently on the nightstand, and wished she hadn't given in to Roger's badgering and promised to check in. She really didn't want to talk to him. Didn't want to hear his pleas. Didn't want him to know how little she cared they were through—though that made no sense considering he had cheated on her.

Sighing, she reached for her cell phone, and placed the call.

****

Logan rinsed the last of the dishes and pulled the stopper from the sink. As the water disappeared down the drain he marveled again over Candace's revelation. He couldn't quite get his mind around the notion she thought he was gay and Eric's lover, to boot. Now that

41

he'd had some time to think about it, Eric's deception struck Logan as nothing short of a betrayal of his twin.

Logan gave the kitchen a quick once-over before flicking off the lights and heading for the stairs. Obviously Eric had told Candace nothing about his relationship with Luke. The question was, why not? Was he simply keeping his past private, or did Luke's death still hurt too much to discuss? That Logan could understand. To this day, it remained the most gut-wrenchingly painful experience of his life.

Come on, Logan. Drive with me to New York. It'll be an adventure. Don't you want to see where I'll be living? Logan cringed as Luke's words came back to haunt him for the millionth time, though he hadn't replayed the scene recently. Hadn't thought of the fatal accident, or of the police report surmising Luke had fallen asleep at the wheel.

Logan climbed the stairs with care, doing his best impression of a cat burglar, in case Candace was already asleep. At the second floor landing, he glanced toward her room. A thin crack of light shone from beneath the closed door.

He meant to head straight to his room. But the sound of Candace's voice reached out and grabbed him like an invisible hand. He stood stock-still, trying not to so much as breathe.

"I told you, Roger, I can't tell you that."

A pause while Roger answered.

"Very well. I won't tell you. I'm not going to argue semantics. I've gone somewhere to work and to clear my head." Another pause. "No." She sounded exasperated. "I told you there's no one else. It's not like that."

Logan experienced a perverse desire to bang on the door and call out in his deepest, manly-man voice.

"Look. I don't owe you any explanations, and I only made this call because you said you'd worry. The bottom line is, I need this separation right now, and...you should be using this time to find a place to live." She broke off briefly, then said, "No. I'm not threatening anything. There's no need. As far as I'm concerned, we're already over."

Logan nodded approval. Clear enough even a moron like Roger couldn't mistake the meaning..

"Yes, I'm thinking about what you said. Yes, yes, I'll let you know."

Let him know? Let him know what? She needed to stick to the part where she didn't owe him anything.

"Can't we just leave it for a while, Rog?" Roger must've answered in the affirmative because a few seconds later, she said, "And Roger? Don't expect to talk to me anytime soon, okay? I-I need time to think."

Logan thought he heard the sound of a man's voice booming from the earpiece of her phone all the way to where he stood in the hallway.

Logan grinned and moved toward his bedroom, somehow managing not to whistle.

Chapter Eight

Logan rose early, deciding to give up on chasing sleep when the clock struck six a.m. Perfect, he thought sourly. Just in time to catch sunrise.

He threw on some drawstring pants and tripped lightly down the stairs. No reason to wake Candace just because he couldn't sleep.

He rounded the base of the stairs, and stopped in his tracks. Closing his eyes, he inhaled deeply, savoring the unmistakable aroma of fresh brewed coffee. Nothing tasted better than coffee someone else had made. With a grin on his face and a skip in his step, he followed his nose to the kitchen.

He poured a cup of joe and, not seeing the coffee angel, wandered to the living room in search of her. No Candace in sight.

His gaze skimmed over the empty room, the equally empty formal dining room, through the single-paned French doors leading out to the back patio and pool, and finally landed on her. She sat at the glass-topped table. Her hair was pulled back and light from her open laptop illuminated her face. Already, piles of books surrounded her. She had one leg tucked under the other and was staring into the screen as if it held the hidden answers to the universe. Beyond, the morning sun rose in the sky, splashing shards of pink and blue and gold, and silhouetting the shape of Echo Summit on the south shore.

Logan felt an old familiar quickening of his senses—one he hadn't experienced in a long, long time. Of needing to capture what he saw. Of knowing exactly how he wanted his vision portrayed to the rest of the world. He set his mug down with care, hoping not to draw Candace's attention.

Praying she didn't move, he jogged up the stairs two at a time. Without bothering with the light, he entered the closet, found his duffel tucked in the back of the top shelf. A quick zip—and his fingers closed over the cold metal of his most prized possession. Seconds later, he was back in the shadowed living room.

He took several shots, not using a flash so as not to startle her or change the composition or lighting of the picture. In frame after frame, he captured her angelic profile illuminated only by the light of the computer screen. The myriad colors of the awakening morning sky and the contrasting mountainscape across the lake made a perfect backdrop.

She half-turned, angling her chin toward the house, as if something had alerted her to his presence.

He froze, not even drawing breath. Only after she turned back to the computer did he recognize the flicker of guilt pricking his conscience. He hadn't asked to photograph her. He should—would—tell her what he'd done, and give her the option to delete his work. But first he wanted to see what he had. He went into the kitchen and shuffled through the digital shots.

Great pictures. Beautiful composition. *Beautiful subject.*

Now for the confession. With camera in-hand, he

set out for the patio. He reached the French doors just in time to glimpse the bottom of Candace's running shoes as she disappeared around the back of the house. Out for a morning jog from the looks of it.

He opened one of the doors and did a quick study of the area. The laptop was closed and a pair of long yoga-type pants hung neatly over the back of her chair. He'd missed her stripping them off. Damn.

The clang of the house phone had him jumping nearly out of his skin. Jesus—he covered his heart with his right hand, and went in search of the sure cause of his early demise. Who the hell would call at this hour?

He got to the cordless phone on the third ring. "Logan here."

"Hi! Um…this is Jenna Michaels with the Palmer Agency. I think I dialed the right number. Is this Eric Palmer's residence, and is there a Candace Riley staying there?"

"Yes, and yes." After a pause he added, "I'm Logan Shaw, an old friend of Eric's."

"O-oh," she drew out in a knowing voice.

The gay thing again? He shrugged. "I assume you have a reason for calling," *at this hour of the morning.* "Candace is actually not in at the moment. Can I give her a message?"

"Oh, no. I'd hoped I'd catch her by calling this early. Oh, this is awful."

Logan recognized a damsel in distress when he heard one. "You sound like you've got a problem. Problems are my specialty Jenna Michaels of the Palmer Agency."

Her giggle came across the line. "I appreciate the offer, but unless you have a couple of professionally done photos of Miss Riley which you can miraculously send my way in the next...mmm...five minutes, I think I may be out of a job."

"Is Eric such a task master?"

"I'm exaggerating. I hope. The thing is, I was supposed to copy the publicity shots of Miss Riley onto a thumb drive, and didn't. Now the computer the pictures were saved on is fried and the photographer who took them is MIA, so I can't get any duplicates there, and I have to submit the photos and a blurb on Candace to the publishing house's marketing department like an hour ago. They're doing a big publicity push for the debut of her new book. Mostly the web ads will feature the book's cover and its trailer, but they wanted some pictures of her, as well. Readers love to see their authors in action."

As she spoke, Logan scrolled through the shots of Candace. In the last few, the sun had risen higher, lighting the deck area and, subsequently, Candace, making her recognizable by anyone who knew her. One corner of his mouth crooked upward. She looked amazing, especially for someone who'd gotten up at the crack of dawn.

"Matter of fact, Jenna, I think I can handle your problem for you. I do happen to have a few photos of Miss Riley. But I'll have to get her approval before I send them your way."

"Great. When do you expect her—in a few minutes?"

"Doubtful. She just headed out for a run."

"Oh, pleeeease." Jenna dragged out the word in a dramatic fashion. "I'm late as it is. I'm sure she won't mind. She's always super easy going and, besides, she approved the last shots without seeing them first hand."

Logan hesitated. He hadn't even told her he'd taken the pictures.

"Please? You'd really being doing Eric a favor." She sounded truly pathetic.

"You say she approved the last pictures sight unseen?"

"Without a blink."

"All right. Give me your email address."

****

An hour and a half later, Candace stared at Logan, trying to make sense of what he'd just told her. He'd not only photographed her, he sent pictures of her to Jenna. Without her knowledge. Dressed like this. Sure she'd approved the last shots without looking at them, but those had been professionally staged and Eric had done the choosing.

She ought to be annoyed. But instead, a small…okay *big* part of her tingled with pleasure at the compliment. The sight of her had inspired him to snap pictures? She bit the inside of her lip to keep a silly grin from plastering itself across her face.

"You're not saying anything. You are angry. Dammit, I should have known better."

He pushed a button several times on his camera, and Candace heard the rapid beep-beep-beep. Was he deleting them? Her own innate curiosity reared its head and she started to ask him not to when he angled the back of his camera so she could see the digital frame.

"Here's one I sent."

She inched a little closer to him. "It's beautiful," she heard herself say. "I mean—I mean the shot. The mountains in the background, not me," she rushed to add. Why did she always turn into an idiot around him?

"Thank you. The composition drew me in the first place. The sky, the light from your computer, and especially your face."

She peered at the image of herself. She saw nothing special. "What about it?" She turned her gaze on him.

His eyes never wavered from the small screen. "You look serene. Completely in your element. All woman. Beautiful." One corner of his gorgeous mouth curved upward in a hint of a smile.

She blinked rapidly and willed herself not to giggle like an imbecile. "Oh."

"I'm sorry I didn't ask permission to photograph you. And as far as allowing Eric's agency to use the shots...I have no excuse." He jammed one of his hands through his thick dark hair. "Hell, I've been in this line of work for years. I know better." His eyes, full of remorse, locked with hers.

What was the point of allowing him to suffer with guilt when she couldn't work up a good temper, well deserved or not? She gave a one-shoulder shrug. "I could be mad, or I could thank you for bailing me out. So, thank you, Logan. And you know what? Your photographs are better than the ones the other photographer took. Definitely more artistic."

He averted his gaze, but not before she glimpsed the flash of pleasure. Because she'd complimented his talent?

A warm, cozy sensation settled in her tummy. "Let's pull up my publisher's website and see how the final layout looks. Hopefully they gave you credit for the shots."

"They did, believe me. Jenna wouldn't hear otherwise."

****

Candace sat cross-legged in the sitting area of the bedroom suite reading over her WIP, and realized she hadn't digested the last several paragraphs. She'd been at it for hours. Time for a break.

She stood, stretched and grabbed her cell phone, then exited the room. As she skipped down the stairs, the cell phone buzzed. The Palmer Agency. "Candace Riley here."

"Candace? Hi. It's Jenna. I don't mean to keep bugging you when you're on vacation."

Logan walked through the front doors as she reached the first floor, looking flushed and delicious, in loose fitting workout clothes, a towel gripped in one hand.

Smiling and waving a greeting, she crossed the living room toward the kitchen, cell phone to ear, and collided with the long table behind the couch.

"Ouch! Jenna? Hold on a sec." She rubbed her hip-bone where it had met the hard corner of wood. Her face burned with mortified heat. So much for getting her head on straight when Logan was around.

"Poor baby. You okay?" Logan inquired from behind her.

She pivoted and found herself almost toe-to-toe with him. Close enough to see the hair at his temples and nape were damp and curling at the ends. Their eyes met. He smiled and brushed the back of her hand, still pressed against her hip, with his fingertips.

Her heart tripped over itself. The sound of a voice in her ear brought her back to earth. "Miss Riley? Are you hurt?"

"Uh, no. Not at all." She spun away from Logan, and continued toward the kitchen. "And by the way, this is a working vacation, Jenna. You have permission to bug me at will. What's up?"

Logan's footsteps followed. She leaned on the cool granite of the kitchen island and watched him beeline for the refrigerator. He ducked inside, reappearing a moment later with a carton of organic milk in hand.

"Miss Riley," Jenna hesitated. "I don't want to alarm you. It's just, our inbox has been flooded with mail for you today, which is nothing unusual when we start a promotional campaign, but..." Her voice trailed off.

"But?"

"Usually we receive loads of fan mail. Which we did. It's just...this time we also got, um, I'm not quite sure how to put it."

"I'm on the edge of my seat here. What besides fan mail did I get?"

"Hate mail."

Chapter Nine

Logan poured himself a glass of ice cold whole milk, and leaned against the counter. He brought the glass to his lips, downing the creamy contents in several gulps. Across from him Candace's golden brows furrowed as she concentrated on whatever was being said to her on the other end of the phone.

A prickle of alarm raised the damp hair on the back of his neck. He rubbed a hand over his nape and told himself to cool it with the overactive imagination.

She finished her conversation and hung up, simultaneously lifting her gaze to his. Her sky-blue eyes had a glazed look akin to bemusement. On closer inspection, make that alarm. Her face had paled.

The fine hairs at his nape bristled again as another internal warning went off. The instinct to protect her had him moving to her side in a flash. "Something's wrong."

"I don't know. That was Jenna. The lady you spoke with earlier."

"What now? Jeez, does the place shut down when the boss and you are gone?"

She smiled at that. "Hardly. Actually, her phone call was above and beyond. I just don't know what to make of it."

Logan stared at her, unblinking. Hardly able to breathe.

"I have an electronic mailbox that Eric's staff sorts through for me." She twisted a strand of hair around her pointer finger. "They mark a small amount of mail as urgent, say, if it's from my publisher or something to do with the industry, clear out the junk, and put my fan mail in a separate folder I can read at my leisure, say, when I have time or need a little encouragement. That sort of thing."

He waited for her to continue, the pit of his stomach tightening into a hard knot. What the hell was wrong with him?

She sighed and blurted, "Evidently, I got a handful of hate emails today." She sank onto a stool at the kitchen island, looking like someone had taken her last cookie. "I've never gotten nasty letters before. Romance readers are typically sweet."

Logan pulled out another stool to sit beside her. "How many emails are we talking about? Was there any consistent theme? Did they threaten you in any way?"

Her eyes crinkled with amusement, and a touch of color returned to her cheeks. "Hello, detective Shaw."

He grinned at her and put his hand on her knee—and the pit in his stomach morphed into a new, far more pleasant sensation. Damn, she was pretty.

"They're all from the same person, seemingly. According to Jenna, none are signed, except by initials. And they all say something to the effect…" she paused, and twirled more hair on her finger. "You made a big mistake…" She paused again and offered an apologetic smile before quoting, "bitch. I'll find you and make you regret messing with me."

Logan's blood went from simmer to boil in an

instant. "At least it's obvious who the perpetrator is. We need to call the cops right away."

She looked dumfounded. "It is? Who do you mean?"

"Your ex-fiancé, of course."

She half rolled her eyes. "I ruled him out immediately."

He gave her a *come on, moron*, look, which was the best he could do at the moment.

She held her hands, palms out toward him. "Consider the 'mess with me' reference. That wouldn't make any sense coming from him. I haven't done anything to him."

"Except call off your relationship."

She shook her head doubtfully. "For another thing, the vulgarity isn't like Roger. He's nothing if not proper."

"Hmm. A proper cheat." His sarcasm was probably over the top. But her naiveté could land her in serious trouble. Why couldn't she see that?

"I'm sure the emails are nothing but a fluke. The timing tells me they're a knee jerk reaction to the publicity drive that opened today. Just the ramblings of some weirdo author who read the blurbs of my books and thinks I stole her ideas. Which I didn't by the way."

He stifled a chuckle. She looked so sincere, as if he might actually consider her a plagiarist. He leaned back on the barstool and crossed his arms over his chest. "Have you actually read the emails?"

"Nope. And I'm not planning to."

"Why not?" He spread his arms wide.

His tone seemed to put her on the defensive, which hadn't been his intention. She crossed her arms over her chest and leaned back, putting some distance between them.

He promptly inched forward and covered her knee with his palm.

"Because," she said, drawing out the word, "the nastiness might get under my skin, and that would give it too much power over me. Like staying indoors after terrorism, or paying a kidnapper's ransom. Or hiding out when the weather's bad."

Unable to restrain himself Logan laughed out loud. "You are an author, aren't you?" A moment later he sobered. "But let me play devil's advocate here. Maybe you should be afraid. Maybe the threat's real. Did you even consider that?"

She pursed her lips, drawing Logan's gaze to her mouth. Her lips always looked soft and moist. Begging to be kissed.

She took another moment to consider his question, then shook her head. "You know what? No. No one knows where I am, except you and Eric." She drummed her fingers on the granite-topped island. "Eric's probably just getting to his hotel room after a long flight, so he's out." She lowered her voice to a conspiratorial whisper. "Don't tell me you sent those emails?"

A grudging smile tugged at the corners of his lips.

She laughed aloud. "It hurt my feelings more than anything else. I don't like to be hated. Tell you what, let's forget the whole thing. So..." Her gaze flitted over his body and he felt like she'd feather dusted him. Specifically, his cock.

"I take it you went to the gym? Don't you like the one here?" she asked, referring to the one on the ground floor. "Or did you just need some other adult contact?"

"I like the adult contact here just fine," he said without thinking, then closed his mouth with a snap. Could he not open his mouth without flirting? He cleared his throat and hastened to add, "Unfortunately, Eric's gym doesn't have a rock climbing wall."

"Oh. Rock climbing. That's very...impressive." Her gaze fastened on his chest, and her soft lips parted slightly.

Was she finally admiring the merchandise? Not that he wanted her to. Much. She licked her lips and his lower regions took control of his blood flow. Soon he'd embarrass both of them. He rose, intending to put the island between them.

Unfortunately for his libido, Candace chose the exact moment to rise from her stool. Their bodies collided and the contact felt way too good. God, his erection was straining against his briefs. He jerked back, knocking the stool sideways, just managing to catch it before it hit the floor. He lifted it in front of him, hoping to hide the evidence of his heterosexuality.

"Nice save." Candace sounded breathless.

"Thanks," he muttered. Had she noticed his hard-on? Was that the reason her cheeks were flaming?

She made a beeline for the archway leading out of the kitchen. "I've...uh...got to get back to work." She jerked a thumb over her shoulder. A split second later, she was gone, the sound of her footsteps disappearing as she trotted up the stairs.

****

Late that night, Logan lay on his back, naked except for a pair of boxers, arms crossed under his head, staring blindly at the ceiling. For what seemed like the hundredth time, he closed his eyes and concentrated on relaxing, one body part at a time. Unfortunately, like the ninety-nine times before, his muscles refused to cooperate, re-tensing the moment he lost focus.

This wasn't his usual insomnia. Hell, he'd had regular bouts of sleepless nights since Luke's death. But tonight, he couldn't seem to banish the sense of impending disaster. The last time he felt this way, he woke to find an unbalanced woman standing over his bed with a butter knife in her hand. Butter knife notwithstanding, it hadn't been a pleasant thing to wake to, even if he'd subdued her with no more than a firm grip on her wrist.

But this was different. This time Candace was the target.

That damned hate mail. He wished she'd let him read it. In his opinion, she needed to treat any and all threats as credible. Especially if his theory held true, and her ex had come unhinged since she left.

He'd wanted to discuss it with her further, but he hadn't seen her since this morning. Almost like she was avoiding him. An unwelcome voice, suspiciously like Eric's, sounded in his head. *Why would she do that, Romeo? Maybe because you pressed your erection into her belly?*

He sighed and clicked on the bedside lamp, opening the book he'd randomly selected from Eric's study. He read the first page and realized when he reached the bottom he hadn't digested one word. Slamming the book shut, he flopped onto his back.

How could she be so unconcerned? If the emails came from Roger, the man was a certified nut. And if they hadn't, a nameless, faceless crazy had fixated on her. An image of Julie Braun, his own personal stalker, flashed before his eyes. He hated to think of someone raining havoc on Candace's life the way Julie's obsession had with him.

Julie had run him right out of the magazine. After he slept with her, of course.

He didn't care to think about that, and, he reminded himself, Candace's problems were not his to take on. He reopened the book and started from the beginning. Again.

After rereading the same paragraph for the tenth time, Logan gave up and switched off the bedside lamp. Maybe he could try counting sheep.

"Huh?" Logan jolted awake, his own gruff voice startling him. His gaze shot to the orange glow of the digital clock. 3:50. He had fallen asleep. So what in hell woke him?

Scowling and bleary-eyed, he threw back the sheet and got out of bed. He stalked to the door, yanked it open, and peered into the darkness till, gradually, the outlines of the hall came into focus. At the opposite end, Candace's door was closed, and no telltale light seeped through the cracks. He listened for any sounds of movement. Nothing.

He tromped back to bed and got horizontal, fuming over being awake for no good reason. Then he heard it. A soft whirring coming from the balcony—like the bearings of a sliding glass door rolling, bit by slow bit. And it sure as hell wasn't his door. God, had her ex-fiancé found her? *Dammit*, why hadn't she let him read those emails?

Dire thoughts racing through his head, he flew off

the bed and yanked the door open to peer toward Candace's room. Door closed. Lights out.

Adrenaline pumping, he leaped toward his own slider. Grasping the handle, he slid the door open using the same care the perp next door had used. He hoped. He gritted his teeth as the sound of his door amplified tenfold to his own ears. As soon as he had space enough to squeeze through, he sidestepped onto the balcony, bare feet silent on the cold stone.

The moon was shining bright, reflecting off the gauzy white curtain billowing from Candace's room. He inched closer, scooped the drapes aside, and stepped over the tracks.

His gaze went straight to Candace's bed. She lay enveloped in a mound of bed covers, evidently fast asleep. From the corner of his eye, he caught movement in the open doorway leading to the hall. Open doorway? Jesus. A shadowy figure hovered at the threshold.

Suddenly, Candace's bloodcurdling scream rent the air, fueling another rush of adrenaline, and propelling his body toward the dark figure, now fleeing into the hall.

"Candace, don't move!" he shouted in warning, just before his body slammed into the intruder.

The man jerked backward and swung something at Logan.

Logan twisted his body so the cold, hard object glanced off his shoulder. With a jab of his elbow, he sent the would-be club flying. Then he grabbed the smaller man's hands, and spun him around to smash him, face first, into the wall, using his own body as a lynchpin.

Candace was probably scared out of her mind. If

this bastard had hurt one hair on her head... Logan gulped air and called out to her in as calm a voice as he could muster. "Candace? Are you all right?"

"L-Logan?" came her muffled, very frightened sounding reply.

From directly beneath him.

Chapter Ten

"Is that you, Logan?" Candace could hardly hear her own voice over the blood rushing through her ears.

The very hard, very male body pressing her into a human pancake relaxed its pressure slightly. "Candace?"

Logan's voice. Thank God. It *was* him. Assuming he wasn't a total maniac, she might live through this night. "Wh-what's g-going on?" She couldn't stop shaking, and even her words sounded like she was speaking into a fan. She swallowed hard and tried again. "Is there an intruder?"

Logan braced his arms on either side of her and eased backward. Cold night air rushed over her scantily clad body, and her shaking turned into violent shudders.

"I heard...I thought...after those emails..." His words died in a soft curse. With surprisingly gentle hands, he turned her to face him.

When he let her go, she had to grasp his broad shoulders to keep from sliding down the wall. "Y-you th-thought?" Despite her best efforts, her knees gave out.

He caught her easily and pulled her into his chest. She almost groaned with pleasure as the heat from his body seeped into hers. She dropped her face into his shoulder.

"I thought *you* were an intruder. I was trying to

protect you—from you."

She struggled to absorb his words. "You...you...me?" She mumbled into his skin. His naked, hot flesh. My God, did he have any clothes on? Maybe he *was* a maniac. She jerked her head back and tried to make his face out in the dark hallway.

She saw a flash of white as he spoke. "I'm not sure what you're asking."

"Do you think...could you possibly help me to my bed because I don't think I can get there on my own."

Without a word he carried her into her moonlit room, and laid her gently on the bed. "I'm so, so sorry." He bent over her and brushed hair off her face. "I heard noises on the balcony and I thought someone was breaking into your room." He cursed again, something to the effect of calling himself a flaming idiot.

He seemed to be waiting for her to respond.

"I couldn't sleep. I wanted a little fresh air. I didn't want to wake you." Her eyes welled with tears.

Logan fumbled with the lamp on the nightstand till he found the switch and illuminated the room in a soft glow. "Oh, no, sweetheart, don't cry." He lowered himself to the edge of her bed and pulled her into his arms.

"I ca-can't help it," she choked. She took a shuddering breath and rested her damp cheek against his chest. He smelled good. Like soap and sleep and the subtle remnants of aftershave. Like a man should. He felt like one, too. Solid and warm. Even the coarse chest hairs now tickling her nose seemed exactly right.

"So. You couldn't sleep," he said, his deep voice rumbling in his chest. "What were you doing out in the hall?"

"I went to the kitchen for something to drink."

"You grabbed a bottle of water, I take it?"

She could hear the smile in his voice. "How did you know?"

"If I'm not mistaken, you hit me with it."

"Oh."

"I think you need a few lessons in self defense," he said, still smiling.

Candace sniffed. Lessons or no, she didn't think she'd fare too well against a villain of his size and strength. "I think I'm all right now."

Logan waited half a beat and then released her. Candace scooted backward till she could lean against her headboard.

Logan's eyes slid over her, making her conscious of the fact she wore only a silky shorts set. As for him…she flicked a glance over his lower torso. Over the thin line of hair running from his navel to his blue and white striped boxers. Her pulse had only just resumed a halfway normal speed and now it slammed back into high gear. Was she experiencing aftershock from the scare of her adult life, or was Logan's unconscious sexual energy doing a number on her? Oh, she was so not right. Pinching her eyes closed, she said the first thing that came to mind. "If I thought I couldn't sleep before, I'll never sleep now."

"Ouch. If it makes you feel any better, I don't think I can sleep at this point either."

She slanted him a glance and grinned. "It does. A little."

"So. What should we do instead?"

Though he'd obviously spoken the words in complete innocence, his heavy lidded eyes and the velvet texture of his voice put ideas in Candace's head that made her face burn. She shook her head as if she could jostle the thoughts from her mind. "I'll do what I usually do in these circumstances."

He arched a brow. "You find yourself accosted by madmen in the middle of the night on a regular basis?"

She grabbed the nearest pillow and flung it at him. "I meant what I do when I have a hard time sleeping."

"Does that happen to you often—insomnia?"

She nodded. "More than occasionally."

"Me, too." He studied her briefly. "So, what is it you usually do?"

She shrugged. "I work."

Logan scrubbed a hand over his stubble-covered jaw. "God, I feel awful. Like a complete and utter fool."

Candace laughed softly. "Good. Then you won't mind doing me a favor."

"Anything. Give me any task."

Candace chuckled at his boyish zeal. "Let's start with my laptop. Can you get it for me? It's in the sitting area on the table."

He retrieved it from the connecting room. "You're going to work from bed?"

Candace nodded, already inching her legs under the bedcovers.

A loud pop sounded from outside, echoing across the lake. She gave a yip and flung her laptop into the air.

Logan caught it with one graceful move. "It's just kids setting off fireworks." He handed it back to her.

"Oh," she breathed, tearing up again. "I thought...at first it sounded like thunder."

Logan's eyes narrowed. "Nope. Just fireworks."

Candace scrubbed at her eyes and tried to send Logan a relaxed smile. "Right. Are there...often random firework displays?"

He cocked his head and studied her face. "It's a fairly regular occurrence around here. Why?"

Candace bit her lower lip, wishing she hadn't said a word. She pushed hair off her face and opened the laptop. "Let's just forget it, all right? It's no biggie." She stared at the computer screen and wished him out of the room.

He planted his feet and crossed his arms over his chest. "You have something against fireworks?"

Another thing she wished Eric had warned her about. Logan's perceptiveness. "I feel kind of stupid talking about it."

"*You* feel stupid? How do you think I feel? I just tackled you in the hallway."

Perceptive *and* persistent. Candace peeked up at Logan and the utter ridiculousness of her situation struck her. She was dressed in nothing more than her nightie, in bed, in the middle of the night, talking to a gorgeous, half-naked man whom she'd only just met, who happened to have just attacked her. And somehow he had her on the verge of confessing one of her most private, most embarrassing idiosyncrasies. Irresistible laughter bubbled up inside her.

He opened his arms in a beseeching manner. "Now what? C'mon. Throw me a bone here."

She swallowed the laughter, but her smile remained in place. "I...since I was a kid, I've had a slight...problem with...thunderstorms."

"You're afraid of thunder?"

She scratched her head and stared at the dual

mounds made of her toes under the blanket. "Not so much thunder as thunder and lightning. And, not so much fear as…anxiety. Fight or flight. I had a bad experience as a child. The doctors say it's a sort of a syndrome, like post traumatic stress. One I was supposed to outgrow."

"Sometimes things take longer than we expect."

Candace nodded.

"Still, I'm guessing you wouldn't have reacted so strongly to the fireworks if I hadn't freaked you out tonight."

"Probably true."

Logan tucked his fingers under his armpits and rocked back on his heels. "Would it help if I stayed here, just until your nerves settle?"

"Oh, I don't think—"

"Let me get the book I'm reading." Logan disappeared into the hall.

A few seconds later he returned, book in hand. He'd donned a white V-neck t-shirt. The undershirt didn't do much to conceal his broad shoulders and washboard abs.

He walked to the opposite side of the bed and turned on the bedside lamp before plopping on top of the covers. He flashed her a smile and opened the book.

A few minutes later his body slid down the covers till he was lying flat. From the corner of her eye she saw him roll onto his side, and prop onto one elbow, facing her. "You probably want to murder me."

She resisted the urge to grin and kept her eyes on her computer screen. "Mm," she murmured, non-committal. "I thought I'd wait till you fell asleep."

****

Light assaulted Logan's closed eyelids. He burrowed his face into the pillow and struggled to hold onto the vision in his dream, but it was too late. The insistent chirp of birds outside the window had yanked him from the most compelling, deliciously erotic dream... It had felt so real.

He rolled onto his back and drew one hand automatically to his throbbing cock. A soft moan of protest sounded to his right.

Logan's eyes flew open, revealing to his conscious mind what he'd conveniently chosen to forget. He hadn't made it back to his room last night. He'd slept in Candace's room, in Candace's bed, and he'd just removed his hand from the curve of one shapely, warm hip clad in pink satin shorts. She lay on her side, facing him. One leg was hidden beneath the sheets, the rest of her sprawled atop the twisted covers. Her satin tank had ridden halfway up her midriff and her sexy sleep-tousled hair cascaded across the pillow like golden silk. His penis throbbed insistently against his palm.

He jerked his hand away from his boxers, belatedly concerned his movement might awaken her. Still, better that than have her catch him with his hand down his pants. Keeping a cautious eye on the woman lying beside him, inch by slow inch, he slid his legs over the edge of the bed.

When his feet hit the floor, he levered himself from under the sheets.

Candace gave another indecipherable moan, and stretched like the proverbial cat.

Logan bit back a moan of his own and backed toward the hallway, never taking his eyes from her prone body. She rolled onto her stomach and her satin shorts crept high on her hips, exposing the curve of her sweet ass, tempting him to run his hands over the enticing roundness. Calling on all his willpower and integrity as a man, Logan retreated to his room.

A short while later, a cold shower pelting his still aroused body, Logan tortured himself by replaying some of the more vivid images from the previous night's dreams. The touch and taste and feel of the woman hadn't seemed much like a dream.

The woman. Hah.

He'd been exploring Candace Riley to his heart's content. The question was, had it all been a dream? Or had he been drawn to her during the night, like a damn stray dog to filet mignon?

He ought to regret his accidental sleepover. Only, he couldn't. Sexually charged dreams notwithstanding, he'd slept like a baby for the first time in years. He'd *slept*. Unbelievable.

Chapter Eleven

Candace waited for the beep following Eric's voicemail recording and left a brief message. No one could say she hadn't tried to reach him. She couldn't help it if he was out of the country and still unavailable. And there were perfectly valid reasons she hadn't phoned him since arriving at the Reno airport.

She didn't call the first night because he'd been flying over the ocean. Then last night, before bed, she'd... Why *hadn't* she called? Oh, yes. Because she hadn't wanted to disturb him before the start of the conference.

More like you didn't want to reveal your silly crush on his boyfriend.

"Ridiculous," Candace muttered as she peeked out her curtains to glimpse the rippling pool and the lakeshore. Not that she was looking for Logan. And she hadn't been earlier when she spied him wandering toward the water's edge with a coffee mug.

She didn't have a thing for Logan. In fact, she was going out of her way *not* to cross paths with him. At least not until she could act normal in his presence, which wouldn't even be an issue except...last night. Those dreams. She got hot thinking about them.

After Logan gave her the fright of her adult life, and those fireworks exploded, she'd expected the worst. The usual bone-deep dread she'd gone through years of therapy to vanquish. She'd fully expected to stare at her monitor, beating back anxiety till her eyelids got heavy. But the dread never materialized. Instead, she found herself in *the zone*. Awake, invigorated, yet oddly relaxed. The perfect mix for her writing to really flow.

That's where last night got hazy.

One minute she'd been writing, making great progress. The next...she was dreaming about Logan. About *doing* things with Logan, and about him doing things to her. Her dreams had been so real they almost seemed like memories now. She could practically feel his warm breath on her cheek, his lips tender on her nape. She smelled his shampoo, and felt the rough stubble of his jaw scraping her cheek. The memory of arching her back, her bottom pressing into his hips, his hips fitted against hers, his erection hot and heavy even through their clothes.

Jesus, it had been a dream, hadn't it? Of course it had. Logan was gay. And he hadn't been anywhere in sight when she awoke. He had obviously slipped out after she dozed off.

But knowing that didn't stop her breasts from tingling with the false memory of his fingertips playing over them. Pathetic!

She tromped into the adjoining sitting room and plopped on the small sofa. She needed to approach this logically. Obviously her dreams had nothing to do with Logan. They merely highlighted a sexual deficit she'd been trying to deny.

Eric had been right, as usual. She'd needed this break. After only a few days, she'd not only unearthed the truth of her lackluster feelings for Roger, but had discovered she'd been selling herself short in the physical department by staying with a man she didn't really love. She'd never felt such...exquisite lust for her fiancé. Their lovemaking had been nice. At least, it had always *seemed* fine.

Until this morning.

Candace covered her face with her hands and groaned.

Going with plan A, which entailed hiding in her room all day, had done nothing but free her to replay her dream life fantasies till she needed nothing so much as a cold shower. Since she'd already had one of those... She marched to her door, yanked it open, and—

"Eek!" She lurched backward, stopping only when her rump banged into the dresser. "Oh, for crying out loud!" she gasped, hand over her heart.

Logan stood just outside the door, hand poised to knock. He stared at her dumbfounded for a moment before lowering his hand and following her into the room. "Are you all right?"

"You scared the life out of me," she said, still catching her breath.

"This time it was sheer luck." He grinned, not looking the least bit repentant, and stepped close, placing two fingers at the base of her throat. "Checking your pulse," he said in a smoky voice. "You'll live." Without removing his fingers, he raised his turquoise eyes to hers and gave her a lazy smile.

Candace's heart skittered wildly, and this time the irregular rhythm had nothing to do with fright.

He withdrew his hand and took a leisurely step back while his gaze grazed over her body. "What you're wearing should be fine. Maybe you want to grab a sweater, though."

Candace glanced down at her pink striped gingham wrap dress. "Excuse me?"

"After last night, I wanted to make amends. I remembered you asking me about the local attractions. Meet your tour guide." He opened his arms wide.

He looked utterly masculine in his snug fitting gray t-shirt that read *I Shoot People with my Nikon,* and a pair of low hung jeans.

Was it the jeans or the thought of spending the day with him bringing fresh heat to her cheeks? "Oh, Logan, you really don't need to do that."

"Of course I do." His mouth turned down at the corners. "Unless…I hadn't considered you might have other plans. Or maybe you have too much work."

"It's not that."

"Good." Another flash of those perfect white teeth. "We'll leave in five minutes."

Chapter Twelve

"An Aston Martin? Is this yours?" Candace's blue eyes were bright with gratifying excitement.

Logan pulled the car from the garage, and parked it in the forecourt. It gleamed, gunmetal gray, in the California sunshine. "Got the registration to prove it. Want to drive?" He dangled the keys on his pointer finger.

"No, thanks. I'll just enjoy the ride."

Logan grinned and swallowed the reply her words had brought rushing to mind. He opened the passenger door and waited for her to settle into the leather seat before walking around to the driver's side.

In a matter of minutes, they purred along Highway 28, Lake Tahoe peeking in and out of view through the lush foliage.

"I always thought of Tahoe as a ski destination. But I might actually prefer the summer here. It's absolutely breathtaking. All these gorgeous flowers, with the ice-capped mountains as their backdrop, and all that sparkling blue below." Candace turned her gaze on Logan briefly before resuming her study of the landscape.

Speaking of sparkling blue.

"This road loops around the entire lake, doesn't it?"

"Yep. Seventy-two miles, approximately." Logan's

attention shifted between her profile and the road. "And I agree. The view is breathtaking."

He hadn't intended to take her on an outing this afternoon. But the day had ticked by without Candace putting in even a cursory appearance, and he'd found himself looking for any pretext to knock on her door.

Sightseeing had seemed like a perfectly reasonable excuse. The more he thought about it, the more he became convinced Eric would want him to familiarize Candace with the area.

"I've heard how scenic this drive is, but probably wouldn't have ventured out on my own. This is really great of you."

He gave her a questioning look.

"I'm horrible with directions."

He chuckled. "It's a circle. You can't get lost."

"Can't I?" Candace smiled wryly.

"Then it's especially lucky I'm the navigator today, since we're going to venture off the beaten path."

"Really? I love adventures."

Logan felt his lips curve up in a contented grin. Damn but he enjoyed her company.

A few minutes later, he took the exit ramp leading to Highway 89. "Ever been to a real mining town?"

"Not even a fake one," Candace said with mock seriousness.

"You're in for a treat." Logan paused. "So. How's Rudy? I assume you spoke to him this morning. Or last night. Or both." He was rambling. He hadn't even meant to broach the subject, and now he wished he'd kept his mouth shut.

"Rudy's fine," she said with a musical laugh.

"Really?" The thought irritated him for some

reason. He cast her a sideways glance in time to see her bite her bottom lip.

"No. Not really. Not as of two nights ago. I thought it would be easier that way."

His ire vanished in flash. In fact, he felt downright pleased she wasn't communicating with her ex. Especially after last night. Not that last night encompassed anything other than his own fantastic imagination.

"Eric called last night but I didn't check my voicemail till this morning after my shower."

A mental image of Candace, naked and dripping flashed before his eyes. He cleared his throat. "Oh?"

"I wish I'd returned his call last night. Now it'll be impossible to reach him, except by email."

Logan nodded sagely though he had no idea why she thought Eric wouldn't take her calls.

"That European writing conference." She shook her head in dismay.

"Right," Logan uttered knowingly. He hadn't had a clue about the conference. He hadn't spoken to Eric since receiving his call double checking Logan would be leaving Tahoe on schedule, and warning him off Candace.

Logan took the *Donner Pass Road* exit and turned right toward the main drag of Truckee. A few minutes later, he pulled into a parking spot under a familiar red and white marquee.

"*Wild Cherries Coffee House.* How did you find this place?" Candace eyed the building's simple stained wood siding and the cluster of people with their untethered dogs patronizing the small, sunlit patio.

"Early one morning on my way to hitting the

slopes. Do you ski? Hold that thought." He jogged around the car to open Candace's door.

She smiled and allowed him to help her out of the bucket seat. "Thanks."

Her grip was surprisingly firm, while her skin was as silky smooth as his false memories.

They started for the shop entrance. "Okay, so back to my question."

"I skied every year with my folks. Even through college. But then things changed, and life got too busy."

He swung open the café door and was greeted by the smell of freshly roasted coffee and toasted bread. He stood aside for Candace to enter.

"Too busy to ski?" he asked in mock horror, even though he knew the feeling all too well. The last two years had felt like a marathon photo shoot of a party that never ended. Something he hadn't realized was wearing on him until his recent leave-of-absence from the magazine.

"I know. It's crazy. Seeing the mountains makes me want to ski *yesterday*." She inclined her head toward the blackboard menu. "What do you suggest?"

He looked down at her and one corner of his mouth kicked up. He could think of a couple things. Once again, Eric's off-limits warning chimed in his brain. "How about I order for us?"

"Hmm," she answered noncommittally.

Logan sent Candace a devilish grin. "Trust me?"

Chapter Thirteen

The girl behind the counter did a double-take when she spotted Logan. Candace slid Logan a covert glance to see if he noticed. He hadn't. The man was utterly oblivious to his effect on women. She hid a grin at the girl's slack jawed, wide-eyed stare. Nice to know she wasn't alone in her fascination with the man's…everything.

"Hi," the girl said, never taking her eyes off of him. "What can I do, I mean, get for you?"

Logan shot the cashier a lazy smile as he leaned over the counter to rest on his elbows. "What looks good today, Lisa?" he asked in that velvet-soft voice.

Lisa fingered her nametag and giggled.

Maybe he wasn't *totally* oblivious.

"You have any of those turkey paninis left back there?"

The girl giggled again. "Sure."

"My friend and I'll each have one, plus one medium latte, and one small black coffee, please."

"I'll bring it right out," she answered with her teenaged attempt at a sultry smile. The girl sashayed to the kitchen.

"I see your effect on women is universal." She hadn't meant to say that aloud. She could've bit out her own tongue.

Logan didn't respond.

When he put his hand on her lower back and led her to an empty table on the patio, she decided he hadn't heard her quip, and she was home free.

He pulled out a chair, waiting for her to settle before seating himself. "I think there's a compliment in there somewhere. Unless I misunderstood." His mouth curved in a grin, and her brief discomfort vanished.

"I know you'll find this shocking, Logan, seeing as how you're so hideous, but I think our little cashier has the hots for you."

He opened his mouth to reply, then closed it with a snap. Was that a red flush staining his cheeks? If Candace didn't know better, she'd think she'd flummoxed him.

Seconds later the cashier appeared with their drinks.

"Which is which?" Candace asked after she left.

"The latte's for you, the *negro para mi.*"

"How'd you know I like lattes?"

He shrugged. "Just a guess. You look like a sweet-latte kinda girl."

"I see." Candace added a couple of packets of raw sugar to the cup then took a cautious sip. "Delicious. I needed it, too. I never had breakfast this morning."

"You should've said something. I would've fed you long before now. Breakfast's the most important meal of the day."

"Yeah, yeah. So. Your shirt?"

Logan angled his head to read the words aloud. "I shoot people with my Nikon." He raised his eyes, shrugged, and sipped his coffee.

"You don't like to talk about your work."

"Why do you say that?"

Candace gave him a *Come. On.* look.

Logan chuckled softly, and gave a brief nod.

"Are you any good?"

"Some people say so."

"What sort of photography do you do?"

"It varies. Mostly magazine stuff, these days."

"I see." She'd never met a man so reticent about discussing his work. His life for that matter. Most men couldn't talk enough about themselves.

Lunch arrived. The sandwich was delicious, but Candace refrained from telling him what a great job he'd done ordering. She felt almost like—if she kept complimenting him—he might get the wrong idea. *Or the right one.*

"I always had an interest in the arts. Both Luke and I did," Logan all but blurted.

Stunned by his outburst, Candace stared into his turquoise eyes and nodded.

"As we got a little older, Luke leaned toward painting: landscapes and architecture. I always had an interest in photography—from variations of light to portraits. But we both had an undeniable passion for the arts. My brother was making a real name for himself. Before he died, two New York art galleries were vying for his work."

"New York? For some reason I had the impression you both lived in San Francisco."

Logan's gaze dropped to his coffee. "We did. Luke was moving to New York when…" He shook his head like he was brushing off a bad memory. "What was I saying before that?"

"That you always had an interest in photography?"

"Right. Mind if we continue this conversation

79

while we walk?" Logan reached into his back pocket and withdrew his wallet. He tossed a generous tip on the table then rose and pulled her chair from the table.

It had been a long time since she'd been the focus of a gentleman's pampering. Opening doors, pulling out chairs, ordering for her. She'd forgotten how much she liked it. She pictured Roger running around the car to open the door for her. Maybe in the beginning...she couldn't be sure though.

They started down the sidewalk and Candace remained quiet, hoping he'd resume their conversation.

The painted store fronts revealed an eclectic mix of modern and old, a unique blending of Victorian England and Western ghost town. "Truckee, huh? I love this place."

"Me too." He smiled down at her.

She decided he needed some prodding after all. "You were saying you had a natural passion for art?"

One corner of his mouth curved in wry amusement.

"No one ever said I was patient. Or subtle."

"I'd never have guessed."

"Did you major in photography? Um, that is..." Maybe she shouldn't assume he went to college. Many artsy types opted not to.

"Yes, I majored in photography," he said, reading her mind. "I did a lot of black and whites. I always thought I'd be a serious artist, like Ansel Adams, only with a more political bent."

"Used to? What do you mean—aren't you a professional photographer?"

"Let's just say snapping photos of rockers for *Rolling Stone Magazine* isn't my idea of the height of intellectualism or art."

Her mouth fell open and her feet refused to take another step. "Wow. Really? *Rolling Stone?*"

"Ye-es," he said slowly, as if he already regretted revealing that much.

"For how long?"

Logan shrugged. "Somewhere around five years now."

"Five years. You must have met some amazing artists."

"After a while the faces all look the same."

"So what does a photographer have to do to land a job at *Rolling Stone?*"

He slanted her a look. "I can see I won't get any peace until I satisfy your curiosity."

She nodded.

"It's not magic, and really not all that interesting."

"Mm hmm."

He rolled his eyes heavenward as if searching for inspiration, and took her arm, propelling them into forward motion again. "Let's see. You major in photography with the aim of becoming a great artist whose bird's eye view might change the world. At around eighteen, you get lucky, and one of your photos wins several photography contests, which culminates in the piece getting hung in a hot San Francisco gallery, where you meet Annie Leibowitz."

Candace put a hand over her heart. "Really—you met her?"

Logan's smile actually met his eyes. "An incredible artist. Incredible human being."

"I agree. Go on."

He sighed. "You work your butt off as a freelance photographer looking for the next great shot to sell to

Vanity Fair. All the while you plan your move to a third world country or a war zone where you can take photos that might actually change peoples' lives. Then something happens that makes you realize you can't change anything." He finished on a rough note.

Candace waited.

When next he spoke, his tone was flat, void of even a speck of emotion. "You sell a photo to *Rolling Stone* that gets Ms. Leibowitz's attention, who just so happens to remember you, and when she pulls strings to get you an interview with the magazine editor, you get a job offer—and take it."

"That's it?" Candace asked dryly, her brow arched.

"That's it," Logan replied matter-of-factly.

"Nothing magical about it, you say. Oddly enough, I agree with you. Other than meeting Annie Leibowitz, that is. To me it sounds like your talent and hard work got you where you are. And why do you think you have to put yourself in mortal danger to change lives or produce art? *Rolling Stone Magazine* does plenty of socially relevant articles."

"Candace?" Logan draped an arm around her shoulders and smiled lazily down at her.

She stared into his sea-blue eyes for a timeless moment before realizing she hadn't responded. She cleared her throat. "Yes?"

"Let me know if you want to stop at any of these shops."

She laughed aloud. "Don't think I won't be grilling you for details about some of your assignments."

They'd been walking in the shade of the store awnings, and without Logan's story to distract her, Candace realized the mountain breeze had turned chilly.

She signaled for Logan to stop while she tightened the sash of her long cardigan.

Logan's gaze rose from the knot at her waistline to the v-neck of her dress. He stepped close, grasping her sweater lapels and pulling them around her neck. "You should've told me you were cold," he said in a whiskey-gruff voice. "You want to head back?"

To Candace, it appeared his focus never left the vicinity of her cleavage, igniting a coil of heat low in her belly. Of course, she was imaging things. *Imagining? Or wishing?*

"I'm fine," she said in a rush, starting forward. Reflexively she turned into the open doorway of the next shop. "I want to try this one." Belatedly, she glanced overhead at the marquis. *Truckee Mountaineer*.

"No, not cold at all. Just looking for snowshoes," Logan said, dryly.

Better he think her cold than know standing toe to toe with him was turning her insides to melted wax. "Smarty pants."

Before he could reply, the store clerk, a twenty-something year old approached. He smiled at Candace, tossing his long hair slightly to clear a path for his eyes. "Can I help you?"

"Just looking, thanks." Candace replied.

The clerk fell into step beside her. "You're not from around here, are you?"

"No. Florida."

"I didn't think so. Visiting long?" He flashed her a bright, hopeful smile.

Before Candace could reply, Logan crowded into the narrow aisle flanking her other side. He wrapped his arm around her waist and fitted her body to his. "We're here for another month. Any suggestions for a romantic dinner spot?"

The clerk's twinkling gaze swept from Candace's face to Logan's. His grin disappeared, replaced by a slack jawed gape. "I'll think about it and let you know what I come up with, sir. Uh…let me know if I can help you find anything." Then he made himself scarce.

Confused, Candace studied Logan.

He stared after the clerk, a menacing, wolfish grin on his face.

He had run the poor guy off. Why? And why hadn't Logan's hold on her relaxed? He must've sworn an oath of protection to Eric. Better to focus on that, rather than how her breast tingled where it met Logan's hard chest.

She tilted her head and looked into Logan's eyes. In the florescent lighting, his irises shimmered a cacophony of blues, like the sea before a storm.

Candace batted her eyelids at him and drawled, "Are you my personal knight? Or have I just inherited a big brother?"

As he looked down at her, the corners of his mouth softened, curving up in a slight smile. "Just looking after you. For Eric."

Just as she thought. Candace looked over her shoulder. No sign of the hapless clerk. "Poor kid."

Logan raised his hands to her shoulders and turned her toward the door. "That poor kid looked like he wanted to eat you for dinner." He urged her outside.

"I have no idea where you men come up with these things."

"I guess a knockout like you gets hit on constantly."

Candace flushed in surprise and undeniable pleasure. "I think there's a compliment in there somewhere," she said, aping his earlier comment.

"Definitely."

They started back toward the car. Logan took her hand, entwining his fingers with hers. His hand was warm, his fingers slightly calloused, his grip firm.

Candace gave herself a mental shake. They were strolling down a lovely street and he was holding her hand. And he'd all but chased the cute sales clerk away. What had he said earlier? Looking after her for Eric.

Now if only *she* could remember that simple fact.

Candace gave Logan what she hoped passed for a sisterly smile.

The slow, sensual smile he gave in response didn't bring to mind any sisterly feelings, and he sure didn't look like any brother she'd imagined.

At the parking lot, he released her hand and dug keys from his jeans pocket.

"Where to now?" Candace asked, breathless. She could still feel the warmth of his palm against hers.

"Unfortunately, to the house." Logan narrowed his eyes at the sky. "I had wanted to show you one more area—but it's an outdoors thing and it looks like we might be in for a storm." He flicked a glance over her face and frowned. "Ah, Candace," he said gently. "What happened?"

"What do you mean?" She wrapped her arms around herself.

"Just now I mentioned a storm and you tense like you're ducking a punch. Last night you jumped at what you thought was lightning. You said when you were a child, something happened. Something that made you…" He faltered, searching for the right words.

"You want to know what caused my irrational fear of electrical storms?" Her mouth twisted in a self-deprecating smirk.

Logan shook his head and looked away. "I shouldn't have asked such a personal question." He placed his hand on her lower back, guiding her toward the car. "It's none of my business. It's just, I can't seem to help wanting to know you."

Candace blinked in surprise. Something sweet and poignant bloomed inside her as she realized his words expressed exactly how she felt about *him*.

She stared straight ahead and forced her mind back to that terrible day she didn't like to think about, but still remembered like it was yesterday. "When I was nine I went to the golf course with my father. He was—is—a pretty skilled golfer and he wanted his only child to know the game as well. A storm caught us by surprise, but Dad refused to quit. He wanted to finish all the holes. He—a lightning bolt struck him and put him into cardiac arrest. He almost died and I"—she shrugged helplessly—"didn't know what to do."

"Damn," Logan whispered. "Poor baby."

"Mother didn't think so. She used to—" Candace shook her head. "Never mind. I don't know why I'm getting into all this."

"Because I asked you to. I want you to," Logan said softly.

They'd reached the car, but Logan seemed disinclined to unlock the doors.

"It's no big deal. It's just, I think—*know*—my mother blamed me for what happened. Later, when she realized I had developed my little problem, she told me it was my guilt manifesting itself. She said when I faced what I'd done, I'd get over my irrational fears."

Logan's mouth turned grim. "She told you that? Where'd she get that idea—Dr. Spock?" He pressed the auto unlock button on the remote and the sound of both doors' locks rising in unison seemed an exclamation point for his words.

Logan opened her door, his face set.

The leather made a sh-shing sound as she slid into the bucket seat. She waited, but he didn't close her door. Instead, he leaned in slightly, hand on the chrome frame.

Candace resisted turning her face to meet his gaze as long as she could, but her crumbling will proved no match for his magnetic stare. She locked eyes with his, and sucked in a breath as an internal riptide pulled her into an eddy of unchartered emotion.

"Don't worry, sweetheart. If it storms tonight, I'll take care of you."

"I'll be okay."

"I'll take care of you," he repeated, his voice close to a whisper.

She gave a small smile and nodded.

He grinned, tapped the doorframe with his knuckles, and closed the door.

They lapsed into a comfortable silence on the drive back, as if they'd known each other for years and words weren't necessary. Feeling relaxed and pampered, Candace snuggled into the rich leather seat and drank in the view of the mountainside at dusk. Ominous, untamed, beautiful.

After a while she turned to gaze at Logan's profile. One tanned forearm rested easily on the steering wheel, the other settled over the stick shift inches from her upper thigh. Long, denim covered legs stretched out in front of him in an almost leisurely sprawl. It struck her she couldn't remember ever feeling so utterly feminine, and so totally safe, in a man's presence. Being with Logan felt so…*right.*

The peace inside her snapped in the face of her inappropriate affection for a man she hardly knew. A man involved with one of her best friends—who also happened to be a man. She dragged her gaze away, pinching her eyes closed and fisting her hands in her lap. What in the world was wrong with her?

"Everything all right?" Logan's words pierced the silence. She shot him a look and saw his eyes flicking over her clenched hands. Did the man miss nothing?

She forced her hands to unfurl. "Just thinking." *Over thinking.* So she enjoyed his company. That was no crime. Besides, it was already Wednesday and he'd be leaving sometime this weekend. How much trouble could she possibly get into?

Chapter Fourteen

From the corner of his eye, Logan studied Candace. "Just thinking," she'd said. He weighed the options, neither of which he liked. Either he'd upset her by dredging up her childhood trauma, or she was contemplating *Roger*.

He cleared his throat. "I'm sorry."

Even before she spoke, the snap of her head told him he'd surprised her. "For what?"

"For bringing up your father's accident."

"Oh, that." She waved a dismissive hand. "Please don't apologize. I wouldn't have told you if I hadn't wanted to. Anyway, I wasn't thinking about that."

Okay. So that left Roger. Somehow her thinking about her ex didn't sit well with him. He tamped down a surge of...what—jealousy? Nah. More like protectiveness. "Want to share?"

"Nothing in particular. The scenery. Mostly."

Right. The scenery. That was why she'd been white knuckling it a few minutes ago. Although—he shot her a sidelong glance—she seemed fine now, studying the aforementioned scenery, arms folded under perfect breasts.

Not that he'd noticed her breasts. Much. *Pig.*

As if responding to his thoughts, Candace unfolded her arms and wrapped them around the headrest of her seat. Her breasts pressed forward, enticingly.

Eyes on the road, Shaw.

"Let's see," Candace mused. "So far you've cooked me dinner, washed up, driven me around the lake, taken me to lunch, and shown me Truckee."

"Don't forget the mugging."

"Okay." She laughed. "Not your best moment." She sighed. "Still. I want to do something for you. How about tonight I cook?"

Something like warm honey flowed through his veins. "That sounds like a deal."

"What do you fancy?"

Logan took his time answering, as he had to first banish the highly sexual response that sprang to mind. Her face was decidedly flushed. Had she guessed the direction of his thoughts? "Pasta?"

"Perfecto." Candace pinched her pointer finger and her thumb together like an Italian chef. "But, Logan?"

"Yes?"

"Can we stop at the grocery?"

The call from his editor came as they waited in the checkout line. "Hold on a minute, Alex." Logan tucked the phone under his chin, pulled his wallet from his back pocket, retrieved his debit card, and tried to force it into Candace's hand.

She shook her head, crossing her arms and tucking her fingers under her armpits.

After a futile attempt to give the cashier his card, he sent Candace an ominous look that said he'd deal with her later and exited the store. "Logan here."

"Thanks for taking the call, Logan. I wasn't sure you would."

"My beef isn't with you, Alex. I'd never screen my favorite editor's calls."

"Good to know, charmer."

Hearing the smile in her voice caused a nostalgic half smile to lift a corner of his mouth. "Why the call?"

"I'd almost forgotten how direct you are."

"I find the direct approach works best, most of the time."

She snorted.

They both knew he was referring to Julie Braun, the copy-editor turned photographer turned stalker that landed him here, on indefinite leave.

"She's gone, Logan. Larry Braun came in two days ago and said he'd convinced her to check herself into a clinic."

"O-kay." He drew out the word. "And you thought I'd want to know, precisely why? Thought maybe I'd want to send flowers and a card?"

Candace stepped through the automatic sliding doors carrying two sacks of groceries. He grabbed them both with one hand and they fell into step beside each other. *My editor,* he mouthed to her.

She nodded.

"Very funny. I think you're being deliberately dense."

"Let's assume I'm not and you have to spell out the relevance of…" he glanced at Candace, "…this news flash."

"You can come back now, and right away. Larry Braun's on board. He's willing to forget the whole incident."

"I see."

"How soon can you be in New York? I have an assignment with your name all over it. It's—"

"Hold it, Alex. I'm not sure I'm coming back."

Out of his peripheral vision he saw Candace's head snap toward him.

"What? I thought I'd talked some sense into you when we agreed you'd take a leave rather than quit."

Candace was still staring at him, wide-eyed and mouth agape.

"I'm sorry. I've thought a lot about this over the last month."

"And? What are your plans, Logan?"

"Nothing concrete yet."

"Then let's just leave your imminent return on the table for now. Okay? I'm banking on the hope you'll come to your senses." Taking his silence as acquiescence, she went on. "How about we talk again in another few weeks? After you've had a chance to think about it some more. And Logan? Promise you will think about it?"

"Word of honor."

"And you never break a promise," she said before hanging up.

Logan slid his phone in his back pocket and popped the trunk. He placed the bags inside and closed it, all the while aware of Candace pinning him with her stare.

He sighed and walked to her side of the car. He swung the door open and gestured for her to climb in.

"Let me guess." She tucked her skirt under her legs as she sat. "You don't want to talk about it." She flashed him an impish grin.

He burst out laughing and closed the door.

After he put the car in reverse he said, "There's not much to tell. My editor asked me to return to my old position. I declined."

Candace gave him a speculative look. "Your leave happened as a result of something, and now that something's changed?"

She was the most damnably perceptive woman he'd ever known. "Anyone ever tell you you should've been a reporter?"

Her blue eyes twinkled with mischief and all the tension in him fled.

"I have no idea what you mean."

"Mm hmm." He eased his Aston into the flow of traffic.

"So?"

"I don't want to bore you with the details. Let's just say you're right, and the main catalyst behind my decision to take a leave is no longer an issue." That was one way to put it.

"But you don't want to go back?"

"Not now. I didn't ask for this crossroad in my life." *Strictly speaking that wasn't exactly true,* "but now that I've reached it, I'm re-examining my goals."

"That sounds very wise."

Her praise warmed him from the inside out. His gaze slid to her face, seeking...something he couldn't name. Their eyes locked for an eternal moment before he forced his focus back to the road. He had no business imagining things, *wanting* things from Candace he couldn't be trusted to reciprocate.

****

Logan followed Candace from the dining room into the kitchen carrying the serving platter and their empty plates.

"I still say you aren't supposed to have any cleanup duty," Candace said over her shoulder. She grabbed the man-sized apron off the wall hook as she passed and slipped the strap over her head. The garment all but covered her flowered halter dress.

"Tell you what, you get started on the dishes and I'll work on the sundaes."

"Deal."

"I still can't get over what a fabulous cook you are. You make my efforts look amateur. Which they are."

"Methinks you're fishing. You're no slouch." Candace slanted Logan a glance as he set their dinner plates on the counter beside the oversized copper sink.

Logan flashed a cocky smile. "Maybe I am. Fishing, that is."

Candace sent him a chiding grin as she wrapped the apron strings around her waist to tie them in the front. She'd made lemon chicken and pasta, using pre-made penne from the freezer section, but she'd created the sauce from scratch. A little olive oil, a little garlic and herbs, some sun dried tomatoes, et voilà. The prep work had taken some time, but Logan's raves of delight had made the effort well worth it.

Waiting for the water to warm, she craned around to eye Logan's V-shaped back as he made his way to the refrigerator. As if sensing her scrutiny, he glanced over his shoulder and raised a querulous brow.

She jerked around to face the sink. "A few minutes ago you said you were stuffed," she murmured, mostly for something to say.

"Candace," Logan drawled.

"Mmm?" When he didn't answer immediately, she turned.

He looked like a damned cover model again, standing there, one corner of his sexy mouth quirked in a grin. He gave a slow wink, and reached for the freezer handle. "There's always room for dessert."

Chapter Fifteen

Candace faced the sink and pinched her eyes closed as liquid heat pooled low in her belly. Inside she vibrated like a woman who'd been thoroughly, expertly kissed, and he'd never laid a finger on her. She'd met attractive men before, and had managed to control her libido perfectly well. *Always.* Till now.

Less than a week in the company of the most ineligible man on the planet and she was a walking sex-powder keg, about to go off.

Candace gritted her teeth and forced attention on the dirty dishes. While she scraped the plates, Logan hummed and rustled in the cupboards.

She absolutely refused to notice his smoky baritone.

Using more force than necessary, Candace squirted dishwashing soap into the copper basin and aimed the water sprayer onto the cleanser. Droplets of sudsy water ricocheted into her face, and on instinct, she stepped back.

"Candace, do you like—"

Logan's voice, so unexpectedly close to her ear had her spinning around, sprayer in hand. In a nanosecond she released the lever, cutting off the water. But the damage had been done.

Logan stood, mouth agape, eyes closed, water dripping from his thick black lashes and down his nose onto his black t-shirt. The words *Don't be Negative,* printed under an unraveling roll of film, clung to his impressive chest. He brought one hand to his face and swiped before opening his eyes.

A giggle escaped Candace's lips. She clamped her free hand over her mouth.

"You think this is funny, do you?" Logan asked, calm and deliberate.

Candace stared, wide-eyed, hand still covering her mouth, and nodded.

"I see." He looked down at his hands and Candace realized he held a small glass pitcher filled with chocolate sauce.

She had the presence of mind to toss the sprayer in the sink. Putting her hands out in a plaintive gesture, she offered an apology—most likely belied by the merriment in her eyes. "S-sorry," she choked out, just barely containing her laughter. "You surprised me and—"

"Like this?" Logan dribbled warm chocolate on her bare upper arm.

Candace's mouth fell open.

Logan's lips twisted in a satisfied grin, but he wisely began a slow retreat.

"Yeah, you better run," she said in a mock threat. She scanned the kitchen for a weapon—and spotted it. A can of whipped cream.

Logan's gaze followed hers. Their eyes met for a timeless moment. Then they both lunged for the can.

Candace had the advantage, being closer, but Logan had the arm reach. Even so, she beat him to it by inches. "Ha HA!" She flicked the nozzle with her thumb.

Still armed with his chocolate, Logan fled the kitchen. "Now, Candace, be reasonable. We don't want to get sticky stuff all over Eric's living room."

Candace raced after him, but he was too fast and his height and athleticism gave him an unfair advantage. In one leap, Logan jumped over the back of leather couch to land in front of it.

Candace glared back and forth between the obstacle and her quarry.

"Candace?" Logan's blue-blue eyes twinkled. "Fair's fair, right? You shot me with the water, I got you with the chocolate."

"Mine was an accident," she replied.

She went left; he went right.

She went right; he went left.

"Look, I'm putting down the chocolate." His unblinking eyes locked with hers. Bending at the knees, he placed the pitcher on the coffee table behind him.

Undeterred, Candace shook the whipped cream can, arming her weapon, and narrowed her eyes menacingly.

"You know," Logan stared pointedly at her chest, "you look adorable with all that chocolate dripping off you."

Frowning, she peered down the front of her apron. She didn't see any chocolate.

Candace yelped as Logan flew over the couch. Before she knew what was happening, he'd grabbed the can and grasped her wrists, holding them behind her back with one hand. He smiled triumphantly as he scooped her feet from under her with one deft slip of his bare foot. Together they tumbled over the back of the couch, landing on the cushions in a heap.

Logan lay on top of her. The cocky smile told her he wasn't in any hurry to get off, either.

She'd see about that. Neither spoke, but the sound of her labored breathing filled the air as Candace struggled to free her hands while simultaneously bucking her hips and torso against Logan's weight. Her best efforts couldn't budge him, but she wasn't giving up.

At least Logan was breathing hard now, too, and his smile seemed a little strained.

"Remember what I told you? You really need to take some self-defense classes. I could teach you," he said, his tone taunting.

She tried and failed to turn her grin into a frown as she twisted beneath him. "Let. Me. Go," she gasped between giggles.

"I wouldn't do that," he said in a singsong voice.

She aimed a head-butt at his chest and missed.

"You asked for it." He pressed the nozzle once, and following a *shh* sound, a dollop of cream landed on the tip of her nose.

Candace stared at him in stunned silence.

Logan eyed his handiwork with satisfaction, before throwing his head back to roar with laughter.

Damn the man. His laughter proved contagious. Candace laughed so hard she couldn't breathe for several seconds. But as soon as she had her bout of hilarity under control, she started bucking again.

"Ah ah," Logan said, playfully warning her. This time he held the cream threateningly over her lips. "Give up?"

"Never."

He shook his head piteously and pressed the

nozzle, this time a bit longer. *Shhhhhh.*

Candace turned her head side to side, squeezing her eyes closed, but there was no avoiding the creamy sweetness covering her lips. With a moan she stilled, licking one corner of her mouth, then the other. She peeked at Logan's handsome face, expecting to see his eyes brilliant with laughter.

But the laughter was gone. His turquoise eyes had darkened to a smoldering blue, intent on one thing. Her mouth. His forearm rested against the back of the couch. The can dangled in his hand. A pregnant moment passed during which Logan's unblinking gaze never strayed. Was it her imagination, or did his breathing grow more ragged with each passing second?

The area between her legs responded with a will of its own, filling with a heavy, aching need. Unable to stop herself, she relaxed her thighs allowing them to fall open just a touch.

Far from flinging himself off of her in disgust, Logan's body seemed to settle more surely onto hers, his hips nestling more snugly. Heat emanated from him in waves. Candace's skin burned wherever their bodies met. With every breath he took, his chiseled chest grazed the tips of her breasts sending tiny electric shocks through her. She barely restrained herself from arching beneath him to bring more of him into contact with more of her.

His face drew closer. His lids lowered to half mast and his breaths came in hot little puffs, almost as if…God, was he as turned on as she was?

One way to find out.

She was so going to hell for this.

She parted her lips, and eased the tip of her tongue

from her mouth. Slowly, channeling as much sex kitten as she could muster, she moistened her upper lip. At Logan's hissed intake of breath, her heart threatened to burst through her ribs.

Logan tossed the can over her head with a dismissive flick of his wrist. It landed on the cushions with a soft thud and rolled to the carpet. The rich scent of chocolate and vanilla reached her nostrils as he touched his fingertips to her cheek, all the while staring at her with the concentration of a neurosurgeon. With one finger he scooped the whipped cream on her face. He slipped the cream-covered finger into her mouth, probing gently into the slick, soft underside of her lips, urging her to suck.

She did.

Logan's expression grew pained. He lowered himself until his lips were almost touching hers.

Candace thought she might burst into flames at any moment. She couldn't think, couldn't concentrate beyond the urgency of her all-consuming need. She bit back a moan.

"Candace," Logan rasped. "I'm—"

The sound of spilling water—lots of it—cut off his words. Abruptly he released her wrists, planted his palms on either side of her and pressed himself upward. He peered over the couch toward the kitchen and held himself perfectly still, listening with the keen concentration of a watch dog on high alert.

A half second later Logan closed his eyes briefly, blew air out of his cheeks, and hoisted himself off her. He padded toward the kitchen.

With her freedom restored, reality crashed back with the force of a tidal wave. This was Logan—Eric's

Logan—and she was out of her mind. Candace hefted herself off the couch and went in search of the source of her lunacy.

She arrived in time to see Logan shutting off the faucet. The cascade of water over the sink's beveled granite edge, slowed to a trickle.

Candace took in both Logan's rigid back, and the disaster in dumb silence. Considering what was about to occur on the couch, whereby she would surely have made a total fool of herself—it was a timely disaster.

"I'll get a mop and bucket." Logan turned toward the utility closet without raising his eyes.

"I thought I'd turned it off," Candace offered weakly.

"Uh huh." He disappeared into the closet.

The house phone rang as Logan reappeared. A glance at the caller ID had her mouth curving in a humorless smile. With dread churning in her gut she took the cordless phone from its cradle. "*Eric*," she mouthed to Logan. "Hello, stranger," she said with forced brightness.

"Hi, beautiful."

She picked up some of the towels Logan had set on the kitchen island and squatted. As she sopped up the water, she leaned forward so a wall of hair shielded her face from Logan—not that he was looking at her. All his attention seemed focused on the damned mop.

"What's that noise? Why are you breathing hard? Is everything okay?"

"I had a little spill," she answered. "I'm just wiping it up."

"I see. I think. But everything's all right? It seems like I haven't talked to you in a year."

"I know." Candace tried to muster some enthusiasm in her tone. She caught the phone between her head and shoulder, freeing her hands to squeeze several soaked towels into the bucket. "We've been playing phone tag. Where are you?"

"Paris. This call is going to cost me a fortune—but I wanted to hear for myself you'd made it to the house from the airport and were keeping it together."

Between the two of them, the bulk of the water had been absorbed and with a grunt and a wave Logan gestured for Candace to leave the rest to him. She sniffed at the brusque dismissal, rose and turned her back to him.

"Yes, I'm good. Great, in fact. Work's going well. The place is great. The weather's been perfect."

"How's lover boy?"

Candace blanched. "Who?"

"Roger?"

Candace folded over with relief.

Unfortunately, Eric noticed her hesitation. "You haven't broken your promise, have you?" he asked sharply. "You didn't let on where you're staying?"

"No!" she answered with a bit too much verve. She cleared her throat and tried again. "No. I haven't and I won't. He's pretty bitter about it, though."

"Screw him."

That made her smile for real. "How's your trip going?"

"The conference is great. Lots of prospective clients and…prospectives, if you know what I mean."

Candace frowned and looked at Logan. She hoped he couldn't hear Eric. "Eric," she said in a warning tone.

"I can't hear you, love. What'd you say?"

"Nothing important."

"I'm proud of you, sweetheart. I know it's difficult for you to be a hard ass, even when people deserve it."

"I can be a bitch," she defended.

Eric's laughter rang over the line simultaneously with Logan's soft chuckle behind her.

"I know, darling. Speaking of being a bitch, what are you going do about those emails he sent you?"

Her brows knitted. "Jenna told you about those?"

"I'd have canned her if she hadn't."

"I think they were just a fluke. More importantly, I don't think they're from Roger."

"Please. Who else could it be? And humor me by telling me one more time you're absolutely sure you didn't leave your ex any clue as to where you are."

"Positive."

"Good. Assuming he is the lunatic behind those threats, they're probably nothing but hot air. It's creepy though. Promise you'll be careful?"

"I'm always careful."

"I can't argue that, so I suppose that'll have to do. You getting work done?"

"Yes, mother. In fact, I expect to be done slightly ahead of schedule."

"That's my girl. Listen, if anything comes up, more threats, writer's block, whatever, email me. Otherwise I'll plan on calling when I'm back in the states."

Candace agreed and was about to say goodbye when Eric said, "You haven't mentioned Logan."

"Logan?" she repeated, her voice coming out more like a squeak.

"Tall, brooding, extremely good looking. Anyone

like that roaming around?"

"Oh." Candace forced a laugh. "Him. Yes. He's very…nice." Candace felt heat flood her face.

"He better be. Is he behaving?"

Behaving? "Oh he's been great," she said, her speech coming too fast. "He took me around Truckee, he showed me the grocery store, he…" *almost licked cream off my face.*

"Sounds like he's been a regular boy scout. Has he said anything about leaving?"

Candace didn't want to talk about Logan leaving. For that matter, she didn't want to talk about Logan, period. Especially not with him listening to her every word. "He's right here. Would you like to speak with him?"

"He's standing there—with you?" Eric sounded suspicious.

Oh, goodness had she given herself away?

"Bye, Eric. Love you. Thanks for calling." She took the phone from her ear. "Here." she thrust the receiver at Logan.

Logan scowled and pointed to the floor as if finishing mopping was the most important job in the world. Candace raised a brow and reached for the mop handle.

Logan smiled thinly and made the exchange. "Eric, how's it going in the old country?"

Candace wrung out the mop. Logan had tackled the worst of it; a good wipe down with a dry towel ought to do the trick. She picked up the bucket and carried it to the utility closet to dump into the sink. She returned in time to see Logan retreating to the living room, phone in hand. Evidently he didn't want her listening to his conversation.

She sighed and approached the sink to finish the dishes she'd been about to wash before… Her stomach twisted into a knot. Before she made out with Eric's boyfriend. What had she been thinking? What would Logan tell Eric? For that matter, should she confess herself?

Candace bit her lip and tackled the stack of plates beside the sink. In truth, nothing had actually happened. Maybe…maybe she was making a mountain out of a molehill. Imagining things. Maybe Logan hadn't been about to kiss her.

Logan was leaving this weekend. She would just have to avoid any potential sticky situations until then. Speaking of which. Candace grabbed the two bowls of melting ice cream Logan had dished out and dumped them into the sink.

Chapter Sixteen

Friday morning Logan awoke in a foul mood with a headache to match. He'd hardly slept a wink the last two nights, which explained the headache. But the bad temper had a root all its own.

Tomorrow was Saturday. The day he'd planned to leave. The day he promised Eric he would leave. And damn, but he didn't want to go.

Logan stalked to the shower and switched on the water. At least his not wanting to leave had nothing to do with Candace. He'd proven he could stay away from her. Look how he managed to entertain himself all day yesterday. Not popping in on her once. Not lounging at the pool in the hopes she'd come down. Even leaving for several hours. Granted, returning home to find evidence of her presence downstairs—the coffee pot cleaned and drying, a pool towel hanging on the drying rack, the organic peanut butter she'd bought slightly emptier than when he left—had thrown him off track. He'd almost marched up the stairs to bang on her door and...what—demand she come out and play? Instead, he poured himself into a tough workout downstairs, which eventually restored his self-control.

Not inviting her to eat dinner with him last night had been the hardest, but he'd managed, taking off for a local fish joint around seven where he enjoyed a perfectly cooked sea bass. Every last tasteless bite.

He turned his face into the streaming water still unable to believe he'd almost blown it two nights ago. What a moron. What had he been thinking, painting chocolate sauce on her and basically challenging her to a physical confrontation?

He grinned despite himself. He hadn't had that much fun in years. His smile faded as he remembered what had come after the fun. The feel of her soft body under his had been like sinking into heaven, especially to his groin. He'd had to force himself to stay still so she wouldn't notice the telling bulge in his jeans. He didn't know if he'd been successful on that front.

Logan stepped from the shower and scrubbed the fluffy white bath towel over his dripping body as if he could wipe the thought of those curves and her sensuous mouth, covered with whipped cream, from his mind. Dammit. He was hard again. He should never have touched her. He couldn't get the memory of her out of his head.

He pulled on a pair of black exercise shorts and running shoes. A long run ought to clear his head.

He opened the bedroom door.

Down the hall, Candace was closing hers. She had her hair pulled up in a ponytail, and wore a curve-hugging pair of black yoga shorts and a white exercise tank. He closed his eyes and breathed in the subtle, utterly feminine scent drifting from her side of the hall to his. Before he knew what he was doing, he heard himself ask, "Hey there. Looks like you're heading out for a run. I was just planning to do the same. Mind if I join you?"

****

"That was awesome. What a hill workout. I had no

idea you ran." Candace mopped her face with one of the hand towels they had left on the pool deck for their return.

Logan took a long drink from his aluminum water bottle. Candace watched his adam's apple bob, and tried not to follow the trickles of sweat coursing down his bare torso.

He flashed that glamorous smile and shrugged. "Like I said. I'm not a natural. I just bang out a few miles here and there to stay fit."

She slid him a look. "Mmm hmm."

"What?"

"Sand bagger."

"Who me?"

"Yeah, you. We just banged out, as you say, five miles, and you weren't even breathing hard."

He raised his brows at her, all amusement gone. Had her teasing struck a nerve? She opened her mouth to backpedal.

Logan cut her off. "You know what happened the last time someone called me that?"

She stared at him blankly.

"This."

The next thing she knew, Logan had her in his arms, off the ground, and he was moving like a freight train toward the pool.

Candace could only cling to him for dear life, while she held to one unalterable fact. No way was she going in alone.

They hit the water locked together and sank toward the bottom briefly before splitting apart to kick to the surface.

"I...don't believe you...did that!" Laughing

helplessly, Candace shook her head to clear the water out of her eyes.

Logan treaded water a foot away. His raucous laughter alone might have put her over the edge, but his Adonis good looks definitely did. He had no business looking like a cover model while she undoubtedly looked like a drowned rat.

She launched herself onto him with all her might. Hoisting herself off his shoulders, she aimed to dunk him. Logan didn't sink an inch, but she did manage to thrust her breasts into his face before sliding down his wall of a chest.

The contact felt way too good.

She decided to beat a hasty retreat.

"Oh, no you don't." Fast as a snake, he gripped her waist with both hands and maneuvered her like she weighed no more than a doll toward the shallow end of the pool. Once her rump hit the concrete wall, he released her. He did not retreat. Instead, he bracketed her body with his arms and leaned over her, nearly blinding her with his dazzling, victorious smile.

How could she not respond with an ear to ear grin?

As the moment stretched on, Logan's gaze flicked over her face, and slowly headed south. His leisurely study stalled at the general vicinity of her breasts. His smile faltered.

Oh, no. Just like that, her nipples hardened.

Logan's expression changed from something playful to…something that looked an awful lot like…the way a man looks at a woman he wants. Something hot pooled between her legs, even submerged in the cool water.

If he looked at her like that one second more, she'd

have no choice but to launch herself at him again, this time with a different purpose in mind.

Lucky for her, he did an abrupt backwards dive and swam like the devil toward the deep end.

Candace glanced down at herself. At her now see-through white running tank. At her clearly visible rose-colored nipples. Her face burned as she hoisted herself from the pool. Jeez. He hadn't been in lust. She'd embarrassed him.

Well, she was embarrassed, too, she thought in a huff. And it wasn't like she had carried *him* to the pool. Without a backward glance, Candace snatched a towel from a chair and stomped toward the house.

Logan reached her just as she gripped the knob, his large tanned hand covering hers. She couldn't bring herself to turn, just kept her eyes locked on their hands.

"Are you angry with me?"

Gooseflesh sprang up over her skin at his velvet soft tone. "No. I just want to get changed."

He stood behind her a few seconds more. The only sound was the drip of water from their clothes hitting the deck. Finally he removed his hand.

Candace opened the door to a blast of frigid air-conditioned air.

"Brrr." She snugged the towel tighter around her.

"Hey, you gonna ignore me all day again?"

Candace looked over her shoulder at him.

Logan had moved toward one of the deck chairs. He grabbed a towel and slung it around his neck. "I'm leaving tomorrow. I hoped you'd...I don't know. We can have lunch or hang at the pool. Or something. That is, if you're not scared." His mouth twisted into a crooked smile, and his eyes glittered with mischievous challenge.

Candace's irritation vanished. Palpable dismay took its place. "Tomorrow?" She cringed inwardly at her forlorn tone, then forced herself to brighten. "Scared? We'll see who's scared." She squinted in playful menace. "I've got to change since *someone* got me all wet. Then I have to eat something. I'm starved."

"I'll meet you in the kitchen in…fifteen minutes?"

"Ten."

"Deal."

Candace disappeared into the house. He waited a few minutes, giving her a good head start, before heading to his own room to change.

He was in serious trouble. When he was with her he felt happy, and always on the verge of laughter, and like he could just gobble her up. That was probably what prompted the big dumb move to dump her in the pool. That free, happy feeling she brought out in him.

That and her hot little body. He shook his head in self-disgust as he stepped into the shower for the second time that morning. Since when hadn't he been able to keep his hands off a woman?

He closed his eyes and let tepid water run over him. Damn, but she had nice breasts. When she pounced on him in the pool, she practically offered them to him on a platter. It all happened so fast he hadn't even realized he had an erection. That was when he made the second big dumb move, cornering her and getting up close and personal with those hard, pink nipples showing through her wet clothes. His throbbing erection had made itself known, then, loud and clear.

Just like now. Very deliberately, Logan turned the shower temperature to its coldest setting. Good thing he asked her to spend the rest of the day with him. A little self-torture never killed anyone, right?

Chapter Seventeen

Candace slipped on her swimsuit, a red halter with matching bikini bottoms that tied on either hip. She checked her body in the mirror and immediately chastised herself. *He likes men. He won't notice your body one way or another.*

Even so, she applied strawberry lip-gloss. Just for the SPF 30, of course. *Schmuck.*

What the heck. She searched her jewelry bag, choosing a set of diamond studs and matching pendant necklace. Tying a sheer sarong around her waist, she stepped into the hall. The ring of the cell phone from the bedside table drew her back into the room. Distracted and acting on autopilot, she pressed the answer button before reading the caller ID. She winced. "Hi, Roger."

"Hi, yourself. I'm surprised you answered."

She said nothing since she would have let the call go to voicemail if she'd been thinking straight.

"How are you, Candace?" he asked in a dull voice.

"Fine. Is something wrong?"

Silence.

"Roger?"

"What do you mean, is something wrong? My fiancée has disappeared from the face of the earth, leaving no indication of where she is. What isn't wrong? I'm going crazy without you, dammit."

She'd asked.

"Candace, where in God's name are you?"

She didn't respond. Her mind had gone to the acerbic, threatening emails telling her to go home now and implying knowledge of her whereabouts. Both Logan and Eric seemed convinced Roger had been the author. "Are you sure you have no idea where I am?" she drew out slowly.

He gave a bark of laughter. "Am I camped on your doorstep?"

If he was lying, he was convincing.

"Tell me where you are. I'll drive, fly, or swim—anything to give us a chance to work things out."

This time she didn't hesitate. "I can't."

"What is this can't? Why can't you? You're a free woman, aren't you? No one's holding a gun to your head, are they?"

"No. But…" She toyed with the pendant at her neck.

"Leaving's not going to make this work, babe."

Candace didn't want to explain, didn't want to talk to Roger, and certainly didn't want to hear him calling her babe. "Nothing is. Roger, I've been thinking. I—"

"Don't say another word. Just don't. You need time, fine. Take it. Just don't make a knee jerk reaction from…wherever you are. Don't forget the life we had together." His voice lowered. "Unless…there's someone else, isn't there?"

An image of Logan lying over her, whipped cream can in hand, flashed before her eyes. "Of course there isn't."

Roger blew out a long breath. "All right, then." He sounded pleased, and way too hopeful. "Candace, we have something good. We're a team. Promise me you'll think about that."

She ended the call feeling sick to her stomach, and, God help her, relieved. Relieved to be off the phone and free from worry that Roger might just happen to show up.

"You okay?"

Her head jerked up.

Logan leaned against the doorjamb, a bronzed god in low-hung swim trunks, arms crossed loosely over his chest.

How long had he been standing there? How much had he overheard? Her eyes met his and the sympathy she read in their blue depths told her he'd heard plenty. Candace's eyes welled with tears. Was it because she was realizing just how little her relationship with Roger meant after all this time? Or was it because of the man standing in her doorway? Her best friend's lover who had somehow found a place in her heart, and who would be leaving in the morning.

He crept into the room, as if any fast movement might cause her to bolt.

She swiped at her eyes. "I'm fine. And I'm not crying." A patently false statement, of course. "I just…" She shrugged.

The bed dipped as he sat beside her. Like it was the most natural thing in the world, he wrapped her in his arms, cradling her head on his shoulder. "Sweetheart." Logan smoothed a hand over her still-damp hair and down her back to settle at her waist. He locked eyes with her and brought his free hand up to caress her cheek. "I don't like seeing you cry," he whispered. "It does something to me."

And he was doing something to her. A combination of panic and pleasure swirled inside her. On instinct, Candace flattened her palms against the warm wall of his chest and tried to push away. Nothing happened— unless she wanted to count digging herself in deeper. Now she knew how good it felt to touch him.

"No you don't. Don't you ever let anyone take care of you?"

Candace closed her eyes. Was *that* why she was resisting his embrace? Or was she fighting another demon altogether? Part of her wanted to flee the room. Another part wanted nothing more than to turn into his arms and plaster herself onto him. Both were the wrong things to do, right? Ah, hell. She gave in and let him hold her.

She had to admit, being gentled by him felt like a little bit of heaven.

"There you go," he said in a low voice.

Candace didn't know how much time went by before Logan kissed the top of her head and leaned back to stare into her eyes. Before he spoke, he traced her cheek with his fingertips. "It might help to talk about it. Did he confess to sending the emails?"

Her insides quivered, quietly reacting to the intimacy of his tone, his touch, the honesty in his eyes. "Emails?"

"The ones where he told you to go home or else?"

She chuckled at his doggedness, grateful for something else on which to focus her attention. "Let's just say I'm more convinced than ever he isn't the culprit."

Logan gave her a skeptical frown. "Something's upset you."

117

She bit her lip. "I think…I think Eric was right. I'm not in love with Roger. I don't think I ever really was. And that makes me feel bad."

"Why should you feel bad, beautiful?" he asked, his gaze intent.

"Because I…" She shook her head. She needed to think. And she couldn't do it with this man looking at her so lovingly and touching her so intimately. She closed her eyes and smiled tremulously. "I know one thing."

"What's that?"

She slid off the bed, and onto her feet. "I'm starved."

Logan laughed and took one of her hands. He rose and started for the door. "Let's go, already. Were you planning on keeping me here all day?"

"Brat."

"The worst." He dragged her into the hall.

Chapter Eighteen

Logan worked the kitchen like a professional line-order cook, Candace decided as she finished her frittata. "I don't think I'll need to eat again for a week. I certainly can't sit by the pool now. Not unless I put on a one-piece."

Logan smiled and took his time eyeing her up and down. Candace somehow managed not to squirm under his scrutiny. "They're overrated. And you look great."

One corner of her mouth turned up. "Thank you, Mr. Warlock. Are you trying to fatten me up to have me for your supper?"

Logan's eyes crinkled at the corners. "Hmm. An excellent idea." The amusement faded from his face. He gave her a steady look. "Let's walk off our breakfast down by the lake."

"I'd like that."

Strolling along the shore, Logan broached the subject on the fore of Candace's mind, and the one she least wanted to discuss. "You know I'm leaving tomorrow, right?"

Her hands balled into fists at her sides. She wished she had on shorts, or jeans, or anything with pockets so she could jam her hands inside. "Yep. Going anywhere exciting?" Candace asked, trying for a light tone.

He shook his head.

Then don't go.

"The truth is, I have obligations to see to. Some work I promised to do. Old business."

"Did you decide to go back to work after all?"

"No. It's not that kind of work."

"Aren't you afraid the magazine will replace you if you put them off too long?"

He sent her a cocky smile. "When you're the best, you get to call the shots."

"Lucky you."

"Yeah, right. The truth is, I am taking a chance by refusing the offer flat. I just can't see myself going back."

"Ever?" she asked.

He shrugged. "If I had to give a definite answer right now, it'd be no."

"Is it such a bad life?" Candace turned to study his profile. The late afternoon sun's rays burned through the leaves, silhouetting Logan's gorgeous face and making his expression unreadable. She held her hand to her brow, blocking the glare.

Beside her, he frowned, his gaze steady on the ground before them. Self-reproach, and something like bone-deep weariness seemed to emanate from his soul.

"I sound like a first class whiner, huh?"

"Not at all. Although I confess to having a hard time understanding your distaste for your chosen career. To me it sounds glorious." She stopped walking, touching her fingertips to his shoulder. "Logan, tell me what it's all about. In there." She tapped the area above his heart for emphasis.

Logan gave her a long look as if weighing a heavy decision. "After Luke died, things changed for me. In here." He tapped his temple, and smiled down at her. "I started shooting things I'd never considered photographing before. I call it Pop photography. Before that, I made art, or tried to," he added with a self-deprecating smile.

"I see."

His eyes searched her face.

"The other day you said something happened to change your focus. Luke's death—that's what happened, right?"

He looked away but not before she saw the flash of pain in his eyes. "Yes. Everything just got…blurry. I didn't know what I wanted to shoot anymore—or why. Mostly I just went on autopilot. Listen to me," he said, with a smile that didn't come close to reaching his eyes. "Don't get me wrong, it hasn't been without its perks. Hell, for a long while my work filled that gaping part of me Luke's death left—or it seemed to. Now? I don't know. It's just…I'm dealing with some issues I thought long behind me."

"Oh, Logan," Candace wished she could take his pain away. "Why don't you tell me a little more about Luke. Please?"

His eyes grew distant, as if he was looking directly into the past. "I was always the big brother. Even though I was only a few seconds older, I always looked after Luke. But in the end, I failed him. He asked me to help him do something and I refused. Too busy, I told him. If I hadn't refused…" He left off, unable to finish his sentence.

"You blame yourself for his death, is that it? You think your work got too much precedence?"

"I should have put him first."

Candace took Logan's hand and tugged, urging

him to face her. "Logan. I'm so sorry for your loss, and for what you carry around inside you, and I want to understand. Didn't you say Luke died in a car accident?"

He nodded tersely, his eyes shielded by a thicket of tangled, sooty lashes.

"Were you driving?" she asked softly.

He shook his head in denial. "I wasn't there."

"Then how can it be your fault?"

He raised his gaze to meet hers and his eyes blazed with self-recrimination. "Because I *should* have been there."

Candace wrapped her arms around his waist and held him, hoping to comfort him like he'd done for her earlier. Except that she was a foot shorter and so had to settle for pressing her cheek into his chest.

After a while, by mutual, unspoken agreement, they made their way back poolside. For the rest of the day, again by unspoken agreement, Candace and Logan put the serious talk aside.

Just before sunset, she announced her intention to go back to her room to get some work done. She had to, or else give in to the urge to pounce on him she'd been fighting for the past several hours. All right, *days.*

"I'll miss you," Logan said softly from the lounger. He wore a pair of reflective sunglasses, and Candace couldn't read his expression, although, of course she knew he was teasing.

"Try not to lose too much sleep over it," she threw back over her shoulder.

She thought she heard him snort.

Ensconced in the cozy sitting area in her room, Candace set to work. Her roiled emotions proved fruitful. Page after page flowed from her fingertips and before she knew it, she'd passed the dinner hour, evidenced by her stomach's rumbled protest.

Though there had been no discussion on the matter, Candace assumed she and Logan would dine together, especially in light of the fact he was leaving tomorrow. She felt a little guilty for keeping him waiting. Logan, she'd noticed, had a big appetite. If she was this hungry, he was probably starving.

She closed the notebook and unfolded herself from the chair. She linked her hands overhead and stretched, then wandered to her bedroom door. Just as she opened it, she heard the unmistakable thump of the front door closing, followed by the scrape of the key turning in the lock. A minute later, Logan's car purred to life, its well-tuned motor fading as he pulled down the drive.

Huh.

He'd gone out. Alone. Disappointment that felt a lot like hurt feelings swamped her. Now what? Her stomach growled answering her unspoken question. She plodded morosely to the kitchen to grab some carrots and peanut butter.

Ah, screw it. She put the carrots away and scooped out a generous portion of vanilla ice cream. She spooned little bites into her mouth as she wandered, forlorn, back up to her room.

A bubble bath might make her feel better.

She soaked. Listened to her mp3 player. Finished the ice cream. Sulked.

After her bath, she crawled into bed and opened a romance novel by one of her favorite authors. She started the Regency again and again, but couldn't seem to stay focused long enough to get past the first page.

She kept thinking about Logan, and the fact he'd gone out without her on his last night in town. He'd probably gotten tired of her prying into his personal life.

"Give it up," Candace muttered. She closed the book, and turned off the bedside lamp.

And slept. Unfortunately, only for about three hours, calculated after a bleary-eyed glance at the bedside clock. Midnight and wide awake. She rolled onto her stomach, pounded her pillow and squeezed her eyes closed.

A half hour later, Candace flung off the covers and tromped through the darkness toward the sitting room where she'd left the laptop. She aimed for the shadowy lump she assumed was her armchair, hands outstretched.

Thunk. She gasped. That would be her now-blackened big toe as it attempted to penetrate the table leg. She grabbed her injured digit, balancing precariously on the one foot. Why hadn't she turned on the light?

A knock sounded on the bedroom door.

"Candace," came Logan's muffled voice from the hall. "Are you up?"

Her heart lodged in her throat. Throwing caution to the wind, she dashed to the door, swung it open, and found an empty hall. Had she imagined Logan's voice?

She peered down the dark corridor. Relief flooded her senses as she made out his shadowy form hovering at the threshold of his room. Her mouth curved in a wide grin she didn't bother to censor since no one could see her shameless glee. "Logan?" Candace called in a sleep scratchy voice.

"Hi," he whispered.

"Hi."

He gave a low chuckle and her heartbeat skittered in an uneven rhythm as he started toward her. "I couldn't sleep. I heard a bang in your room and wondered if you were having the same trouble," he said in a velvet voice.

"I managed to fall asleep for a while. But as of a few minutes ago, I'm wide awake. I thought I'd—"

"Work," he finished for her, crossing his arms over his chest. He stood just in front of her now, wearing boxers and nothing else. His scent, a tantalizing mixture of soap, aftershave, and warm male skin floated over her.

Her toes curled into the carpet. "Right," she said, sounding breathless.

"I'm surprised you have any creative energy left after working so diligently today. All day long. You were working earlier, weren't you?" he asked, his tone almost accusatory.

"I was. Um…do you want to come in?" She gestured inside her room.

"Yes."

His rough voice made Candace's skin tingle.

Chapter Nineteen

Dammit, Candace cursed herself on the way into her bedroom. The man had no idea what affect he had on her. That sexy voice. That Adonis body—shirtless more than half the time. That illusive, masculine scent. She should be ashamed of herself, lusting after him like so much meat.

And she was ashamed.

She was just *more* happy to see him—one last time.

She sat on the edge of the bed, feeling it shift as Logan plopped himself at the foot. She switched on the bedside lamp and belatedly gave her nightwear a cursory glance. A powder blue string tank with the words *sleep tight* imprinted on the front, and matching shorts with multiple zees printed on them that left very little to the imagination. She shrugged inwardly. Logan *had* no imagination where she was concerned. *She* on the other hand, could drum up all sorts of scenarios involving Logan.

She took in his brilliant turquoise eyes, his sleep-mussed hair, the dark stubble covering his jaw. His naked, muscular torso. Lust uncoiled in her belly and spread all the way to her toes.

She needed a distraction. Candace plumped a couple of pillows, placed them against her headboard and leaned into them, all the while replaying an inner mantra. *Think of him as a girlfriend. A very masculine girlfriend.* "Why couldn't you sleep?" She tried not to stare at his chest.

He shrugged. Lowered his lashes. Stared at the bed covers. "Doesn't take much of a reason. Although..." He smiled, a bashful, little boy smile, and shrugged again.

She waited for him to elaborate, which, of course, he didn't. "Yes?"

"I was..." he hesitated, then blurted, "I didn't want to leave without saying goodbye."

"Really?" she asked, sounding way too hopeful. "Me neither. I didn't know what time you were planning on going and..." She bit her lip, not wanting to reveal how hurt she'd been over his decision to go out solo on their last night together.

"And?" Logan stretched diagonally on her bed, leaning on his elbow and propping his head in his hand. He eyed her expectantly and at the same time pulled a couple of pillows to his chest as an armrest.

"I was just hoping I'd see you before you left."

His mouth formed a slight frown and his eyes lowered to the bedspread. "I kept waiting for you to come out of your room. And waiting. I didn't knock because Eric threatened me with bodily harm if I interfered with your work. Finally I went out and picked up Thai takeout for us. But," he sighed, "you never emerged."

"I thought you'd gone out. I picked a bit in the kitchen and took a long bath."

"Must've been some bath."

"I didn't know you'd come home. I fell asleep reading, and the next thing I know, it's midnight and

I'm wide awake." She paused. "I love Thai."

"I figured you would."

"Why's that?"

He gave a one-shouldered shrug. "I do." Logan had somehow made it up from the foot of the bed to lie beside her. "Can't believe you thought I'd leave without a word. I would never have done that. Are you hungry?"

She shook her head.

"What'd you eat?"

She grinned at him. "Ice cream."

"Candace, Candace. Who's gonna take care of you when I'm not here to feed you? Promise me you'll eat better than that." He reached over and tucked a lock of hair behind her ear.

She shivered.

He raised his brows and slid off the bed. "You're cold. Where's your laptop? I'll get it while you crawl under the blankets." He blew out a breath and ran a hand through his hair, mussing it some more.

Candace started to tell him not to bother, but his unblinking stare aimed straight at her chest had her crossing her arms in front of her breasts. Her nipples were hard as rocks.

If she had any doubt as to whether he'd noticed, she had none now. Before her eyes, his bronzed skin tinged pink, and he suddenly had a great interest in the ceiling.

"Thanks. I…um…left it in the sitting area. You can't miss it." She scrambled under the covers, pulling them to her chin.

"Do you need the power chord?" he called from the other room.

"No," she called back.

He dropped the computer on her lap and resumed his position beside her on the bed, sprawling flat on his stomach. "I hope you don't mind I came in here."

"I'm glad you did. I was disappointed I didn't get to see you last night." The understatement of the year.

"Really?"

"Really."

He closed his eyes and sighed in pleasure. "Good."

She opened her laptop, but didn't open her work. Instead she let her gaze roam over his perfect profile, his chiseled, V-shaped back, his nicely rounded derriere.

"Candace?" he began, not opening his eyes.

She started guiltily. "Yes?"

"Can I lay in here with you for a little while? I promise not to bother you while you work."

She opted not to mention he'd already made himself quite at home. "Aren't you worried you'll oversleep for your flight?"

"Driving. To San Fran."

"Oh." Candace watched his torso rise and fall in a steady rhythm. Just like that. The man had fallen asleep on her bed.

She yawned. Not a half bad idea. Would it be so wrong to take a catnap with Logan beside her? He had fallen asleep on top of the covers, and she was fully beneath them. Setting her computer aside, she reached for the bedside lamp and snapped off the light.

Snuggling under the sheets and burrowing into her pillows, she told herself she probably wouldn't sleep a wink. In five minutes, she'd be up, typing away. Another one of Logan's soft, contented sighs reached her ears and she smiled into her pillow. That was her last thought before morning.

Chapter Twenty

Logan slowly opened his eyes. Morning light filtered through the drapes, illuminating the silky blonde hair on the pillow inches from his.

Candace lay on her back, one arm flung over her head. Someone had pushed the bedcovers down, leaving Logan bare to the waist. Candace lay uncovered past her hips. He reached down, half reluctant to deprive himself of the view, and pulled up the covers. He didn't want Candace to be cold.

Speaking of bedcovers...Logan frowned. Hadn't he purposely refrained from getting under them? Guess his brain forgot to tell his body.

Right now that brain was screaming at his body to keep its hands—and other parts—to themselves. The other parts were doing a little screaming of their own. Matter-of-fact, his throbbing cock had probably been what had roused him. Now it urged him to sift his fingers through her hair, to slide his palm over her flat belly, to remove her torturously revealing nightshirt and...damn Eric for putting these restraints on Logan.

Except...

The truth was, Eric was right to warn him off Candace. She already had one lowlife man to deal with; she didn't need to get messed up with Logan.

Beside him Candace murmured. His erection reacted like a long lost lover called home, straining against his boxers, unmoved by his moral struggle.

And then she rolled toward him, so close her breath tickled his face. His guts churned as lust spun through his veins like a drug. He couldn't remember ever wanting any woman more than he wanted Candace right now.

She shifted again, kicking down the bedcovers, and giving Logan a perfect view of her cleavage. Her nipples were pebbled against her silky top. He swallowed. Torture had never tasted so sweet.

He should get up and get out of here. Take a cold shower. Only he couldn't peel his eyes off her perfect breasts. What was she? A C-cup? A D?

"Hi," Candace breathed.

Logan's gaze flew to her face. Her expression remained soft with sleep, but her face was crimson. So much for hoping she hadn't noticed where he'd been looking. All right, staring.

"Hi, yourself." Logan tried for a casual tone. Forced a grin. "I slept great. That's twice now."

Candace smiled shyly in return, before lowering her lashes and pulling the covers to her chin. Then she lifted her arms and arched her back in a languid cat stretch.

Fully covered or not, Logan's body reacted. Dammit. Why hadn't he left while he had the chance to make a clean escape? When he finally did get up, it was going to blow the hell out of the gay theory.

"What's wrong?"

"What do you mean?" he asked, though he figured his sexual frustration was written all over his face.

"You're scowling."

She looked so taken aback. Logan searched his

mind for an explanation other than, *You make me want to jump on you and not let you up for an entire day.* "I…uh, was just thinking about the drive ahead, and the work my mother has planned for me."

"Oh? You're going to see your family? How lovely. I'll bet your mother is thrilled."

Diversion. Good. Keep talking. "You bet right. She's been hinting for a year she wants me to come help her and Dad tackle the attic. She wants to sort through all the crap they've accumulated over the years and she needs a lackey to help."

Candace laughed softly and batted her lashes sleepily. "And I guess you're it?"

"You guess right."

"I think that's wonderful." Candace's eyelids drifted shut. "Your parents are still married?" Her voice was almost a whisper.

Logan drank in the sight of her face. "Thirty-seven years. Thirty-eight? Some ungodly number."

Candace's lips curved in a sex-kitten smile.

"Are your parents still…"

She shook her head without lifting it off the pillow. "Nope. They split when I was in college."

On impulse, Logan combed his fingers through the fine hairs that had fallen across her cheek. He'd meant the gesture to be comforting. Maybe it was—for her. For him…touching her made him burn. Her lips parted and her eyes opened, locking with his. He knew she could probably read the longing eating him up from the inside out.

Hell with it. He was just going to tell her the truth. He wasn't gay, and he would die if he didn't…

Candace rolled to her side of the bed and swung

133

her legs over the edge. "Mmmm." She stretched her arms over her head. "I'm going to make some coffee. Want some?"

Logan closed his eyes. "Like you wouldn't believe."

****

Candace hastened to the closet and donned a short velour robe. She squeezed her eyes shut and took a deep breath before emerging to give Logan a brief smile and dash from the room.

He looked like a sexy cover model lying there. An edible underwear model she wanted to roll on top of and lick all over. She was one sick puppy.

Ten heaping scoops later, she hit the brew button and sat on the barstool to wait for the pot to fill.

Logan was leaving today, and she didn't want him to, which meant it was past time for him to go. Her feelings for him were totally inappropriate. His mere presence left her weak, and addle-brained, and kind of sex-crazed.

Even in her dreams, like the ones last night. Lascivious dreams of Logan. His mouth. His hands. His body.

When she woke to find him eyeing her breasts with what looked like real enjoyment, she'd had to fight the urge to *accidentally* roll on top of him.

It was definitely a good thing he was leaving.

So why did the thought fill her with what she could only describe as an all-over toothache? She skulked to the fridge and pulled out the creamer.

Candace was on her second cup of coffee when Logan arrived in the kitchen.

His scent: soap, aftershave, and something

uniquely *Logan,* hit her like a shock to the senses. His dark hair, still damp from the shower, curled around his neck and over his sport's jacket collar, and his strong jawline gleamed from a recent shave.

He held a loosely filled backpack in one hand. He was really leaving. *Buck up, camper.*

Candace poured a mug of coffee and handed it to him. She grinned at his t-shirt. *It's a camera not a magic wand.* "Ouch."

"If the shoe fits… Present company excluded, of course."

Candace rolled her eyes. "It looks like you'll have nice weather for your drive."

One corner of his mouth curved upward. "Yeah, it does. Before the rains come in tomorrow."

"I'm going to miss your car." Candace forced a light tone to her voice.

"In that case, maybe I should stay."

"Oh, no. I don't want Mama Shaw to give me the evil eye for stealing her lackey."

"You've met her then?" Logan's twinkling eyes were more blue than turquoise this morning.

"Are you hungry?" She picked up a sleeve of bagels.

Logan gave her a long, considering look. "Hungry?" He chuckled softly and lowered his eyes. "I'll get something on the road."

"In that case, you must have more bags than that. Let me help you."

"I'm…uh…all packed and ready to go." He gestured vaguely to the front door and said in explanation, "Last night."

"Oh," Candace said, sounding as pathetically

forlorn as she felt.

"I've written down my cell number." He reached into his pocket, thrust a small sheet of paper toward her awkwardly. "If you need anything…"

"Thanks." An uncomfortable silence passed. "I'll write mine for you." She scrawled the number on a sticky note and handed it to Logan. He glanced at it, and tucked it into his jeans pocket.

"How long do you think—"

"I'll walk you to the—"

They both stopped talking. "You first," Candace said.

"I wondered how long you're planning on staying."

"Probably till the end of the month. Maybe longer depending on how things go with Roger's house hunt."

Logan tensed visibly at her ex's name and sent her a serious frown. She guessed he was still worried over those emails.

"Can I walk you to the car?"

He looked like he was still deciding whether or not to lecture her about Roger. Finally his expression cleared. "I'd like that."

She followed him out. His Aston Martin sat under the covered space next to the garage where he must've parked it the night before. He went to the driver's side door.

Candace crossed her arms over her middle, trying to quell a stab of hurt. He hadn't even given her a hug goodbye.

He pulled the door open, paused, and fixed her with a somber stare. "I've really enjoyed spending time with you, Candace. Eric is a lucky man to have you in his life."

"Likewise, Logan. Not sure what I'll do with myself now that you won't be here to entertain me."

"Don't be surprised if I call and check up on you from time to time."

Candace smiled and waved. Seconds later, he was gone.

Chapter Twenty-One

Candace sat on the floor of the balcony peering out the iron slats of railing at the cheerful, glistening ripples on the lake. They didn't offer much salve for the ache in her chest.

She missed Logan. She'd dreamed of him the last two nights—when she'd slept, that is. Her insomnia was in full bloom.

It had to be a chemical thing. Logan must exude hormones, or pheromones, or whatever sexy-as-hell men gave off. But she knew in her heart it was more than sexual attraction she felt for Logan.

She dragged a hand through her hair and glared at the waves. Could she be any more of an idiot? How could she have allowed herself to become infatuated with the man? Sure, he resembled a Greek god, and saw the world through an artist's eye—and what woman could resist that combo? Plus he made her laugh, and pampering her seemed to be his normal modus operandi.

But he also happens to like men. Oh, yeah, *and* he and Eric are lovers.

Her cell phone rang in her bedroom. She listened, noted Roger's new ring tone, the refrain from *Leave Me Alone,* and ignored it.

Maybe the longing in her had nothing to do with Logan, per se. Maybe Logan was simply a metaphor for a newfound appetite for…the richness of life. Dammit, she no longer wanted to play it safe with the Rogers of the world. She wanted to live.

She just wasn't sure how to go about doing it.

Her phone chimed, signaling Roger had left a message.

Candace rubbed her eyes with the heels of her hands. The relief she'd felt last night after gently, yet firmly, informing him their relationship was absolutely over and he needed to find a house by the end of the month was rapidly fading at his flat-out refusal to accept her decision. Today she kept replaying the conversation in her head, wondering if anything else she might've said could've made a difference.

"It *is* over, Roger."

"You're just angry. You're punishing me."

"No. I'm not. I've thought this through. It's better for you, too. You deserve more than I can—"

"No, Candace. Don't say it."

"—give. I don't love you, Roger. Not like a wife should love her husband."

"Dammit. You shouldn't have left. We needed time to work this out."

"I think it's all turned out for the best. Plus, with me gone, you have more time to find a proper place to move. Think you can find a rental by the end of the month?"

A charged silence ensued. And then Roger's clipped reply. "I'm not going anywhere. Whenever you finally decide to grace our home with your presence, I'll be here waiting. This isn't over. Better yet, tell me where you are."

She ignored that. "Roger, one of us has to go, and

it won't be me."

"I don't see it that way."

"I'm getting off the phone."

"Not before you tell me where you are. We need to discuss this face to face."

"Goodbye, Roger."

At midnight, the calls started and did not cease. After the first, Candace stopped answering. Around three, she powered off the phone. Now she wondered why she hadn't left it off. She really didn't want to listen to any more of his frantic, angry messages.

Because you want to hear from him*, and* he's *never going to call.*

Candace stepped into her room and closed the slider. She picked up her cell phone and pressed the power button until the screen read, *goodbye.*

Thank God Roger had no idea where she was staying. Eric's instinct to keep it a secret had been more than prescient. For the first time in two days, a real smile spread over her face.

Just as rapidly, it disappeared. What in the world would she say to Eric when they finally spoke? "Hi, Eric. I broke it off with Roger. Oh, and by the way, I've fallen in lust with your boyfriend." She shook her head in disgust. She just needed time. In a day or two, she'd forget all about Logan Shaw.

In the meantime, she'd go for a run. A good, long run never failed to clear her head.

****

Logan stood, hands on hips, and surveyed the now nearly empty attic. Only one box left to lug down the stairs, the last of the Goodwill items. The myriad winter clothes, decorations, books, and miscellaneous junk had filled at least ten boxes, and as many bags of trash. Then there had been the canvases, some still brand new, and Luke's paints.

The setting sun slanted in through the dormers, illuminating a storm of floating dust particles. Logan smiled wryly. Remnants of his family's past. For a moment he imagined photographing the play of light and shadow. It had been a long time since he thought of his camera as anything other than a means to a paycheck. When had photography become nothing more than a job?

Around the time Luke died.

Everything came back to that, didn't it? Before and after.

He and Luke had dreamed of opening an art gallery together—Shaw and Shaw's. They'd devote half the gallery space to paintings, the other to photography. Luke would specialize in modern abstract—Andy Warhol style. Logan's photography would alternate between portraits and abstracts of light and geometric shapes. His specialty was the evening sky when the stars came out and the moon was full. Add a craggy tree and a lightning bolt and it was even better.

But that was *before*. He no longer thought of himself as an artist. No, he was a burned out shooter for *Rolling Stone*. Sure, a bit of talent and a lot of luck had landed him on top of the heap. He could now pick and choose his subjects, and he could name his price. But something was missing, and had been for a long time.

Deep down he'd known it, but hadn't been willing to face his shallow lifestyle head on—until his last meaningless sexual fling blew up in his face, catapulting him out the door and onto indefinite leave.

He knew now he wasn't going back. Perhaps he'd redeem himself in the war-ravaged deserts and caves of Afghanistan, or in the desperate streets of Darfur, or in poverty stricken Moscow. Surely somewhere on this earth he could find the meaning his life had been missing for so long.

Logan glanced at his watch. Straight on six o'clock. The tantalizing aroma of his mother's cooking permeated the attic from the open hatch. The homey scent of rich meat and slow cooked vegetables reached inside him, dredging up unwelcome emotions. Yearning, guilt, dread, sorrow.

Why had he thought this visit would be different? Ever since Luke's death, every time Logan looked at his parents, every time his eyes met theirs... He gritted his teeth. They never said anything, never uttered one accusation, but they knew. Knew he'd failed all of them. If Logan had gone with Luke to New York, Luke would be alive today.

"Logan?" Logan's father's head emerged from the hole in the attic floor. "You all right up here, son?"

"Yeah, Dad. Just giving the room a once-over."

His father hoisted himself through the opening and shuffled toward him. He looked tired, the lines around his eyes more pronounced than the last time he'd been here. "Your mother and I appreciate you coming to help clear this stuff out."

"I know you do, Dad."

"But we could've taken care of it ourselves."

Logan frowned, confused.

"Do you know why we asked for your help, son?"

Logan shook his head. Let his dad finally say it, once and for all.

"Logan, your mother and I love you very much. We're worried about you."

Logan looked down at his father with furrowed brows. "Why?"

"You've changed. We keep hoping and praying you'll find peace, but it seems you're going headlong in the opposite direction. First there was all the wild carousing with your job. You traded in your art for a playboy lifestyle."

"I knew you didn't approve," Logan muttered, his voice tinged with bitterness.

His father shook his head. "It's a fine career choice. An achievement most photographers will never see. But it doesn't seem like it's brought you any satisfaction."

Logan couldn't deny the truth of his father's words.

"And now this Afghanistan thing."

A humorless smile curved his lips. "At least it's a change from the playboy lifestyle."

"Son, you're deliberately missing the point. We're very proud of your work. But we'd also be proud if you snapped photos for a department store, or if you worked at a fast food restaurant. Anything, as long as you did it to the best of your abilities, and more importantly, it brought you happiness. We just can't help but think this is another one of your attempts to…" His voice faded.

"Yes?" Logan demanded.

His father looked at him with sage, weary eyes.

"You don't have to make amends, Logan. It wasn't your fault."

Logan stiffened. "Dad…don't."

"You've been avoiding this conversation for six years. Enough's enough."

"How can you say that? It'll never be enough."

In a flash, his father's arms came around him. "You're my son, Logan. I love you. Do you hear me? You've got to stop blaming yourself."

"I should have been there," he choked through the sudden lump in his throat.

"It wasn't your fault. Please believe that, son. Please. We need our son back. We need you to move past the grief and rejoin the land of the living. It's what Luke would want, Logan. Don't you see?"

"You don't...you don't hate me, Dad? You and Mom?"

His father drew back and regarded him with something akin to shock in his eyes. "Never, Logan. Not for anything you could ever do, much less something you had nothing to do with at all."

"Logan? Lars?" His mother's voice called from the attic's floor level entrance. She peered up at father and son. "Oh, Logan."

For so long, Logan had kept himself apart from his parent's warmth and love, not wanting to ask it of them, not feeling he deserved it. He didn't know if he deserved it now. But, he realized, it didn't really matter. Because they needed him as much as he needed them.

****

For the first time in years, dinner at the Shaw house was a happy affair. By the time he headed into the den to watch the ten o'clock evening news, Logan felt more relaxed and at peace than he had in years, save for the brief time spent with Candace.

He wondered what she was doing. A terrible ache filled him at the thought of her, as unexpected as it was poignant. An almost overwhelming urge to call her flooded him. But he couldn't. Not at this hour. Plus, what would he say?

Jamming s hand through his hair, he sprawled on the sofa and grabbed the remote. Time for a little TV therapy.

He dozed through most of the national news. But when scenes of flash flooding and intense showers filled the screen, Logan pulled himself upright. At first he wasn't sure what he was watching. Then he heard the anchor: *Lake Tahoe hasn't taken this kind of a pounding since the late eighties. Authorities say they have plans to open the gates to the dam to avoid overfilling of the basin...*

Logan's eyes remained glued to the television as his hand reached for the cell phone in his back pocket.

He'd entered her number into his contact list before he even got on the highway out of Tahoe. He felt foolish at the time. Now he thanked God he'd taken the time. It meant he didn't have to waste time rummaging through his dirty laundry searching for it.

Residents are requested to stay indoors as severe lightning has been reported in multiple locations...

Logan peeled his gaze from the television to scroll through his contacts. He found Candace's information, and pressed Send. The call went straight to voicemail.

Trying not to panic, he dialed the landline at Eric's house.

Many of Northern Tahoe's residents are without power as several transformers have been struck. Power companies say they hope to have the power grids up and running within the next forty-eight hours. Logan listened to the broadcast, even as he digested the prerecorded message playing in his ear. *We're sorry.*

The number you're dialing is temporarily out of service.

Logan cursed under his breath and muted the television, his useless cell phone gripped in his hand. He wanted to throw the damn thing across the room, and only refrained from doing so because he didn't want to startle his parents.

He'd feel better if he thought she'd kept up with the weather forecast—not that the climatologists predicted anything this severe. Regardless, he doubted it. He hadn't seen her turn on the television or radio once while he was there.

Think, Logan. Candace seemingly had no phone, definitely had no car, and possibly was without electricity. In all probability, she was stranded in the dark, in the midst of a raging storm, scared out of her mind.

What were his options? Only one. He took off for his bedroom at a run. In swift order, he repacked his bags, dashed off a note to his parents explaining he had an unforeseen emergency to see to at Eric's, and beelined for his car.

Five minutes after seeing the news broadcast, he slammed his car into Reverse. "I'm coming for you, babe. Hold tight."

Chapter Twenty-Two

Candace sat on the bedroom floor hugging her knees and staring out the sliding glass doors. The whitecaps on the lake glowed like neon in the moonlight. The massive trees surrounding the house shimmied and swayed under the mighty gale-force winds and pounding rain. The lightning bolts, thank goodness, had lessened in frequency and seemed to be traveling across the lake, away from her.

Not that she truly feared a deadly rogue lightning bolt would shoot through the walls. No, tonight she suffered just the standard unreasonable paranoia every electrical storm heralded. At least the power had waited to go out until after she returned home, soaking wet, from her run. She wasn't sure when the phone lines quit.

Her cell phone still had some juice. She just didn't want to turn it on and waste its battery life.

A blinding flash of lightning lit the sky. "One one thousand, two one thousand, three—"

A loud crack of thunder interrupted her count. Every muscle in her body tensed.

She willed herself to relax, comforting herself with the notion that, yep the storm was definitely farther away. Last time she'd only counted to two one thousand.

How long had she been sitting here, anyway? Her

tailbone felt numb, like she'd been perched on it all night. It couldn't be near morning yet, could it?

Candace crawled to the nightstand and grabbed her cell phone, pressing buttons randomly until the screen lit up. One a.m.? That was it? She stared at the screen until the light faded.

She ought to turn on the phone and check messages. But she really didn't want to listen to any more of Roger's rants. Who would've guessed her suave ex-fiancé would turn into such a psycho?

Still. Her mother may have tried to call. Or Eric. If they'd heard about the storms they'd be worried. Doubly so if they called and only got her voice mail. Heaving a sigh, Candace pressed the power button.

Almost immediately the phone rang. Candace expected Roger's name to pop up on the caller ID. But it wasn't Roger's ringtone. And the number was local.

"Hello?" Candace answered tentatively.

"Candace?"

Her heart slammed into her ribs. She'd know that voice anywhere. "Logan?"

"Are you all right?"

He sounded annoyed. It had to be her imagination. "I can barely hear you over the noise. What is that?"

"It's the sound of rain pounding the roof of my car. You didn't answer my question."

His question? Oh, right. "I'm...fine."

"That doesn't sound very convincing," he practically shouted.

She smiled in the darkness. "Well, other than getting caught in a storm while on a long run, and returning here in time to lose power and phone service—that is, other than my cell—"

"Speaking of your cell, I've been trying to call you for hours. What the hell is wrong with your phone?"

"I turned it off. I had to. It was ringing off the hook after—" She bit her lip. She didn't have battery power to waste getting into the nitty gritty concerning Roger. "Never mind. With the power out, I didn't want to kill my battery. Which reminds me. I need to hang up, unfortunately." She *really* didn't want to. "I don't know when the power will come back on, and I don't want to be completely isolated. Just in case."

"Good idea. Look, Candace, I'm about six miles away."

"You are?"

He hesitated a beat. "I was worried about you—"

"About me?"

"Yes. When you didn't answer your phone—"

"Oh, Logan. I'm so sorry. I had no idea you were trying to call. So you're coming here? Now?"

"That was the plan, yes. Unfortunately, I hit a snag. Or rather, I almost hit a fallen tree and ended up skidding off the shoulder. Now I can't muster enough traction to get back on the road."

"Oh my Lord! Are you all right?"

"I'm fine. I've put a call into OnStar. They said the roads are out at Truckee River, but they should be able to get to me within a few hours."

"A few hours!"

"It's no big deal. I can afford to wait now that I'm not worried about you."

"About *me*?" she squeaked. "You're stranded on the side of the road…" Lightning briefly illuminated Candace's room. Then came the thunder. She raised her voice to be heard over it, annoyed with the interruption.

149

"…and you're worried about me?"

"I'm fine. I'm safe and dry and can easily wait for OnStar."

"Like hell. I'm coming to get you."

"No." His clipped tone said he expected to be obeyed. "Stay where you are and I'll see you in a few hours."

"I'm coming to get you." She was already racing to the stairwell.

"It's pouring out here. And there are tree branches littering the streets. Have you forgotten you have no vehicle?"

"I do, too. I have Eric's scooter."

"That. Is. Ridiculous. Even if you could get here, you have no way to get me up the hill."

"What hill?"

No reply.

"Logan?"

He sighed. "I'm kind of…on a drop off."

And he wanted her to wait? "Are there any trees around?"

"Yes, but—"

"I'll bring a rope."

"Candace. You. Aren't. Coming," he ground out.

"I take it you're on Highway 28?"

No answer.

She opened the front door and stared across the expanse of land separating the main house from the garage. She would get soaked in about two seconds flat. Again. "Logan, I'm hanging up because I have to cross the yard to get to the garage and this rain will destroy my only means of communication. I *am* going to get on that scooter, and I *am* coming for you. You can cooperate, or not. But if you don't, I'm likely to die of exposure."

"Has anyone ever told you you're a stubborn little fool?"

"Are you going to tell me where you are or am I going to leave here blind?"

He didn't immediately reply, and Candace feared she really would have to go hunting for him in the darkness.

"Dammit." Logan inhaled deeply. "Take Highway 28 westbound to Highway 89 south."

"Did you say eighty-nine? As in eighty-nine above Truckee Canyon? *That* drop off?" A cold fist of fear having nothing to do with the raging storm settled in the pit of her stomach.

"According to my GPS, I'm three point two miles north of the intersection. Look for a massive tree in the road." He broke off, cursing softly. "Dammit, Candace. I really don't want you to do this."

She ended the call, and sprinted across the driveway.

Ten long minutes later, armed with her pillaged rescue gear, Candace piloted the scooter out of the garage. Raindrops pierced her skin through her long sleeved t-shirt like tiny, frozen darts, but she didn't care. She kept seeing Logan's car tumbling down a slippery ravine. She would die if anything happened to him because she didn't reach him in time.

Unfortunately, Logan hadn't exaggerated about the debris littering the road. Fallen branches blocked every turn. But there was nothing like the gashed guardrail, and huge tree in the road that told Candace she'd found the site of Logan's crash.

She parked the scooter and forced her numb legs to carry her toward the mangled railing. Leaning forward, she finally spotted the Aston. No wonder he hadn't wanted her to come. Precarious didn't begin to describe his situation. His car hugged the rocky incline, nearly on its *side,* on a thin ledge that jutted out before another vertical drop off. He was lucky to be alive. When she got him safely off that cliff—and she would—she would kill him.

****

Logan's phone buzzed, and Candace's number appeared. She'd gotten here fast.

"Logan here."

"I'm tossing a rope to you now."

"Okay, boss."

She hung up.

Logan wiped at the fog covering his window and looked down the length of the steep incline into the swollen ditch below. He hated to admit it, but he was damned lucky Candace had insisted on coming. Minutes after he hung up with her, his car had begun an intermittent slide down the mud-eroded hill. A couple more lurches like the last one, and he would topple all the way to the bottom of the gorge.

The telltale thump of rope sounded against the uphill facing passenger window. Now or never. He inched toward the window, knowing any movement might affect the precarious balance of the car.

Fantastic. The rain was picking up again. The drops pounded the car like so many elephants stampeding past. He reached the passenger door, held his breath and pressed the button to lower the window. The slight vibration caused the car to shudder and slide further down the ravine.

After what seemed an eternity, the end of a ski rope toppled inside the car, as well as a bucket full of freezing cold rain. Logan grabbed the rope, twisted it several times around his forearm.

He gritted his teeth and using mostly upper body strength, dragged himself out. Once clear of the vehicle, Logan dug his heels into the mud and rocks. He made it a few feet before his running shoes slid over the scree, stealing most of the progress he'd made. He peered upward through the sheeting rain and saw a beam of light. The scooter's headlight. Candace had pulled it to the edge of the street to guide his way, and she was there waiting. He started climbing again.

Lightning illuminated the sky in three short bursts and Logan redoubled his efforts. He calculated the vertical climb to the top at eight, maybe nine yards.

Another bolt of lightning struck, followed by a fierce yet very feminine voice shouting, "Move your ass, Shaw!"

Anger and plain bruised male ego kicked his determination into high gear. His biceps ached with the effort of dragging himself upward, but Logan didn't lose any more ground. All because he couldn't wait to reach the top and give Candace a lecture she'd never forget.

The end was in sight. A few more feet and…her hands reached out, grasping him under his arms and tugging while he used the last of his strength to haul himself up and over the edge.

Exhausted. Soaked. Muddy. Hair plastered to his forehead, blinding him. He dug his elbows into gravel and dragged himself further from the drop off, then rolled onto his back and closed his eyes. He would definitely lecture Candace. Just let him catch his breath first.

"Logan, are you all right?" Candace wasn't content to wait for him to recover his strength. She crawled onto his chest and put her ice-cold hands on either side of his face, pushing his hair out of his eyes. "Logan, answer me."

He cracked his eyes open. Her fair hair was soaking wet and plastered to her skin. Water droplets slid down her cheeks, and off her nose.

"You told me you were safe, you silly man," she half-yelled, half-sobbed. "You're lucky your car stopped where it did instead of crashing into the gorge." She gestured wildly behind her.

Shivers wracked her slight frame. Was she frightened? Cold? He lifted one exhausted arm and swiped her hair back from her cheeks. "Let's get you home," he said.

For a moment she stared at him with the blankest expression—then laughter burst from her lips. "You're crazy."

"*I'm* crazy? You just took a joy ride in the middle of a tropical storm."

She sat back on his stomach and smiled at him. A big beautiful smile that lit her whole face. Something warm and wonderful filled Logan's chest and he did the only thing he *could* do at that moment. Grasping her nape with one hand, and her shoulder with the other, he dragged her down and kissed her.

Chapter Twenty-Three

The moment Logan's hands tightened on her, Candace knew he meant to kiss her. No, the moment just *before* that. Something about the intensity of his expression, and the tempo of his breathing. And in that moment, that millisecond in time, nothing ever felt more natural than to melt into him, and revel in the sweet, salty taste of his mouth.

And then *poof,* she came to her senses. This was Logan. Eric's Logan.

He must have had the same realization, because his kiss ended as abruptly as it began.

"Let's get back to the house before the rain starts again," Logan said without inflection. He helped her off his lap, got to his feet, and offered Candace his hand.

She forced herself to meet Logan's eyes. How was it he looked so normal—as if he hadn't just rocked her world with that heart-stopping kiss?

He held out his hand, palm up. "Keys, please."

Damn right he'd drive. She didn't think she could manage, the way her body had begun to shake. From the cold, she told herself. "The keys are in the ignition."

Logan righted the bike. He swung one wet, skin-tight, jean-clad leg over the seat to straddle the bike and clipped on the helmet she'd brought him. "Climb on and hold tight."

Candace buckled her helmet and resisted the urge

to paste herself onto his solid frame. Instead, she put a hand on either side of his muscular waist and held herself erect. She was freezing, soaked to the bone, and ever so slightly worried about flying off the back of the scooter, but she had her pride.

Logan twisted to face her. Though she couldn't be sure, she thought he was glaring at her through the helmet shield.

A moment later, he faced forward, grasped her hands with his, and tugged her forward on the seat until her chest met his back. The steamy heat emanating from his body through his wet t-shirt made her want to moan first with delight, then embarrassment as her nipples hardened into pebbles against his back. She could only pray Logan was too preoccupied with their predicament to notice.

He took off, maneuvering around the debris like a pro. Candace held on tight.

At the house, Logan guided the scooter to the front stoop and turned off the engine. Candace gracelessly climbed down, yanked off her helmet and raced for the door. "I'm fr-freezing."

She darted inside. The house was silent and dark. A bubble of laughter rose up inside her as she stood in the foyer dripping water, her rain-soaked shirt and jeans molded to her body like a second skin.

"Something's funny?" Logan asked in his velvet voice, closing the door.

"I was thinking about the last time I entered a house soaking wet in the middle of the night. The night I found Roger. I don't know why…it just struck me as funny."

She could feel his intense stare. "I'm glad one of us

finds some humor in this."

Candace blinked at his rigid tone.

"That was a damned foolish thing you did coming after me."

"Wh—"

He cut her off before she could frame a reply, ticking points off his fingers. "Number one, you don't know the area, and don't think I've forgotten how you once admitted to me you're not good with directions. Getting lost in this kind of mess can be catastrophic. Number two, driving a damned scooter in the rain through all that debris is plain foolhardy. Number three, what the hell were you thinking not turning on your cell phone? You had to know people were worried about you."

He'd been worried about her? A funny little flutter tickled her stomach. "I had a perfectly good reason for having my phone off—"

"Number four, you shouldn't go digging around in a dark garage looking for things. You could've easily gotten hurt."

Enough was enough. "Just one minute. Do you want to be the kettle or the pot?"

Logan crossed his arms over his chest.

Candace fought a losing battle to quell the tremors coursing through her. "You had no business driving out here in the middle of the night when you knew very well a storm had already wreaked havoc on the area. And you must've been driving pretty darn fast to go over the edge of the road like that. Talk about self inflicted danger. You could've gotten yourself killed." To her horror, her voice began to quaver as the truth of her words hit her. "Even worse, you lied to me, telling me you would be perfectly safe waiting for Lone Star—"

"OnStar."

She ignored him. "What if I'd believed you? If you would have tumbled to your death, I never would've forgiven you, L-Logan Sh-Shaw." She gritted her teeth, hating her loss of composure and unable to do anything about it. "Never mind. You're welcome!" She squared her shoulders and turned, fully intending to make a grand exit.

In a lightning move, Logan grasped her shoulder in a grip both gentle and firm. Candace stilled. She heard Logan's intake of breath, as if he were about to speak, but then thought better of it. His obvious discomfort softened her anger toward him. Slightly. She started to tell him to forget everything she'd just said, but the words lodged in her throat when he placed his other hand on her opposite shoulder. He gave her muscles a quick squeeze and lowered his mouth to her ear. "Thank you."

His strong fingers moved rhythmically over her tense muscles. "I just—" He broke off. "I feel like a jerk. The whole reason I hightailed it out here was because I was worried about you. Then, like an idiot I ran off the road. I didn't tell you how bad it was because I didn't want you to come rescue *me*. But you did anyway. I guess I've been acting like an ass ever since because I feel like one. And," he heaved a sigh, and removed his hands, "I really wish you'd look at me, Candace."

Candace bit her lip uncertainly. She turned and found him standing a lot closer than she'd imagined. In the moonlit darkness, she could just see his sheepish grin as he asked, "Forgive me?"

"There's nothing to forgive." Distant thunder rumbled, setting her thoughts spinning in a different direction. "Oh my goodness. Oh my. Am I remembering right?" She concentrated a moment. "I am."

"Mind telling me what you're talking about now?"

She sent him a beatific smile. "You know something really...neat? I wasn't afraid. Tonight. Out in the storm. With all the excitement, I only just realized it. I knew I had to find you and I wasn't afraid. I was worried about you, but as far as the lightning," she shrugged, "it was more like background noise."

He stared into her eyes. "That's great."

Candace got caught in his gaze. She couldn't make out the mesmerizing blue of his eyes, but she could feel the draw of his stare, pulling her in like a magnet. She said the first thing that came to her. "I, um...I really need to change."

"Out of these wet clothes? Yeah, we do." He stripped his long sleeved tee over his head and dropped it on the floor. It landed with a splat.

Surely he wasn't planning to strip right here, right now. Apparently so, and evidently he intended her to do the same. In stunned surprise, she watched like a sideline spectator as he grasped the bottom of her shirt. The feel of his warm fingers sliding over the damp skin of her belly sent a rash of gooseflesh over her.

"Um...Logan," she said in a breathless voice. Delicious heat roared through her veins even as she attempted to put distance between them by backing away.

Logan matched her movements, step for step, never

releasing his hold on the hem of her shirt. She ceased her half-hearted retreat when her backside collided with the front door.

"What? Don't you think we need to get out of these clothes?" he asked, the playful glint in his eyes, belying his innocent tone.

Farfetched as it seemed, Candace could only conclude he was trying to seduce her. And succeeding. She turned away from his hypnotic gaze and lowered her lashes. It—this—was all wrong. Not that she tried to dissuade him shimmying her shirt upwards.

"Arms up, please," he whispered.

She complied.

He bared her belly. Her breasts. Her neck. When her head slipped from the neckline he stopped tugging, leaving her arms overhead, ensconced in her shirtsleeves. He twisted the loose material around one of his wrists, squeezing drops of water onto her head, and pinned her wrists against the door.

In the stillness, Candace heard the telltale rasp of his breathing. He wanted her.

She wanted to purr.

She peeked at him through her lashes and felt her own breath catch. He didn't just want her. Logan stared down at her like he wanted to have her for dinner. He licked his lips and her breasts tingled as if he'd licked them. By sheer force of will she resisted the urge to arch her back and close the distance between their bodies.

After a few, excruciating moments, Logan finished the job of removing her shirt, flinging it away. However, he opted not to release her wrists. Instead, he held them in place over her head with one hand, as his other hand dropped to the waistband of her soaked jeans. His fingers released the top button.

"What are you... Logan what's happening?" she managed to get out.

"What's happening?" He lowered his head toward hers, closing the distance between them in the same steady pace as he unzipped her fly. Slowly. So slowly. Her lips trembled in anticipation of the touch of his mouth on hers, just as the area between her legs grew hot and heavy with the awareness his fingers were separated from her most sensitive skin by a zipper and silk panties. Candace couldn't breathe much less bring herself to utter one word of protest. She couldn't even remember why she might want to.

While his parted lips hovered just over hers, his naked chest grazed her breasts through her sheer lace bra. Her nipples puckered reflexively.

His warm, sweet breath tantalized her senses for an endless moment. Finally his whisper pierced the silence. "Let me taste you?" He waited a heartbeat for her refusal before brushing her lips with his in the softest of kisses.

Her insides twisted with a terrible need that balked at Logan's slow torture. Unable to stay still a moment longer, she tugged against the restraining hand holding her arms captive. He opened his fingers. Her hands fluttered in the air as she pondered their destination, finally settling, feather light on his shoulders.

Her touch seemed to snap his restraint. "*Candace.*" In one fluid motion, he surged forward, pressing her pliant body into the door with his masculine frame and claiming her mouth in a voracious kiss. Her arms slid up and around his neck and her hands curled into his thick damp hair. She tilted her head back, opening to him, greedy for more of him.

A growl sounded in the back of Logan's throat and he tore his lips from hers. He trailed hot kisses over her cheek, until he reached the column of her neck. He paused there to feast while his hips pressed rhythmically into hers, leaving her in no doubt of the direction of his thoughts.

Her body answered with a quivering, wet response of its own. She heard a soft whimper, only dimly realizing the sound came from her.

"You taste so good. Just like I knew you would," he said in a hoarse whisper. His lips stilled and he drew a ragged breath. "I want you."

A statement. A question.

God, how she wanted him, too. Like she'd never wanted any man. Over her, under her, between her legs. But…She searched her muddled brain for the source of the nagging doubt still assailing her conscious—albeit dimly.

Oh, no. *Eric*.

His lips had been at work on her earlobe, alternately nibbling and suckling. Abruptly he drew back, pressing his forehead against the door with a thump. "You don't…you don't want me, do you?"

He sounded so forlorn. If she hadn't been beside herself in a tangle of guilt and lust she would've laughed aloud. "It's not that."

"Then *what*?"

"What about Eric?"

Logan straightened. "Candace. Listen carefully. There is no me and Eric. Not now, not ever. Do you understand?"

"But I thought…"

"Yes. You thought."

"You mean…"

"I'm not gay, Candace. And you are driving me mad," he finished hoarsely.

She groaned. "Thank God."

He touched his forehead to hers, staring into her eyes. "Now that we have that out of the way," he whispered.

"Yes?"

"I really think we should do something about these wet clothes. Don't you?"

"Oh, definitely."

Not wasting another second, he released her zipper and tugged at the waistline of her jeans. They refused to budge.

She smiled.

"A little help, here?"

Obligingly, she wrestled the wet material down until she could finally kick the offensive denim toward the growing heap of clothes. Logan stood before her in nothing but a pair of black briefs. V-shaped torso. Washboard stomach. Muscular thighs and calves covered with just the right amount of hair. Sex personified.

But it was his eyes that captivated her. Intense, and full of sensual promise.

He approached her with halting steps, his gaze sliding over her. "I don't know where I want to touch you first." Then his eyes fixed on her chest and one corner of his mouth quirked upward. "On second thought, I see I still have some work to do undressing you."

He hooked two fingers under one white lace bra strap, slipping it from her shoulder, then repeated the process on her other shoulder. Her fingers itched to explore his body, to stroke and caress every tempting inch of him, but the sheer magnitude of his focus held her still.

With practiced ease, he unsnapped the front clasp of her bra, then, using both hands, sent the garment tumbling to the floor.

The night air washed over her damp skin and she shivered.

He cupped both her breasts with his warm palms.

They both groaned.

His eyes locked with hers as one of his hands left her breast to slide over her ribs and down her stomach. One fingertip circled her belly button before continuing south to skim the lacy front of her panties. "Such a shame these have to go, too."

But he didn't immediately strip them off. Instead he grazed the silk fabric covering her curls, as he made his way down. Coaxing her legs apart with the barest of pressure, he insinuated his fingers between her legs to nestle in her damp heat.

She whimpered with need. Only one scrap of silk now stood between her most sensitive flesh and his touch.

He closed his eyes and inched the edge of her panty aside. Sucking in a breath, he froze. "You're soaking wet," he whispered, and unhooked his fingers. The thin fabric moved back into place, covering her quaking flesh.

"I know," she said in husky, desperate voice.

"Slick and wet."

"I know," she said again, her tone pleading. Unable to resist the compulsion, she parted her legs in a silent demand for more.

A wicked smile lit his eyes in the moonlit room. Taking his time, he leaned forward to take her mouth in a deeply sensual kiss, his tongue at once plundering and seductive.

He wrapped one arm around her waist and pulled her into him. Meanwhile his fingers taunted and teased her through her panties, coming close to her most sensitive area, but never quite touching.

She would die soon if he didn't touch her.

She'd just have to help him along. Wrapping one leg around his rigid thigh, she plastered herself to him. He felt so good, every steely inch of him.

"Touch me," he commanded against her lips.

She didn't hesitate, though her fingers danced around his erection. Two could play the teasing game. "Here?" she asked, her nails scratching the straining material of his briefs.

He nodded.

She smiled against his lips and rocked her hips into his. "Right here?"

"Oh God."

With one hand she reached behind him and eased his briefs down far enough for her to squeeze his tight glutes.

"Can't...wait," he said between his teeth and slid one finger into her.

Her breath caught in her lungs and she almost shattered right then. "Oh, Logan, oh yes," she sobbed.

The teasing had gone on long enough. She slipped her hand under the elastic band of his briefs, encircled his engorged cock and squeezed.

Every muscled inch of him froze except for the tiny shudders wracking his body. Pure feminine satisfaction coursed through her veins. She ran her hand down the length of him over the tip of his erection, then encircled him again, squeezed again.

His turn to whimper.

She laughed softly and nipped his jaw. "You like that."

"I'm not sure. You better try it again," he choked out hoarsely.

She laughed and complied. She was on fire. Never had she felt so confident of her own sexual power—or so consumed with her own sexual need.

She rode up his hips, sliding her softness over the length of him. It felt so good she did it again. God how she wanted him inside her.

She started her climb once more, and he grabbed her hips, stilling her. "Baby, wait." He laughed, sounding self-conscious.

"I don't want to wait." She pulled herself up his chest.

"Jesus." He picked her up with both arms till she straddled him mid-air. The tip of his erection teased her opening through her lacy panties and she mewed softly.

"Hold that thought," he ground out. He crossed to the stairwell, taking the steps two at a time.

Chapter Twenty-Four

A moment later, Candace felt herself being dumped onto a bed. A quick glance around told her he'd taken her to his room. A drawer opened then a foil packet crackled. She propped herself on her elbows and watched him sheath himself in the latex.

He stood beside the bed and watched her watching him, a lazy smile lifting the corners of his mouth. Lightning flashed in the sky, brightening the room for a split second. No thunder sounded, just the steady sheeting of rain on the balcony.

A moment later, the bed shifted with Logan's weight as he kneeled over her and hooked his fingers under the elastic band of her panties. Slowly he rolled them down, pausing to kiss one hipbone then the other.

He continued peeling the panties back till the thin strip of material covered only the apex of her thighs. He caught her eyes as he dropped a kiss on the meager scrap of material.

"Logan," she begged, her head lolling back.

"Yes?" He sounded relaxed and nonchalant. Only the trembling of his hands as he resumed stripping her gave him away.

Finally he slipped the material over her toes.

She rose to her knees, bringing her body into contact with his, thigh to thigh, chest to chest. She wrapped one elbow around his neck and pulled his mouth to hers. Her tongue slid between his lips; she shifted her hips side to side in an erotic dance reminiscent of her dreams these past weeks.

"I want you," he whispered against her lips. "I want you so bad. I've ached for you from the first day." His fingers dipped into the heat between her legs.

She shivered. "Right now?"

He groaned in answer.

Without another word, she took his cock in hand, raised her hips and sheathed herself over him.

His sharp intake of breath was like an electric jolt to her core. "Ho, God. Oh, yes." He pulled her down until he filled her completely. For a long moment neither moved, spoke, breathed.

Then he began inching out, only to fill her again and again.

In the moonlit room his face was hard and masculine and unspeakably sexy.

Candace's insides coiled like a spring tightening. She could hardly breathe, couldn't think at all beyond Logan. His intense eyes. His hard body. Filling hers.

Faster. Harder. Deeper.

And then she came apart, hanging onto Logan for dear life while the world around them imploded into a thousand shards of light.

She could only cling to him as his answering release and male shout of triumph filled the room. Together they spilled onto the bed. Boneless. Replete. And, for Candace, exactly where she wanted to be.

****

A fire alarm blared into Logan's ear, dragging him awake. Wait. Not an alarm. A ring. A telephone. The phone was ringing. Logan didn't open his eyes, just groped the nightstand for the receiver till he found it and dragged it to his face. "Yeah?"

Silence.

"Hello-o?" Logan drew out.

"What the hell are you still doing there?"

The irritation in Eric's voice registered in a heartbeat. Followed swiftly by the more important realization Logan was in bed. Alone.

"Actually, I'm not *still* here. I'm back."

Silence greeted this important distinction.

"I came last night when I learned the area's phone and power lines were down. To check on Candace," Logan added.

"Mmm," Eric said, noncommittal. "I called last night from New York. The phone lines were down."

"I know. That's what I just said."

"You know about Candace's, er, fear of storms?"

"She mentioned it." Logan looked up as she came into the room carrying two steaming mugs of coffee. Apparently all the utilities had been restored.

She wore a cotton t-shirt and denim cut-offs, and her hair was damp, like she'd just showered. He wished he hadn't missed that.

"That's not really like her, talking about things like that."

"Mmm." Logan's turn to be noncommittal. He sat up letting the sheets fall away as Candace approached the bed. The cold morning air rushed over his naked chest.

She handed him a mug and he accepted it with a smile of thanks. He sipped the hot brew, never taking his eyes off her.

"So you left, and showed up again last night. I

suppose I should thank you."

Logan's gaze slid down Candace's smooth tanned legs. He wanted to touch her silky skin, but holding the coffee in one hand, and the receiver in the other ruled that out.

"Thanks." Eric sounded anything but grateful.

"You're welcome." Logan set the mug on the nightstand. He beckoned to Candace, patting the edge of the bed and scooting to make room for her.

"Well?"

"Yes?"

"How is she?"

"Last time I talked to her, she was fine. More than fine."

"What the hell is that supposed to mean?" Eric snapped.

"Just that she seemed to be handling the weather like a champ."

Candace perched beside Logan and frowned.

Eric, he mouthed.

She nodded, and remained silent.

"Is she around? I've tried her cell phone, but she's not answering, and her voicemail box is full."

"I'm sure she's around here somewhere." Logan let his gaze slide idly over Candace's body.

Her lips twitched.

"Have her call me, all right?"

"Sure. Where can she reach you?"

"At my office in New York. No, tell her to call my cell."

"So you're back in the States?" Logan frowned. He hoped Eric wasn't planning on paying any surprise visits.

"Yes. Why?" Eric sounded suspicious.

"Just curious."

"I'm curious, too. How long are you planning on staying?"

Logan slipped his fingers into Candace's damp tresses. "Probably just a day or two. I need to look the place over—make sure everything's tip-top."

Candace slipped off the bed and walked to the slider. She stood with her back to him as she took in the view and sipped her coffee.

"Logan," Eric hesitated, "It's not that I don't appreciate the offer, but I can get someone out there—"

"It's no trouble." Logan purposely ignored Eric's not-so-subtle attempt to give him the boot. "Besides, I'm sure Candace would rather not have a total stranger roaming around the place."

Eric hesitated before conceding. "True."

"Besides that, my car's in the body shop and won't be delivered for two days."

"You got into a wreck?"

"A little fender bender." Logan glanced at Candace's perky backside and decided he and Eric had been on the phone long enough. "Okay, then. I'll have her call you."

"Logan?"

"Yes?"

"Nothing's going on there that I need to know about, right?"

Nothing that concerns you, Eric. "Nothing at all."

"And you do remember the promise you made?"

Logan gritted his teeth a moment. "Yep."

"And Luke always said, you never break your promises."

The moment Logan replaced the receiver, Candace pivoted to face him. "That was Eric?"

Logan eyed her. "Yes. He wants you to call him."

"I see."

"I get the feeling he wants me out of here."

Candace met his gaze squarely. She opened her mouth to speak, and Logan got the distinct feeling she was ready to dismiss him.

He spoke up before she could. "You look fresh. You showered. I wish you'd waited for me."

The corners of her lips tilted up in a slight smile.

"Come here," he whispered, sounding strange and gruff to his own ears.

She hesitated.

"Please?"

Candace inched forward.

"I'm not going to eat you. Not entirely," he said with a lazy grin. He reached for her mug and set it down, then pulled her into his arms. "What's going on in that head of yours, Candace? You trying to get rid of me? A quick cup of coffee, maybe a shower, then my hat and the door?"

"Of course not," she said, sounding satisfyingly breathless.

Logan rolled with her until he lay half on top of her, tangling both of their legs in the sheets. "Good. I would have felt cheap."

She laughed, and his stomach did an odd somersault. His eyes locked with hers, searching for…he didn't know what.

He did know his morning erection had stiffened into a pulsing hard-on, insistent on boring through the covers separating their bodies. He fought the urge to grind himself into her, not wanting to embarrass himself with his intense desire for her—again. They'd made love twice last night, the second time not five hours earlier. And he wanted her like he hadn't had sex in a year.

What if last night was an anomaly? What if Candace didn't share his intense attraction? What if she thought of him as nothing more than a one-night stand?

And what the hell was the matter with him? Since when was he concerned with anything more than the present tense? He gave himself a mental shake. "I'd kiss you, but I'd probably burn your skin off with my beard."

Candace's eyes dropped to his lips. Beneath him, she shifted slightly and he felt his hips settle a little more snuggly between her legs. He almost groaned from the pleasure of it.

He squeezed his eyes shut, trying to distract himself. "Plus I haven't brushed my teeth or showered like you."

Candace grabbed his face with both hands and pulled him down until their lips met, mouths open. She moaned softly and wrapped her arms around his neck.

"Sweet Jesus," Logan whispered. He grabbed a fistful of sheets and yanked them from between their bodies. His hands were everywhere, all at once. He gave a low, frustrated growl. "One of us has too many clothes on." And it wasn't him. He was naked.

Candace gave him a seductive smile and let her arms fall back, next to her head. "What should we do about it?" she asked in a perfect imitation of a southern belle.

All the blood in his body headed south. He wanted

to rip off her shirt, wanted to shove her shorts aside, and get himself inside her. But he also wanted—needed—to know she wanted him as badly as he wanted her. He gave her a wicked smile and slid down her body till his face was even with her waistline. He inched up her shirt and flicked his tongue over the silky skin beneath.

Her thighs tightened around his torso instinctively and her fingers gripped the hem of her t-shirt. She began to pull it upward.

"Uh-uh." Logan placed his hands over hers. "I'll do that." Her breathing was soft and shallow. Good.

His lips found her belly and nibbled their way up her body, sliding the fabric of her shirt as he went. Candace wriggled and arched, making little noises in her throat that threatened to drive him over the edge.

"What have we here?" Logan's throat went dry as he uncovered her sheer pink bra. "You have…" he circled the hard buds of her nipples with gentle fingers, "beautiful, perfect breasts."

She gazed at him with passion-drugged eyes.

"I'll bet you have matching panties on," he said in a husky whisper. "Don't you?"

Candace bit her lip and nodded.

"Let's see." Logan abandoned her breasts and headed back to the waistband of her shorts. He released the button with a deft twist and tugged down the zipper. He parted the material, and sucked in his breath. Sheer pink panties, and a small patch of light colored curls just visible through the material.

He raised himself onto his elbows and tugged her shorts over her hips, down her legs, past her feet, to toss them on the floor. He grabbed her knees using both hands, and spread her thighs.

"Logan," she whispered.

"Shh." He kissed the silky skin just outside the edges of her panties.

Candace's hips wriggled. His tongue skimmed over the thin strip of silk between her legs and she jerked reflexively. He kissed her through the silk, then slipped the tip of his tongue under the lacy edge, tasting her damp heat. Using his fingers, he inched the material to the side giving himself greater access. He gazed at her for a moment, mouth watering in anticipation. Then with one finger, he traced her opening slowly. Drawing nearer and nearer to the small pleasure bud at her apex.

He heard the small, feverish sounds she was making. Even without the sounds, he would know she was close to the edge. She was soaking wet and trembling with need. Perfect. He touched her with the tip of his tongue, soft, gentle flicks. "God, you taste good."

She moaned and arched upward, urging him on.

He was happy to oblige. His tongue played over her while he slid one finger around and inside her. In a matter of seconds she was moaning his name and coming violently into his mouth. It was nearly his undoing. He groaned as her hands frantically tugged at his shoulders and hair, anywhere she could reach.

"Hell, yes!" He didn't think he *could* wait any longer. He rose, kissing her voraciously as the tip of his cock found her tight opening.

She resisted, squeezing her thighs together to stop him.

"Wh...yes... You want me to stop?" he managed, his muddled brain trying to make sense of her

175

hesitation.

"Don't we need?" She pointed to the nightstand.

The condom. Shit. What had he been thinking? He hadn't been thinking.

He broke away, yanked open the drawer to find one of the wrappers and ripped it open. Candace took the condom from his shaking hands.

A minute ago Logan hadn't thought he could want her more. He'd been wrong. She looked like a goddess perched on her knees in the middle of the rumpled bed, still dressed in her translucent panty and bra set. She'd managed to lose the t-shirt, he noticed. She took him in her hands and covered him in the latex.

A moment later he was on top of her. He didn't take the time to remove her panties. He couldn't. He just pushed them aside and slid into her. He heard a whimper as he pulled partly out, and realized it was him. He pressed into her wet heat. His stomach was a jumble of tight knots, his groin wound as tightly as a spring-loaded coil. And still he wanted her. Couldn't get enough.

Again and again he drove into her, each glide more satisfying than the last. When her second release began, his self-control snapped and he gave in to the most intense climax of his life. When it was through, he fell on top of her, unwilling to pull out. Not yet. He was probably crushing her, but he couldn't make himself care, couldn't let her move even one inch away from him.

"Wow," Candace said in a low voice, breaking the spell Logan was under.

A sudden wellspring of mirth bubbled up inside him, and he laughed. A deep belly laugh like he couldn't remember having in a long, long, time. "I couldn't have said it better myself." He raised himself onto his forearms and pressed a kiss on her lips. "Care to take another shower?"

Chapter Twenty-Five

Candace stood beside Logan at the kitchen island, washing and cutting fresh strawberries while he sliced a mango. They both wore their bathrobes and nothing else, having come straight from the shower where they'd worked up an appetite making love yet again.

Logan had turned on the stereo and the soft sounds of jazz filled the air. It all felt very...domestic. And perfect. By rights, Candace should be scared. She *should* be building a wall to barricade her heart against Logan's barrage of tenderness, charm, and sex appeal.

But that was the old her.

"Wonder what's going through that pretty head of yours," Logan said, cutting into her thoughts.

Startled, Candace nearly nipped her thumb with the knife.

"Hey, be careful there, will you? I like your fingers."

"I like them, too." She wiggled them in front of her face to make sure she hadn't nicked herself. "I'd say that's enough strawberries, wouldn't you?" Candace effectively sidestepped Logan's comment about her train of thought. She rinsed the paring knife in the island sink and popped a strawberry into her mouth.

"Why don't you sit down? I'll finish this." Logan scraped the mango slices into a bowl and washed the cutting board as Candace moved to sit at the island counter.

"We need to talk," Logan said, not meeting Candace's eyes.

Here it came. The *thanks for a good time, now I have to go* speech. She could take it. She'd gone to bed with Logan with her eyes wide open. She'd known it was nothing more than a fling. Logan had told her that very first night he didn't commit. Ever. Of course, at the time she'd thought he was talking about men, and Eric in particular. She looked at Logan's rugged profile and wondered again how she could ever have thought he was gay.

"That's what I want to know." Logan shot her a crooked grin.

"Did I say that out loud?"

"Yep."

"Oh. Not that there's anything wrong with it."

"Glad to hear it."

She gave Logan a speculative look.

"Luke. He and Eric were lovers."

"Oh." So that was it. The tie that bound them. "I had no idea."

"How could you have? Obviously it's still too painful for Eric to discuss." He shrugged. "I was trying not to expose Eric's prevarication, as unethical as I found it."

Candace blinked. "Eric's..." Understanding dawned. "Logan, Eric never said you and he were, you know, together. I just assumed when he said he had a special friend staying at his house."

One corner of Logan's mouth curved up. He pulled a hand towel from a small drawer and dried the knives and cutting board. "And here I thought Eric was protecting you from the big bad Logan."

Candace cocked her head. "What do you mean?" she asked.

"He warned me off of you before you arrived."

"I see." Could Candace feel like more of a fool? So Eric had known Candace would fall for Logan's charms? Candace who never dabbled in illicit affairs? Worse still, was Logan some kind of notorious love 'em and leave 'em ladies' man? Well, yes, he was. By his own admission, a small voice chimed inside her head.

Logan gave her a quizzical look. "Based on the myriad of expressions flitting over your face, now I'd really like to know what you're thinking."

Candace pasted her best poker smile on her face. "What did you want to talk about?"

"Are you almost finished with your book?" Logan asked.

Her mouth opened, then closed with a snap. Her book. Her book? Candace prided herself on always being one step ahead, on always being prepared. So why was it with Logan, almost without exception, her plans and conjectures flew out the window? "As in the one I'm currently writing?"

Logan cleared his throat and lowered his eyes to study his neatly trimmed nails. "Yes, that's the one I was referring to."

Confusion furrowed Candace's brows. "Yes. Just wrapped up the editing phase, in fact."

Logan nodded and rolled his shoulders.

"Did you want to read it?"

Logan's mouth curved slightly. He placed his forearms on the counter, hands clasped, and leaned forward. "I was just wondering how much longer you were staying."

Her heart plummeted as Logan's intentions became crystal clear. He wanted her to leave, so he could stay. So much for preparing herself mentally for the brush off. "I was planning on staying another month. Leaving the first week of August—at Eric's suggestion," she finished, sounding sullen and defensive to her own ears.

"Great." Logan flashed his glamorous smile. He walked to the stainless Viking refrigerator and opened it. "So you..." a portion of his words got swallowed by the frigid air as he rummaged inside. A moment later he re-emerged, grinned at her, and said, "Right?"

"I'm sorry. I didn't quite catch that."

His smile froze. "You didn't?"

"Logan." Candace put her palms to her heated cheeks. Why was he dragging this out? "Are you trying to tell me you want me to go home?"

Logan blinked. "No. Hell no. Where would you get that idea?"

"Because if you are... No?"

He walked slowly around the island to stand beside her, his eyes never leaving hers. "What I'm trying to ask, apparently in the most convoluted way possible, is if you'd mind having company."

He wanted to stay. With her.

"Then you asked about my book because..."

"Because I didn't want to distract you from it. I gave Eric my word." He shook his head as if to say *scratch that.* "The point is, Eric would have good cause to bust my...to kick me out then. But since you're all but done, I thought," he shrugged, "why not?"

"Why not?" she aped softly.

Logan cupped the nape of her neck and bent to

brush a kiss on her lips. "Is that a yes?"

"Yes."

"Good." He rubbed the tip of his nose against hers. "Now that's settled."

"Yes?" she asked, half in a daze.

"I'm starved."

Candace was too, and not for food.

As if reading her mind, Logan gave her a tut-tut smile. "I need sustenance, vixen."

After they polished off most of the fruit, Logan made a couple of peanut butter and marshmallow sandwiches. His own creative genius at work there. They'd thrown away most of the refrigerated meats and dairy, as the power had been off for over twenty-four hours.

They sat side by side, nibbling sandwiches over the polished marble counter, and a deep sense of contentment washed over Candace. She stole a glance at Logan's profile. What was it about him? Ever since she'd met him, her outlook on life had changed. Her rigid need for control seemed to have vanished. Look what happened last night when she ventured out into the storm. She'd never been able to quash her irrational anxiety during lightning strikes even while *indoors*. But last night, in the midst of a raging storm, her entire focus had been on Logan, and making sure he was safe.

"So. What are you going to tell Eric?" Logan asked.

Just like that, reality reared its ugly head. "I haven't thought about it."

"Uh-huh."

"What do you think I should I tell him?" Candace asked, lobbing the ball back in Logan's court.

Logan finished the last bite of sandwich and turned his heart-stopping smile on her.

Well, damn. Damp hair curling over the collar of his terrycloth robe. Freshly shaven, smelling of just the right amount of spicy aftershave. Twinkling turquoise eyes.

She didn't realize she was staring until Logan lifted her chin to close her mouth. "Babe, if you want to get dressed sometime today, you'd better quit looking at me like that."

Candace felt the heat radiating off her cheeks. "I have no idea what you mean."

Logan chuckled softly. "To answer your question, I don't think I'd volunteer anything. About me that is— not if you don't want him to worry."

Candace wrinkled her nose. "That would be dishonest, don't you think? After all, it's his house." She replayed Logan's last words in her head and gave him a searching look. "Are you that bad, Logan?"

Logan winked at Candace playfully, rising from his stool. "I'm that good, darlin'."

****

Candace re-read the last page and gave a satisfied nod. She closed the laptop with a click, a thrall of anticipation coursing through her body. Just the thought of seeing him did that to her. Even after three days of spending every waking moment together.

Today she'd deliberately put some distance between herself and Logan, using the very real excuse she needed to work. She'd also harbored another, secret reason for disappearing into her room. She'd wanted to know if she could. Even more importantly, could she clear her mind of the vortex that was Logan.

So now she knew. She could. For the last several hours she'd been totally immersed in Zeke and Kitty's love story—Zeke and Kitty being the characters in her current work-in-progress.

But now. She opened the sliding glass doors and stepped one foot onto the balcony, leaning forward far enough to eye the deck below for Logan. Not there.

Maybe she'd get lucky and find him in his room taking an afternoon nap. Or just out of the shower, fresh from a workout. This thing with Logan couldn't last. The real-life fantasy could only be temporary. But oh how intoxicating this temporary insanity was to her starved senses.

Before she reached the hall her cell phone chimed from its perch on the dresser. A glance at the caller ID took just the tiniest bit of wind from her sails. "Hello, Eric."

"Hello, yourself. Mind telling me why it's been three days and you haven't returned my call yet?"

"I was just about to. I got caught up with my writing and didn't want to put on the brakes. So. You're back? How was your trip?" Candace let herself out of her room and skipped down the stairs. She headed to the back door. This phone call might take a while—she may as well stretch her legs.

"Great. Exhausting. Exhilarating! I came back with ideas for expanding the agency and extending some of my writers' reach to the European market. Yours for instance."

"Really? Oh, Eric, that would be fantastic."

"I thought you'd say that. We'll discuss it after your current project is signed, sealed, and delivered."

"Sounds great. What are your plans now? I suppose

you have a pile of work waiting for you."

"As always. But, Candace, I...uh, actually wanted to talk to you about something other than work. You have a minute?"

Her stomach sank to her toes. This was about Logan. Had to be.

On second thought, maybe he wanted to discuss those hateful emails. Her spirits rose. "Sure. What's up?" She went through the back gate and stepped onto the weaving path leading to the lake below. The stones were smooth, and sun-heated, and felt like heaven to her bare feet.

"Candace, you're one of the most...mm....how can I say...challenging women I've ever known as far as male/female relationships go. What I mean to say is, you're no easy cookie. Your defenses are stacked way too high for the average mortal male to climb. You follow me so far?"

"I...think so."

Eric hesitated. "Logan is no mere mortal."

Damn. "I'm not sure I follow."

"Uh-huh. Maybe I shouldn't assume. Let me back up a bit. Is he still there?"

"Logan? Yes."

"I knew it. All right. Let me just shoot straight. I'm hoping you're not involved with him. I mean, under normal circumstances, I'd be thrilled to see you in an illicit affair. I'd just rather not see you get tangled up with Logan. The man has no heart—at least not one he's willing to share."

Candace waded, ankle deep, into the waves lapping at the shore. The shock of icy cold water momentarily stole her breath; at least that was what she was blaming her sudden shortness of breath on.

"You're not saying anything." Eric sighed. "You're sleeping with him."

She thought about denying the truth, then decided against it. This was Eric. "It's no big deal."

"Oh, shit. I knew it."

"Eric, for goodness sake. It's not like I'm expecting a marriage proposal. Give me a little credit, will you?"

"You have good taste. I'll give you that."

"I *mean*," she said with emphasis, "I'm not in over my head. We're just two adults, thrown together by chance, enjoying some time together."

"Mm hmm. Enjoying yourselves. I want details."

Candace laughed. "Not gonna happen."

"You can't leave me in the dark, princess. I'll worry myself sick. Give me something."

"There's not much to tell. Up until, say, seventy-two hours ago, our relationship was PG rated."

He whistled. "That has to be a world record. You held out longer than any other woman I've known, with respect to Shaw."

She scowled at the phone. "It's not like he set out to seduce me."

"He didn't with the other women, either," Eric said dryly.

"I'm guessing none of those other women thought he was in a relationship with their best friend until the eleventh hour," Candace muttered. She didn't much care for being just another number in a long line of women.

"Say again?"

"Until the day before yesterday, I kind of assumed

you two were, you know, *together."*

A beat of silence passed. "Why on earth would you think that?" Eric finally asked.

"You. You and your special friend."

"I did? Oh. Now I remember. Huh."

"You rarely introduce me to your paramours, and I thought this one must be really something for him to be staying at Eric's house."

"He is that. Did Logan know you thought he and I were lovers?"

"Sure."

"And he didn't bother to correct your mistake? That's not like him."

"He neither confirmed nor denied. He only mentioned the two of you had a long and complicated past, without offering many details." She hesitated. "Then a few days ago he told me about Luke."

"He mentioned Luke?"

"He's talked about his brother quite a bit. About his art. About his death. Did you know Logan blames himself for Luke's accident?"

Silence.

"Eric? Are you still there?"

"Yes. You just caught me off guard. But to answer your question, no, I never knew he felt responsible. I always thought..." His words died in his throat.

"Eric?" she prompted.

"I just assumed he blamed me," Eric said, his voice just above a whisper.

"Why you? My God, Eric, were you in the truck with Luke?"

"No."

"Then that's just as absurd a thought as Logan

taking the blame." She hoped her gentle tone softened her harsh words.

"Candace…" Eric drew a ragged breath before he continued, "I was the reason Luke was in that truck. He was moving to be with me. I should have been with him. Instead, I was working."

A mist of tears blurred Candace's vision at the raw pain in Eric's voice. "You never said anything, Eric. I'm so sorry you lost him."

"It was a long time ago."

Candace smiled sadly. "That's exactly what Logan said."

"Six years," he breathed.

"From what Logan said, I know he was a truly gifted man. You loved him very much, didn't you?"

"He was," Eric's voice cracked, "the love of my life."

"Oh, Eric."

He heaved a great sigh. "Yes, well. Now you know. I have to tell you, I'm shocked Logan confided in you. Really shocked."

"Maybe he's ready to work through the pain finally."

"Maybe. I hope so. Now you see why I couldn't toss Logan out when I offered the place to you. Which reminds me of another thing that's got me scratching my head. He broke a promise to me. Logan never lies—not even when it would save him grief. Just ask the women in his wake. He's the first one to tell them he doesn't do permanent. You do know that, don't you, Candy?"

"Of course. I'm not looking for anything permanent either." She wasn't. But why did hearing the words from Eric feel like a hot poker to the heart? "So what promise did he break?"

"He promised to stay away from you, and normally, his word is gold. That makes this very, very interesting indeed."

Candace was completely lost. "How so?"

"On the night of the storm, he came back for you of his own accord. Unless…you didn't call him to come back, did you?"

"Absolutely not."

Eric laughed. "Don't get your panties in a wad, sweetheart. I'm just wrapping my mind around this. Logan Shaw has a weakness," he said sounding inordinately satisfied.

"What's that?"

"Evidently, it's you."

Candace wished she didn't feel such a rush of longing at Eric's words. "Aren't you calling to warn me off of him? This sounds more like a post-game cheer."

Eric chuckled. "You're right. It's the hopeless romantic in me. The point I should be making, and what I want you to remember, is regardless of whether Logan's acting out of character, a leopard doesn't change his spots."

The wind kicked up a notch and Candace hugged herself with her free arm. "In other words, don't get attached. Got it. Believe it or not, I didn't fall off the turnip truck yesterday. To tell you the truth, I'd expected him to ship out two days ago. I never expected him to ask to stay here with me for a while."

"He *what*?"

"Didn't I mention it?"

"No you did not. What did you tell him?" Eric

asked, sounding half exasperated, half amused.

"I told him he could stay, of course," she said. "I didn't think you'd mind."

Eric chuckled softly. "Alrighty, then. Look, Candy-cupcake, promise me you won't pick this instance with this particular man to finally lose your heart."

Candace smiled wryly into the phone. She may have lost her head, but her heart was only on temporary loan. She could, she was sure, handle it when their fling came to its inevitable end. Sure, she'd be bummed for a short period of time. And then she'd get on with her life. It was all so simple. Why had she been depriving herself all these years? "I promise."

Chapter Twenty-Six

Logan finished his last rep and lowered the weight-laden bar onto the rack. For a long moment he lay on the bench, breathing hard and staring at the ceiling of the house gym. It was the first time he'd been on his own in the sprawling house since he'd popped the big question. The first time he'd had a chance to ask himself what the hell he was doing. To wonder what he'd been thinking, when he'd asked to stay with Candace in Tahoe.

He sat up and scrubbed a towel over his damp face. He hadn't been thinking, that's what. One minute he was cutting fruit, the next he was staring at Candace's cheeks, free of makeup and flushed from their shower, the scene of their last, incredible sexual interlude, and presto. He heard himself asking if she minded the company.

He grinned despite himself. He felt like a kid in the middle of his first crush. He couldn't get enough of her, couldn't get his fill of looking at her beautiful, expressive face, of kissing her sweet, full lips. He was getting hard again. He shook his head. He hadn't been this insatiable since he was eighteen.

Logan stepped onto the treadmill and set the gauge to simulate a 10K. As the belt picked up speed, he stared out the window to the lake and asked himself how, in the span of seventy-two hours, Candace had become an addiction.

Okay, if he were honest, the fixation started the moment he sat beside her at the pool and struck up a conversation. He'd wanted her from the beginning. And now that he'd had her, he needed more and more. So not like him, and he wasn't entirely comfortable with the feeling.

Earlier, she'd rejected his offer to take her sailing for the day, blithely announcing she had work to do. Logan's disappointment had been as startling as it was palpable. But he hadn't argued. That was the deal he'd made with himself to avoid any guilt over breaking his word with Eric. He couldn't interfere with her work.

Still. Something about the way Candace waved and smiled told Logan he was being dismissed. Like she'd needed space as much if not more than she'd needed to work. Another man might have missed the signs, but Logan had written the book on the subtle brushoff. He just couldn't remember ever being on the receiving end.

Logan had let her make good her escape. The fact he hadn't wanted to let her out of his sight would be his little secret. The fact he couldn't keep his hands off her was a little less easy to hide.

Abruptly, Candace came into view at the shoreline. An intense jolt of something between pleasure and pain at the sight of her stabbed him in the gut. He jacked up the speed on the treadmill and watched her wade barefoot into the shimmering water in a pair of hip-hugger khaki shorts and a fitted yellow t-shirt. Her blonde hair, caught up in a long ponytail, glistened in the sun. He couldn't take his eyes off her.

She wandered, back and forth, along the shore, a cell phone glued to her ear.. She seemed tense, hugging herself with one arm while she carried on a conversation with…who, he wondered? Eric? *Roger?*

He swallowed hard against a sudden, metallic taste in his mouth.

He hadn't asked Candace about Roger since he returned three days ago, and she hadn't offered any information. In truth, he hadn't given the matter much thought. He'd been a little busy studying every inch of her beautiful body.

He was probably safe assuming she'd written off dear Roger for good. She wasn't the sort to have carnal knowledge with one man while being even partially committed to another. Not Candace who never dabbled in non-committed relationships.

Which begged the question, what did Candace think was going on between them? His head began to throb, and he forced the thought away. The question was moot. This was temporary. And it wasn't any of his business who was on the other end of her phone line.

Candace ended the call and headed back to the house. Before she reached the gate she paused, tilting her face toward the sun.

God, she was beautiful.

A moment later, she resumed her march to the house. Soon she disappeared from sight.

Dammit, *had* she been talking to Roger? His stomach burned with an unfamiliar, dark emotion. He closed his eyes and concentrated on his breathing. Candace didn't belong to him and the sooner he quit indulging any fantasy notions to the contrary, the better for all involved. What did he have to offer someone like Candace? Other than physical pleasure of the temporary kind, nothing.

He knew it, and Eric sure as hell knew it, which was why Eric made him promise to keep his hands off her. And he had. Their physical relationship began after he returned. Big difference.

He snorted. Even he was having a hard time believing his bullshit. If that had been Eric on the phone with Candace, and she'd fessed up about the two of them, Eric was probably well and truly pissed at Logan right about now.

The treadmill slowed and an alarm clamored telling him he'd reached his goal. He pressed the red stop button and jumped off the belt.

He swiped a towel over his dripping face. Feeling more disgruntled than when he started his workout, he headed for his room. He'd shower. Clear his head. Maybe take a ride to the post office. He hadn't checked to see if any of the feelers he'd put out concerning overseas gigs had come in for days.

No more wondering about Candace's relationship with Roger, and more importantly, no more mental cogitation about the status of their relationship. What did he think—they'd stay together forever? Make an actual go of things?

He'd reached the base of the stairs when *bam,* a fierce yearning the likes of which he'd never known seized him, causing him to stop in his tracks, one hand gripping the railing as if holding on for dear life.

Was that what he wanted? A real future with Candace?

Forget it, Shaw. Don't go blowing things. Don't write checks with your mouth your body can't cover. You don't know how to be in it for the long haul. You buckle at crunch time. You're a player. It's what you're good at, who you are, and Candace deserves better.

"Logan, are you all right?" Candace called softly from above.

Logan blinked up at the landing. He forced a smile. "Just catching my breath before taking the stairs. Tough workout."

Candace nodded, looking unconvinced.

He climbed the stairs two at a time. His eyes never left Candace. "I, uh, saw you down by the lake. On the phone."

She gazed at him with soft eyes. Eyes that seemed to see right into his soul. "Eric called."

Relief flowed through his veins in a rush, almost, but not quite, blotting out his secret shame. He'd asked about the phone call. He hadn't been able to resist. He was a pathetic fool. But he grinned.

"He wanted to talk about you."

Logan's grin vanished. "He drag a confession out of you?"

She blushed.

He laughed, but it sounded forced to his own ears. "He did." Logan waited a beat. "Did he mention the promise?"

She angled her head and smiled a little. "He did."

Logan spread his hands. "Guilty. I'm guessing he also took the opportunity to tell you how I'm no good. Told you to steer clear of me."

She lifted a brow. "He was a little surprised you didn't stick to your promise." She gave him a sidelong glance. "By the way, I would have been ticked off if you had followed his misguided instructions."

Logan huffed out a laugh. "Would you, now?"

"Seriously, though, Logan, Eric didn't tell me

195

anything you hadn't already revealed. I'm not saying he didn't try and warn me off, but I made it clear we're two adults enjoying a summertime fling."

Logan nodded. "And he bought that?"

"Why wouldn't he? It's the truth."

Exactly what he'd been telling himself. So why did hearing her say it leave him annoyed? "Good enough. So what now? Back to work?"

"Actually, I'm famished. I skipped lunch."

He was, too. He touched her face with his fingertips. "Hey, the Aston's back from the shop. Let's go out tonight."

She smiled at him, the corners of her eyes crinkling at the corners. "Like on a date?"

"Almost exactly," he teased. He couldn't remember the last time he'd taken a woman on a date.

Her stomach let out a loud growl and she pressed a hand to her belly. "When do we leave?"

"How soon can you be ready?"

She scrunched up her brows. "What kind of place are we talking? Jeans? Shorts? Or a real dress?"

"A real dress. If you brought one."

She nodded. "Brought, in the likely event Eric would pop in. He likes to go to shi-shi restaurants."

"Shi-shi it is."

"All right. Best-case scenario? An hour."

He grasped her ponytail and wrapped it around his hand, enjoying the silken feel of it as it slid over his palm. "Can you make it that long, sweetheart? I don't want you to pass out in the shower. In fact, I should probably shower with you, just to be on the safe side."

"Just to be safe," she replied, breathless, grabbing his shirtfront and dragging him toward her bedroom.

****

Everything was set, Logan thought with no small amount of satisfaction. He'd obtained coveted rooftop reservations at one of the most romantic restaurants on the North Shore. Being last minute, he'd had to do a little name-dropping. Working for *Rolling Stone Magazine* did have its perks.

He glanced at his Breitling and peered up the stairs. He'd headed to his room after their shower, leaving Candace to dress for dinner in her room. Candace had said she'd be ready on the hour. It was six minutes till. He felt like a nervous high school kid on prom night.

Exactly on time, Candace appeared at the landing. As she descended the stairs, Logan put his lips together to blow a slow whistle of appreciation. "Wow."

Candace ducked her head and a faint blush spread over her already-glowing cheeks. She wore a white dress. Two strings tied behind her neck, serving as a halter and cinching in an O at a heart-shaped bodice. The silky fabric hugged her curves, emphasizing the generous swell of her breasts and her slender waist before falling in loose folds. She twirled in place, flashing him a good bit of shapely leg. "You like?"

"I like *a lot.*" Of course, she would be a knockout dressed in nothing more than her own hair, hanging loose over her shoulders.

"You clean up pretty nicely yourself." Candace came forward to smooth the lapels of his black sports coat.

He glanced at his attire. Black button-down shirt, sports coat, trousers. A typical look for him if and when dressy was called for. "Thank you."

She smiled into his eyes. "You're welcome."

He swallowed at the odd lump forming in his throat.

He put his hand on the small of her back, and guided her out the front door. A UPS package sat on the front stoop. Logan bent and picked it up. "A package for you—from the Palmer Agency. Want to open it?"

"And risk dying of starvation? I'll look at it when we get back."

Chapter Twenty-Seven

"I think this is the most romantic dinner I've ever had. Except for my first night in Tahoe, when you served me dinner al fresco."

"Would that be the night you told me I was dating Eric?" he asked with a chuckle.

Candace waved her hand dismissively. "Details."

"Are you...glad?" Had he really just asked her that?

She gave him a considering glance. "Glad? You mean...that you're not gay, or that you came back to me, or that we went on this date?"

He laughed. "You choose," he said, grateful for the dim lighting as he felt an odd heat flood his face and neck.

"Yes. I am. Very."

More warmth, this time flooding his senses, and causing his loins to tighten. He should be used to being hard by now. Maybe someone had slipped some male enhancement pills into the milk container.

A waiter came by to clear their dinner plates and scrape away telltale crumbs.

Candace gazed at him, running her fingertips idly over the white tablecloth. "You know what I'd really like?"

He rested his cheek in his palm. "What's that?"

She tilted her head. "For you to tell me something

about yourself."

A wry smile twisted his lips. "The last time I agreed to do that, you asked me about my boyfriend."

"Tell me about work, then."

He leaned back in his chair. "Such as?"

"Such as…why are you hiding out here?"

"Why do you say I'm hiding out?"

She gave him a knowing look. How did she read him so well?

He lowered his eyes to study the shiny fork he'd begun rolling between his thumb and forefinger. He didn't want to tell her. He didn't want to see her look at him like the fickle player everyone else saw when they looked at him.

"It's not a pretty story," he said.

"I kind of figured that."

Logan lifted his gaze to stare at her for a long moment.

"Look, if it's too personal—"

"I screwed up," he bit out. "You know the old adage, never mix business with pleasure?"

She slid her gaze back to his and nodded slowly.

"It's good advice, take my word. About a year ago, a woman started at the magazine. Copywriter. I don't know how we met exactly. Mostly she kept turning up everywhere I was. I was working at HQ a lot at the time, rather than off-site. Drinks after work with the gang—there she was. Coffee shop downstairs—there she was again. Sub shop down the street, you get the picture."

"Yes. Clearly more than just happy coincidences?"

Apparently she did get the idea. Logan's gourmet dinner settled like a brick in his stomach. But he was committed to telling her everything now. "Honestly, I wasn't all that interested. She was. I could tell." He curled a fingertip under his collar and tugged. "What happened to the breeze?"

Candace smiled faintly. "You weren't interested in her. So, what happened next?"

"One night, we ended up at a cocktail party hosted by one of the editors. Turned out she's the niece of this particular editor, but I didn't know that at the time."

"Hmm."

"One thing led to another and...I went home with her."

"You mean, she went home with you?"

"No. I mean I went home with her. She happened to leave the same time I did and asked if we could share a taxi."

"Oh, the old share the taxi trick."

"Okay. I admit I knew what was coming. Especially after she asked if I'd come up to her place to take a look at some of her photos. Said she was really into photography." He paused, not wanting to continue.

Candace's gaze held a question—or, rather a dare. Tell the truth. Trust me.

Fine. Logan clenched his jaw, but continued. "She was pretty hot. I thought at the time she was just offering...you know...sex. And I like sex. A lot. So I made a grave miscalculation, and slept with her. No big deal, I thought. Just a one night deal. Not even. I went home a little later."

"I think they call those one-night stands," she said softly.

"Yeah, I guess they do. You hate me now?"

She looked genuinely taken aback. "Why? Because

you had consensual sex with a woman? Logan." She tilted her head and gave him a half smile. "Have a little more faith in me than that. After all, what are *we* doing?"

His insides seized. How had the conversation become about them? "What?"

She waved her hand in an almost frantic gesture. "Not what I meant to say. Forget that last bit. I meant it would be hypocritical of me to judge you for that. Anyway," she added, "I still don't see what your…impromptu sexual liaison has to do with work."

A moment ago, he'd been dreading this revelation. Now he grabbed onto it like a drowning man clutching a lifeline—anything to avoid *the talk*. "Almost immediately she started showing up in my work space. Just to say hi, or because she happened to be passing through the wing. She started calling me, and I hadn't even given her my number. I told her straight up, *before* anything happened, I wasn't interested in anything permanent. Even semi-permanent. So, I repeated the sentiment for her edification.

"For a month or so, the phone calls diminished. And then I went away on location, a really sweet assignment in D.C." He smiled faintly, remembering. "I was working with an ace writing team bent on uncovering a scandal involving some big-wigs on Capitol Hill."

"Just the thing for a crusader like you," Candace said in an admiring tone.

Her words surprised him. He searched her face, taking in the gentle smile curving her lips, the warmth of her eyes. He'd been so sure his less than pristine past would be a total turn off for her. But instead of latching onto the ignoble aspects of his character, she had found something in him to praise.

"You're lovely." He meant it in every sense of the word. If they were alone he'd haul her into his arms. He settled for covering her hand with his.

She inclined her head, brushing the compliment aside. "What happened next?"

"Since she could no longer reach me by phone or pop by my area at the office, she flooded my inbox with love letters. I intended to deal with the situation when I got back. Only, when I arrived, I found she'd made inroads to the photo department. She got herself assigned to me, as an apprentice."

Candace's brows furrowed. "Is that normally how it's done?"

"No."

"How'd she do it?"

"Exactly what I wanted to know. Remember that editor I mentioned—her uncle?"

"Ah. He pulled some strings. What did you do?"

"I said, 'Hell no.' And then the other shoe dropped. My editor called me in. Said something about a sexual harassment suit."

Her free hand flew to her cheek. "Oh, no. But you didn't use your position to hinder her career."

"Just what I told my editor, that our jobs were completely removed from one another. But I was preaching to the choir. After we talked, I realized Alex, my editor, was pissed off on my behalf." Logan's laughter held no humor. "Hell, she even suggested, in a roundabout way, I threaten a lawsuit of my own."

Candace raised her brows. "Sexual harassment?"

"Yep. But that's not me. I just want to be able to go

to work, do what I do, without complications. So I gave my editor my resignation. She suggested I go home and sleep on it. I did." He smiled humorlessly. "And woke to find Julie Christian Braun, naked and standing over my bed with a butter knife."

Candace's eyes bugged. "You mean butcher knife, right?"

He flashed her a grin. "You are an author, aren't you? No. I do mean butter knife. She's crazy, but not necessarily the sharpest tool in the shed."

Candace's smile faded and a frown puckered her brows. "What did you do?"

"I disarmed her, wrapped her in a sheet, and tied her to a chair, all the while with her crying like a banshee."

"Did you call the police?"

"Nope. I called her uncle and had him come get her and told him where to shove his lawsuit. The next day I went on leave."

"You should've called the police," she said, her spine stiffening with indignation. "And you should not have let her push you out of your job."

"The thing is…it just felt like time. Time to move on. To make some changes. And that's what I told my editor. I didn't mention Julie's break in, and I don't think anyone but myself, Julie, and her uncle knows about it. I don't even think he fired her." He shrugged. "Anyhow, my editor refused to take my resignation, and talked me into taking a leave of indeterminate length. More recently she called to tell me Julie's gone and I can come back." Logan didn't know exactly what he expected from Candace, but the mischievous grin lighting her eyes wasn't it. "Something's amusing?"

"I'm sorry. It's not funny. It just reminds me a little of that movie in the eighties, the one where the man cheats on his wife—"

"And then the wife ends up with dead rabbit stew?"

She nodded.

"Thanks."

Candace sobered and reached across the table to wrap his fisted hands in both of hers. Her skin was cool and silky smooth. "It seems to me you've beaten yourself up enough for your temporary brain freeze. I'm not going to jump on the bandwagon, no matter how much you might want me to."

"I was an idiot."

"Probably. But your co-worker sounds like a very determined and disturbed woman who had you in her sights." She lifted one shoulder slightly. "You're only human, and humans err. But even having said that, it sounds like, in the end, maybe she did you a favor."

I'd never have met you. He frowned at the unexpected thought.

"The question now is: what are you going to do to get your life back?"

Safe territory once again. He unfurled his fists and twined his fingers with hers. "I'm leaning toward freelance work. Maybe crossing the pond. I've put out some feelers. We'll see." He lowered his eyes to their joined hands. "Thanks. I hadn't told anyone what happened."

"I'm glad you felt like you could talk to me."

He gave her a crooked smile. "You make it easy." God, he wanted to kiss her. He always wanted to kiss her. "Let's get out of here. I have something special in mind for dessert."

Chapter Twenty-Eight

Logan tipped the valet then helped Candace into the car. The night air was cool and she hugged her arms around her for warmth.

When he got in the driver's side, he removed his sports coat. "Here." He leaned over the console to tuck his jacket around her like a blanket. The fabric still retained the heat from his body. That, and the combined subtle scents of warm masculine skin and aftershave enveloped her.

"Thanks. It smells like you."

He stared, unblinking, into her eyes for a moment before pressing a quick, possessive kiss on her lips, then he sat back and put his seat belt on.

"I have to cry off for dessert. I'm too full to eat anything else," Candace said.

He slanted her a glance as he maneuvered the car out of the parking lot and onto the road. "I've been craving this for a couple of weeks. Can you humor me?"

"I'll watch you eat. How's that?"

He laughed softly. "Almost perfect."

Candace thought about what Logan had told her at dinner. She could almost feel sorry for the woman. She couldn't imagine hunting a man down, stalking him like prey. But she could imagine how hard it would be to accept the idea Logan wasn't interested—especially after being intimate with him.

She didn't like to think of him being intimate with anyone else, but that was another matter entirely. She shoved the thought from her mind and tried to read his expression in the red glow of the dashboard lights.

As if sensing her attention, he placed his big warm hand on her thigh. He began a slow sensual massage that made her toes curl in her strappy sandals. If she was a cat, she'd purr.

"Did I tell you how beautiful you look tonight?" he asked in a husky voice. "Good enough to eat."

He had told her—with his slow, secret smile, with the way his eyes glinted as he looked her up and down when she'd first come down stairs to join him, with that single word, uttered low, "Wow." But she didn't mind hearing it again. "Thank you." She put her hand over his where it rested on her thigh and caressed it lightly.

"I like it when you touch me," he whispered, so softly she wasn't sure what he'd said at first. In a normal tone of voice he added, "Do you mind if we make a quick stop? I want to show you something."

Candace blinked as the car slowed, practically in the middle of nowhere. "Here? Now? Is this when you kill me and drop my body into a ditch?"

"I think you've been reading too many murder mysteries," he said with a teasing grin as he turned onto an almost imperceptible, unmarked dirt road.

She grinned at him. "Romantic suspense novels."

"My bad."

He drove cautiously over the winding, single lane road. Quite suddenly, the road ended on a broad expanse of cliff, marked ominously with a short line of metal guardrails. He stopped the car just in front of the bars and put it into Park. The night swallowed the headlight beams.

"What is this place?" Candace asked.

"It's not this place, it's that." He pointed to the mountainscape across the valley. "It's called Lover's Leap. Ever heard of it?"

"No," Candace said, curious.

"Will you be too cold if we get out?"

"Not if you stay close," she said.

"Not a problem, sweetheart."

He slid out of the driver's side and hurried around the car to open her door, something Candace realized was as natural to him as breathing. He helped her into his jacket. She could just make out his gleaming smile in the moonlight.

"This looks so much better on you than me. All you need to do is lose the dress." Eyeing her legs, he added, "Keep the shoes."

She laughed as he took her hand and led her to the front of the car. He leaned against the hood and pulled her to stand between his legs, her back resting against his chest. He wrapped his arms around her and murmured into her ear, "Are you warm enough?"

She nodded even as his silken voice sent a shiver up her spine.

"Good. I had basically forgotten about this place. I don't even remember how I heard of it, but when we passed the turn off tonight, I thought of you."

"Oh?"

"The legend of Lover's Leap is very romantic. Perfect fodder for a romance novelist. Plus it'll give you some time to digest dinner." She heard his low chuckle. Caught the hint of something deliciously wicked.

Candace tilted her head back to look into Logan's eyes. Heat flared between them, like an invisible flame. He dropped a slow, lingering kiss on her lips, turning her legs liquid so she had to nestle deeper into his hard chest to keep from sinking to the ground. He gave her a lazy smile, as if he knew just what he had done.

"Tell me the story," Candace said, trying to distract herself.

"See that ridge there?" He took her arm ensconced in his jacket sleeve and pointed with it. "They say that's the profile of Chief No-name. And before you say anything, yes, that is what they say he was called, whoever 'they' are."

She studied the ridge. "I suppose I can see a man's profile. Is that his forehead?" She traced the outline of the rock in the air. "which would make that," she drew a circle, "his nose."

"Yes, and the bottom part is his chin."

"Oh my goodness! I do see it."

Logan wrapped his arms tighter around Candace and urged her back till her head rested against his shoulder. "Chief No-name was said to be a very wise man in all areas except his own family affairs. No-name had a very beautiful daughter. His pride and joy. All the boys were crazy about her, but of course, none dared approach her. It was well known No-name would put any buck who tried to court her to death."

As he spoke, Candace took in everything around her. She didn't want to forget a single thing about tonight. The crickets chirping, fireflies flashing like tiny stars, the scent of pine and earth, and the feel of Logan's rich voice rumbling against her back.

"One summer, however, the chief's daughter—"

"What was her name?" Candace asked.

"That I don't remember. What would you like to call her?"

She thought a moment. "Is this a happy ending, or sad?"

"Mmm," he said thinking. "Tragic."

"In that case, we'll call her Blissful Heart."

"That fits with a tragedy, exactly how?" he asked, a smile in his voice.

"It doesn't. It's a counter-balance. I like to think positive."

Logan shook behind her with silent laughter before saying, "All right. Can I call her Bliss for short?"

She nodded once.

"One hot summer, Bliss spent a good many days bathing and frolicking in the lake where she met a handsome young brave from the East. Before long, the two fell madly in love." Logan paused. "Damn, you smell good," he said, his voice a smooth caress in her ear. "I can hardly think."

Her veins flowed with instant, molten heat. She settled against him like a second skin as once again, her legs went wobbly.

"Mm," he said. "Just ignore that."

Ignore the rigid erection pressed into her backside? Oh, sure.

He breathed in a lungful of air. "Where was I?"

"Bliss and Invincible Lion had just fallen in love." Her voice sounded husky to her ears.

His laughter rumbled in the air. "Invincible? I don't think the natives had such a word."

"You don't *think* so. Call him Lion then, if it suits

you."

"When Bliss told No-name about Lion, he flew into a rage and ordered the buck put to death. Naturally, the young couple fled into the forest, where they planned to follow the trail leading to the river, and escape. The chief and his warriors pursued.

"They say a great rain came, brought on by the force of their love. Unfortunately, it obliterated the trail. With Chief No-name closing in, Bliss and Lion emerged from the forest, thinking they would find the river. Instead they stood at the precipice of the Big Gorge."

"That big gorge?" She pointed into the drop-off below.

"Uh-huh."

"What happened?"

"Faced with death at the hands of the chief and his warriors, the couple locked their bodies together and jumped into the abyss. Chief No-name raced to the cliff's edge and screamed to the heavens, perching there for hours in search of the lost couple. When he finally tried to rise, he had merged with the rock."

"You realize, of course, that the lovers survived to cross the river and made a life for themselves." Candace pressed her face into his neck, inhaling the warm, male scent of him.

"That's not generally how I've heard the story told."

"Well, it's true. And Chief No-name isn't sad. He's watching his grandchildren grow-up, and their grandchildren, and so on. He's quite happy."

"Okay, beautiful," he whispered. "Did you like the story?"

"It was lovely," she murmured into his neck. A tremor went through Logan's body. "You're shivering," she said, concerned. "And I have your coat."

"Sweetheart, I'm not cold, but I think it's time to go anyway."

A little while later, Candace recognized the landmarks telling her they were near the turn off to the house. "Did you decide against dessert?"

He flashed his glamorous smile. "Not at all."

Logan pulled to the front door instead of parking in the garage. He got out of the car and hastily rounded the bumper to open her door.

"This is all very mysterious," she said as he helped her from the car.

They entered the house. Logan stopped her when she went for the light switch. Taking her hand, he pulled her into the living room. He turned on one small lamp, leaving the rest of the house shadowed in darkness. "Have a seat. I'll be right back."

Chapter Twenty-Nine

Candace perched on the arm of the couch as he disappeared in the general vicinity of the kitchen. *Someone* had thrown a blanket over the cushions. Interesting.

A moment later, Logan reappeared, dessert tray in hand. On it, a tub of vanilla ice cream, a can of whipped cream, and what looked like fresh strawberries and melted chocolate. "I brought dessert. I think we should get cleaned up first, though." He set the tray on the coffee table and began stripping.

Candace rose. "Wh—"

"Baby, I've been fantasizing about eating ice-cream sundaes off your sweet body ever since I accidentally sprayed whipped cream on your mouth and—"

"Accidentally?" A giggle bubbled up in her throat as he shrugged out of his shirt.

"I never thought a person could expire from wanting until that night. When I watched you lick cream off your perfect lips... Damn." He closed his eyes, pulled his t-shirt over his head in one move then started on his trousers.

She watched transfixed.

With his fly hanging open, he stopped undressing. He cocked his head and crossed his arms over his chest. "Am I eating alone?"

"No," she heard herself whisper. She licked her lips.

"Then take off your dress, woman," he commanded in a low, rough voice.

Candace reached for the side zipper. She untied the halter string and the dress spilled to the floor around her feet, leaving her standing in a nude lace thong and strappy high-heeled sandals. Intense waves of desire shook her body, and he hadn't even touched her yet.

"The shoes?" she asked.

"Leave 'em," he growled, and picked up the whipped cream.

****

Candace came awake to a gentle shake and Logan's murmured, "Come on. Let's go to bed."

Bleary eyed, she lifted her head and took in her surroundings. Though no lights burned in the room, moonlight shone in from the glass wall, illuminating the couch, the displaced coffee table, the blanket spread on the floor on which they lay. She dropped her head onto the cushion of Logan's arm, and, remembering what had taken place a little while ago, sighed in perfect contentment.

His fingers traced her ribs and he chuckled. "Someone's sticky. Your shower or mine?" He levered himself to his feet before hauling her up.

"Mine."

"An excellent choice." He put his hand on the small of her back and followed her up the stairs.

They headed straight for the bathroom. Neither bothered with lights. They waited in silence for the water to heat then stepped into the oversized travertine shower.

She urged him around, soaping his shoulders, his back, and his perfectly contoured glutes. She wanted to pamper him, to treat him to a fraction of the exquisite care he'd poured into her.

At first, she'd found his idea of making body-sundaes extremely erotic—and downright fun. But somewhere along the way, Logan's ministrations took on a whole different tone. At once sexual and tender—he'd turned the playful lovemaking into something she couldn't quite define.

Logan's lingering kisses and reverential caresses had touched her in a place she'd never allowed another person to reach. In return, she'd given all she had. Oddly enough, giving of herself emboldened her, made her want to give more. Candace smiled inwardly. Maybe it was just Logan that made her this way.

With the handheld sprayer she rinsed his back, smoothing her fingers over his slick skin and chorded muscles until all the soap was gone.

He reached for the soap to wash her. "My turn."

She shook her head and pushed at his shoulder. "Let me wash your hair."

He ducked and Candace moved the sprayer over his head, allowing the warm water to spill over him, then massaged shampoo into his scalp. He emitted a low moan. The sound caused gooseflesh to spread over her entire body. She took her time rinsing him, applying conditioner, rinsing again.

When they stepped out of the shower, Logan grabbed a towel and wrapped it around her, drying her with gentle pats. They brushed and flossed without speaking, seemingly in perfect accord. Either that or they were both too tired to speak. She wondered briefly if he would slip back into his room, or if he would stay in her room as he had the last several nights.

He exited before her from the bathroom, padding naked to the bed and sliding under the covers like he belonged there.

She followed, feeling only slightly worried over the sweet ache that filled her at the sight of him. As soon as she stretched out, Logan reached for her, cocooning her body with his. "Do you mind?" he murmured into her damp hair.

She shook her head on the pillow.

"I don't usually like…that is, I'm not into…"

Her eyelids were growing heavy, but she somehow managed to say, "You're not a big snuggler?"

"Not usually. But that wasn't what I was going to say. I was thinking how I've never been a big sleepover person, either. Until you."

"No?"

"Let me know if I crush you."

She wriggled closer and felt his lips brush her nape. "I like sleeping with you, too," she whispered.

****

The next morning, they sat at the kitchen island and ate breakfast in companionable silence. Cereal with fresh raspberries and skimmed milk this morning. Logan finished first. After putting his bowl in the dishwasher, he disappeared for a moment, and returned with the UPS package they'd found at the door yesterday.

"Ah, yes. I forgot about this in light of last night's dessert," Candace gave a sly smile to Logan. She tore open the large envelope, pulled out a letter and another package. "It's from Jenna. She forwarded this gift to me from my quote-unquote biggest fan."

"It can't be from your biggest fan."

"Why not?"

"Because that's me."

She laughed and opened the smaller package. "But you haven't read any of my books."

"Yet."

"A box of Belgian chocolate. Yummy." She unwrapped the plastic cellophane, opened the box—and froze. "That's not chocolate."

"Bastard," Logan gritted out, picking up a handful of torn, graffiti covered pages to examine them.

Someone had printed photos of her from her publisher's website—and ripped them apart, but not before writing obscenities on them.

Beside her Logan stared intently at one particular photo remnant.

"What is it?"

He flattened the piece against his chest, covering it with his hand. "I don't like this, Candace. We need to call the police in Florida and have your psycho ex hauled in for questioning."

"I told you. Roger isn't behind this." She snatched the scrap of paper from him. It was a blow-up of the photo of Candace Logan had taken. In the backdrop loomed the mountainscape view from the deck. Candace's profile had been blacked out and the peaks were circled with a black sharpie pen. Written in large black letters, was the word "Gotcha."

"If not Roger, then who?" Logan demanded.

"I don't know. I can't think of anyone. I admit to being creeped out, but I honestly think it would be next to impossible for anyone to find me here. Don't you? I mean, it's possible someone recognizes the mountain, but how would they pinpoint the exact house?"

Logan rubbed his jaw. "What about someone in Eric's office. Clearly Jenna has your address."

"Unless she's some kind of split personality I can't see it. In fact, everyone there is great."

"Great. Roger's a saint and everyone at Eric's is above reproach. Let's call the police," he said, unmoved.

"And tell them what? That I've gotten some rude letters and a forwarded, I repeat *forwarded* bunch of slashed photos?"

"Will you at least question Jenna?"

"I will."

"When?"

"Soon."

Logan's mouth flattened in a grim line. "Lady, if anything happens to you…"

"It won't. My biggest fan will protect me. Right?"

A reluctant grin tugged at the corners of his mouth. "That's right. I think we'll start with me tying you up safely in the bedroom where I can keep an eye on you."

"Okay. But after breakfast." Candace picked up her cereal bowl and shoveled a heaping spoonful into her mouth.

****

Candace looked up from her computer feeling both refreshed and replete. Understandable in light of another exceptional morning of making love, followed by a productive afternoon of writing. Could the week have gone any better?

She picked up her cell to call Jenna. She'd purposely planned to make this call when Logan wasn't in earshot. The mention of the torn photos tended to send him into a tailspin.

"How was the chocolate?" Jenna asked as Candace identified herself.

"How did you know it was chocolate?"

"Because the man who sent it to you left the box out for me to see it. I wanted to make sure someone wasn't sending you a bomb or something before I forwarded it to you."

"You said man. You're sure the sender is a man?"

"I didn't meet him, per se. But he signed all his correspondence Chris, and his email address had the same first and last name if I remember correctly. I guess Chris could be a woman or a man, now that I think of it."

"Can you forward one of his emails?"

"Sure. Is…everything all right? The chocolate wasn't poisoned, was it? It was from that famous Belgian Chocolatier and I thought—"

"Everything's fine. But I'd like a copy of the email. To send a proper thank you." She wasn't sure why she wasn't being up front with Jenna—other than Logan's suspicions had made her paranoid.

"Sure, Miss Riley. Right away. Oh! You'll be happy to know no more of those, um, hate letters have come in."

"More than you know," she said. That ought to make Logan feel better.

A moment later the email came through. It sounded normal enough. An email from a fan who wanted to send Candace a token of appreciation. His email address looked like it was a direct reflection of his full name, Chris dot B dot Sanderson.

Candace clicked on the reply icon. She typed a single question. "Who are you?" and hit Send. Not surprisingly, a few minutes later, her email bounced back, marked undeliverable.

Candace brightened. Maybe this Chris had closed the account because his or her fixation with Candace was at an end. It could only be a good sign.

Chapter Thirty

"So you've started another book?" Logan took the dish she'd just rinsed and swabbed it with the hand towel. Normally doing the dishes was an effort akin to watching paint dry, or worse. But he actually liked cleaning up with Candace. He liked watching her pink gloved hands sloshing around in the sink, liked watching her blow a stray lock of hair away from her nose.

She handed him another dripping plate. "Yes. I'd been wrestling with an idea for another book—in the series I told you about. But then this story burst in and wouldn't be denied."

"So that's how it works. Interesting. You mind telling me about it?" Logan put the dried dishes away.

She gave him a curious look, as if his interest in her work surprised her. "Not at all. It's about a woman who's a pharmaceutical rep. She works primarily with cardiologists, selling heart stents. One of the docs she coaches in the operating room—"

"The reps actually go into the operating room with the surgeons?"

She nodded. "Sure."

"Wow. How do you know that—more research?"

She shook her head. A lock of hair floated over her brow, and she blew at it ineffectually. "I sold medical devices in a previous life."

He tucked the stray hair behind her ear and kissed her on the tip of her nose. "I never would have guessed. How'd you get into that? Wait, sorry, I interrupted the plot. But don't forget to fill me in on that later."

While they finished drying the dishes Candace told him more about the book, which would be her first romantic thriller. They started up the stairs to Candace's room.

Candace's room, their room, same difference.

"I want to hear more about your old job." Logan crossed the threshold. He took her hand and pulled her toward the bed. They plopped down on their sides, facing each other.

"What would you like to know?"

"How did you get into the field?"

She rolled onto her back and stared up at the ceiling. "It wasn't plan A. Did I ever mention my father is a doctor?"

"No. Let me guess. He wanted you to be a doctor?" Logan asked.

"Bingo. Naturally I went along with his plan. I was always eager to please him—especially as he was so hard to please."

Logan detected hurt, and a tinge of bitterness in her tone.

"I decided on which field of medicine, though. Again, it was about Daddy." Her voice went very soft. "Remember I told you about the…lightning incident—when my dad took me golfing?"

"Yes." A protective urge unlike any he'd ever known compelled him to prop himself on an elbow and lean over her, poised and ready to swoop her into his arms at the first sign of distress. He traced his fingers over the tender skin at the base of her throat.

"I was nine. It was my birthday. From my bedroom I heard Mom trying to talk Dad out of going to the range because she'd seen the weather forecast. He told her to quit fussing and said he'd promised me. Said he didn't want to let me down." A small frown puckered Candace's brow. "I didn't care a whit about golf. I just wanted to spend time with my dad. He wasn't around much." She paused. "I didn't know he was going to bring one of his girlfriends along."

Logan cursed under his breath, but otherwise held his tongue.

"Mom was right about the weather. It was raining, windy, and the sky was black. They left me in the cart at one of the last holes. Said it was too dangerous for me to be out in the rain. I knew they were sneaking around to the other side of the trees to hide from me. I didn't exactly know what they were up to, mind you, but I knew it wasn't good." She took a deep breath and gazed unblinking at the ceiling. "The lightning bolt came from nowhere and...and...hit my dad. That lady screamed holy murder, but otherwise was totally useless."

Logan carefully rolled her into his chest and put his arms around her. "Sweetheart," he murmured, not knowing what else to say.

"My father almost died. Mom never forgave me."

"Oh, baby," he said, his heart breaking for the little girl she had been. The little girl who grew up blaming herself for her parents' screwed-up relationship.

"The...the cardiac arrest damaged his heart. I guess that was why I wanted to go into heart medicine." She sighed and rubbed the tip of her nose against his chest.

"Everything was on track. Straight A student all through my undergraduate degree, pre-med studies. And then, Dad did something that really made me mad. He left Mom. I mean, I'd wanted her to leave him for years, after I figured out what he was all about. But she wouldn't. And then he up and ran off with his partner's daughter."

Logan pulled back to meet her eyes trying to convey a bevy of emotions. Sympathy. Anger on her behalf. And…another emotion he chose not explore too closely.

She gave him a little smile. "After I graduated with my under grad, I decided I no longer wanted to go to med school. I applied for a position selling stents." She lifted her shoulder in a half shrug. "I was still interested in cardiology."

He felt a smile lift the corners of his mouth. "You rebel."

Her answering grin hit him like a ray of sunshine.

"So how did that lead to writing romance novels?"

Her grin widened. "I always wanted to write love stories—always, for as long as I could remember. But," her brows arched, "Neither of my parents liked the idea. Not enough money for my dad, and not respectable enough for Mom."

He tucked a strand of hair behind her ear. "How'd they feel about selling stents?"

Her brows rose a fraction higher. "I made a lot of money. That's how I bought my house and managed to fund several investments that really paid off. In the end, that's what afforded me the ability to gamble with my career."

He spoke without thinking. "Somehow I figured

the house belonged to…never mind."

"Roger? No. It's mine. He moved in with me."

And now? He wanted to ask—but his tongue wouldn't form the words. Instead he muttered, "Lucky Roger."

She rolled her eyes.

"So one day you quit your day job and now you're living the dream."

"That I am."

Their eyes met and held. Something passed between them, both fluid and charged, and building on itself with each passing second.

He couldn't speak. Could hardly breathe. It was as if someone had opened the floodgates of his own emotional dam, leaving him overwhelmed and shaken by need and desire. To go back in time and knock her father out for subjecting her to his selfishness, and then lay into her mother for projecting her own weakness onto Candace. To hold her and protect her. To *never let her go*.

The thought hit him like a two-ton truck slamming into his gut. He had no business thinking like that. They both knew this was temporary, didn't they?

She must have read something in his eyes because her expression softened to one of concern for him. "Logan," she whispered and cupped his cheek. "It's all right."

He turned his mouth into her palm, kissing her. The next thing he knew she'd rolled him onto his back and had painted herself onto him. He chuckled and wrapped one arm around her waist, anchoring her to him while his other hand smoothed her silken hair. "What's it like being with a mad man?"

"Excuse me?" she muttered, her lips against his neck.

A hot sensation shot through his body at the slight friction. "I'm crazy about you," he whispered.

She didn't answer with words. Just lay on him until it seemed their two hearts beat as one.

Chapter Thirty-One

The following morning Logan, dressed in a pair of boxers and a white, cotton under-shirt, crunched his whole-grain toast and stared at Candace across the breakfast counter, a brooding expression darkening his eyes.

She plucked another cherry from the fruit bowl sitting on the counter between them and popped it into her mouth, tugging the stem free.

Still he crunched and stared.

"Is the bread stale?" she finally asked.

"Mmm?"

"You're scowling."

"I'm not scowling." Abruptly a wry smile appeared, replacing the dour expression. "I was concentrating."

"On what?" she asked, in a low, conspiratorial tone.

"It occurred to me I've been sleeping great."

She raised her brows questioningly. "And that's a bad thing?"

"No. Just extremely unusual."

"Oh. I can relate to that."

He cocked his head. "How are you sleeping?"

A slow smile spread over her face. "Great."

"How about the few nights I was gone? How'd you do then?" His eyes twinkled with mischief, as if he already knew the answer.

"Are you fishing, Mr. Shaw?"

"Yes," he answered, completely unrepentant.

She laughed out loud. "I suppose I had a little trouble on those nights. Are you by any chance sprinkling sleepy dust on my pillow?"

He had stopped smiling. Was, in fact, staring at her, an odd light in his eyes.

"Logan?"

He tilted his head this way and that, studying her. He got up from the stool and walked around the counter behind her, a predator stalking his prey.

She craned around. "What are…" she twisted the other way as he continued to circle her, "…you doing?"

"Stay right there." He disappeared from the room.

Candace shook her head and flipped Logan's *New York Times* around to read the headlines without much interest. A few seconds later she heard footsteps.

He entered the kitchen, a large Nikon camera in his hands.

"What? Oh, no—"

"Please? Aside from the last time I shot you, I haven't had any interest in months and then…I don't know, you just look so pretty sitting there in your pink nightie, with that little strap sliding down your shoulder."

Candace glanced down at herself. Like Logan, she still wore her pajamas. They had come straight down after waking. She raised her gaze to Logan's. "But I haven't even brushed my hair."

"You're gorgeous. Come on. I haven't tried to stymie your creative flow."

"Mine didn't involve you half naked."

"I definitely wouldn't have stopped you then," he said with a wicked grin. "Just a couple shots. Nothing pornographic, I swear. And not for anyone's pleasure but my own."

He looked so hopeful, Candace couldn't say no. And, if she were honest, she could admit to being flattered. "Where do you want me?"

"Baby, that's a loaded question."

"Logan."

He laughed. "First pick up one of those cherries. Yeah, like that."

An hour later, he'd moved her from the breakfast nook to the living room where he photographed her on the rug in front of the fireplace. Upstairs, he shot her tangled in their twisted sheets, standing half hidden behind the gauze curtains leading onto the balcony adjacent to her room, and finally leaning against the balustrade.

Just when she'd reached her limit, he'd put down the camera, approached her slowly and pulled her slip-of-a-top over her head.

"I'm not taking any nude pictures, Logan," she said seriously.

"I'm not interested in taking any more pictures right now," he answered gruffly, picking her up and carrying her back into the room.

****

From the shade of her dark sunglasses, Candace's sleepy gaze drifted over the puffy white clouds. She nearly moaned with pleasure at the feel of the warm sun and soft breeze against her skin. She sighed, wondering how long she'd been floating around the pool on the raft Logan had brought home from the grocery store this morning as a surprise. Her toe dipped into the water, and she gave a leisurely kick to start her moving again. No direction in particular. Just floating.

A few feet away, Logan lounged on a chair under a wide umbrella, poring over the newspaper. She'd never known a man more up on current events than Logan. He'd taken to regularly summarizing particularly newsworthy articles, somehow managing to make all the current events intriguing for her, who mostly eschewed the news as too depressing. She felt like she had her own, private, news anchor.

"Hey, beautiful. I'm going in for some cold water. Can I bring you anything?" Logan asked. He squatted at the edge of the pool and reached for the raft, grabbing first it, then her ankle in his strong hand, and tugging her toward him. He bent to kiss her, simultaneously cupping her bathing suit clad breast with a warm palm, sending hot chills over her body.

She reached for him and he moved out of reach. "Uh-uh." He flashed her a smile. "You're not pulling me in again."

"Spoil sport," she complained. "An ice water sounds perfect, please and thanks."

"I live to please."

She listened for the sound of the door closing behind Logan, then with one foot, shoved off the tiled edge of the pool, sending her and her float spinning across the water. What a whirlwind these past weeks had been. A perfect three weeks. She'd gotten tons of work done without a peep of protest from Logan. He was good about giving her uninterrupted time to herself to work.

But when it was time to play, Logan happily

provided the entertainment, from a day spent kayaking and picnicking at Emerald Bay, to an evening of old black and white movies, to a long hike over Lover's Leap, the mountain he'd shown her the night of their first real date. Candace dipped her fingers languidly into the pool and smiled to herself. She wouldn't say she was an exhibitionist by any stretch of the word, but remembering what the two of them had done in a private stretch of woods that day made her skin tingle.

A loud bang vibrated the walls of the house— ripping her from her reverie.

Candace lifted her head and squinted at the house as if doing so would help her ears hear better. Was the sun getting to her? Making her imagine things? She waited a beat and, hearing nothing unusual, started to relax back onto the pillow, and—thumping sounds echoed across the pool deck, like Logan had decided to rearrange the table and chair ensemble in the back of the house by smashing the set against the walls and letting the pieces land where they may.

Candace jolted upright, swinging one leg over the top of her raft and springing into the cold water in one move. Now she was catching fragments of a shouting match. Something was so not right.

She half-swam half-ran through the pool to the steps in the shallow end. Oh God, Logan. Please let him be all right.

She sprinted across the deck, her mind weighing the possibilities in rapid-fire succession. Burglar? Home invasion? Mini-earthquake? She didn't know whether to be relieved or more frightened at the silence now emanating from the house.

An arm's length from the back door, it swung

open, slamming into the exterior wall with a bang.

Logan poked his head out the doorway. His cheeks were flushed an angry red, and his jaw was set. "Candace, you better get in here." He jerked his thumb over his shoulder.

He disappeared inside, and she hastened after him. Utter relief and a sudden lump in her throat threatened to choke her. Logan appeared healthy, if a bit steamed. Anything else she could handle. "What is it?"

"More like who," he growled, his eyes glued to a prone figure on the floor.

She peered around his hulking body. From her vantage point, she thought she recognized the figure of a man. Yes, definitely a man dressed in khaki slacks, a pale pink polo, and...she stared disbelieving at disheveled golden blond hair. It couldn't be. He couldn't be here.

Chapter Thirty-Two

"Roger?" Her voice came out a squeak.

No. She must be wrong. Roger could not simply appear in Tahoe out of nowhere.

Candace leaned down, trying to get a clear look at his face. A difficult task given that he lay on the travertine tiled floor at Logan's feet, cupping his hands over his nose and—she gasped and drew back. Was that blood seeping between his fingers?

The small sound seemed to draw the man's attention, and his head lolled in her direction. She found herself staring into a set of glazed, all too familiar green eyes.

Wordless he reached for her.

She dropped to her knees beside him. "What are you...how did you...what happened to your face?" she finally got out. She glanced to her right, hoping Logan might fill in a few blanks.

Logan's fisted hands hung about at her eye level. His knuckles were scraped and bruised.

Roger lifted one hand long enough to aim an accusatory finger at Logan. "I think he broke my nose. Freaking maniac."

Logan pointed right back. "You're lucky that's all I did. Ah, hell with it. I'm calling the police." Logan strode toward the kitchen.

A sense of unnatural calm came over her. She

grasped Roger's wrists with a gentle yet firm grip, moving his hands out of the way so she could assess how badly his face was hurt. His nose was swollen, and turning an interesting shade of blue, but not unnaturally crooked. Not necessarily broken, then. "I'll get some ice." She rose.

Logan gave a snort of disgust, followed closely by Roger's low mew of pain.

She dashed into the kitchen and laid a hand on Logan's forearm as he pressed the Talk button on the cordless phone. "Can you hold off, Logan? Tell me what happened first, please?"

He hesitated, and for a moment she thought he'd deny her request. Then he depressed the End button, silencing the receiver, and set the phone on the counter. When he spoke, his words were clipped. "When I came in for water I heard a car door slam. I went out front to investigate, and found suntan-Ken sniffing around the side of the house trying to get a glimpse of you in the pool."

"I wanted to be sure I'd found the right house," came Roger's indignant retort from the other room.

"Most people start with the front door," Logan shot back.

Candace ignored the interchange. "And then?" she pressed in a low voice.

"I asked who he was and what he thought he was doing on the property. He told me his name. Claimed to be your fiancé. Demanded to know who I was, and if you were here. I told him to hold that thought, and came back inside to call the cops. The bastard followed me into the house." Logan rolled his shoulders. "I hit him."

"He attacked me." Roger appeared in the archway.

"Get out of here," Logan said through clenched teeth.

Logan looked like he wanted to kill Roger with his bare hands. She stepped closer to Logan, but addressed her words to Roger. "Roger, I think you should lie down on the couch. Now."

She spared a quick check over her shoulder to assure herself he was complying before placing her palms on Logan's bare chest. His heartbeat pounded like an anvil against her fingertips. "Let me talk to him, Logan. Find out what he's doing here."

"What he's doing here?" he erupted with barely contained fury. "What he's doing is showing up here to make good on his threats."

She sighed and threw up her hands. "I'll get some ice. And then I'm going to talk to Roger. And you're going to cool your heels." She retrieved a zipper baggie and clean hand towel from the kitchen island cabinet, and marched toward the refrigerator.

Logan stared after her, hands on his hips. "I can't believe you're actually getting ice for him."

Candace was half in the freezer. "And I can't believe you think I wouldn't. By the way, his nose isn't really broken, thank God."

"Thank God?" Logan aped.

She emerged from the freezer, cupping the ice bag, and found Logan standing in front of her. His breath came in angry huffs, and his eyes glittered like shards of broken blue glass. He looked like a beautiful, hyped-up warrior, ready for battle.

"Yes. Did you ever consider," she lowered her voice, "that Roger might press charges against you?

Logan, you can't just go around punching people." She took a step to the side, attempting to get around him, but he blocked her.

He surprised her by raising a hand to cup her cheek. He smoothed his thumb over her cheekbone. "I can when the person in question is threatening someone I—" He broke off. Swallowed. "Someone under my protection," he finished on a whisper.

Her throat tightened, and her legs threatened to buckle. She closed her eyes. For a second there, she'd thought he was going to tell her he loved her. And she'd be lying to herself if she didn't admit an instant bubbling joy had risen up in her at the thought. It felt as if her heart had literally blossomed like a flower in her chest. *This is no time for soul searching and confessions, Candace.*

She drew a fortifying breath. "Logan, I have to deal with him. *I* have to deal with him." She stressed the word I. "Trust me?"

Logan crossed his arms over his chest and narrowed his eyes, looking for all the world like he would argue the point to kingdom come. But finally he took a step back, gesturing with a jerk of his head for her to pass.

She found Roger on the couch, his legs stretched out lengthwise, his back propped on a throw pillow wedged against the armrest.

"Here." She eased a hip onto the edge of the seat cushion, before laying the wrapped ice bag against his bruised nose.

"Thanks," Roger muttered, covering her hands with one of his.

She pulled her hands free, and glanced over her

shoulder to see if Logan was watching. He was. He stalked toward them, looking every bit the predator.

"I see your friend's still skulking around. That maniac you're hanging with threw a bunch of wild accusations at me, then hauled off and punched me in the nose," Roger said in an aggrieved tone. "If it's broken, you better believe I'll sue him." He glared up at Logan. "Which reminds me. Who is he?"

She ignored the question. "You need to hold the ice against your nose. It should help with the pain, and staunch any further bruising."

He shifted his focus back to her, attempting a smile. "Thanks again." He pointed to the ice. A moment later he sobered. "This isn't how I pictured our reunion."

"Reunion," Logan scoffed under his breath.

He wasn't making it easy for her to get to the bottom of this.

Candace gave him a pointed look before turning back to Roger. "Roger, what are you doing here? How did you find me?"

"Exactly what I asked him," Logan growled from behind her.

"Again, who is that maniac, Candace? Here I was, minding my own business, working up the courage to ring the doorbell, and the next thing I know, I'm being attacked by a half naked gorilla for—what was it he said? Threatening your safety, or some such nonsense. Meanwhile, the only person who's being accosted is me. Just look at what he did."

"Candace, why are you listening to him? Why are you nursemaiding him? It's obvious he's the one who sent you those threatening emails, and that package.

How do you explain how he found this place? I don't know what I'm waiting for. I'm calling the police."

"Logan, no." Candace twisted around to face him. "Please. I need—can we have just a moment to sort this out?"

"We as in the three of us, or we as in the two of you?"

She let her eyes do the answering.

He stiffened. After a long moment, nodded. He strode toward the stairwell, then disappeared from view, though she continued to stare after him. She had the definite sense she'd handled that all wrong.

Roger lowered the ice bag to gape at her, accusation clear in his eyes. "So that's how it is, huh? So much for there not being someone else."

A prick of guilt stabbed at her, making her tone sharper than she intended. "What are you doing here?"

"Isn't that obvious? Trying to work things out with my fiancée."

"There's nothing to work out, Roger. I made that very clear, on numerous occasions."

"And now I begin to understand your vehemence," he muttered. "By the way, what is all this talk about emails?" Roger winced. "Ouch," he barked, and reapplied the ice. "For the record, I did not, by word or deed, threaten you."

"I believe you."

"So what's his problem?"

"Let's just say he doesn't know you as well as I do." She drew back to study Roger's face, adding, "It does seem odd, you showing up here. I know I didn't give you any idea of where I'm staying."

"No, not you. Let's just say a reliable source told

me you were staying at one of Eric's vacation homes. I took the ball from there."

The truth hit her like a whack to the head. "You called my mother."

He grinned as much as the injury to his face would allow. "She didn't want me to worry."

She'd specifically asked her mother not to tell Roger where she was, and her mother had agreed to keep quiet. But she hadn't hidden the fact she thought Candace jumped the gun breaking things off with Roger. It wasn't a stretch to assume she'd give Roger enough information to placate him, and totally disregard Candace's wishes in doing so. Some things never changed.

"Don't be mad at her, okay? She just wants what's best for you."

"She had no right. She completely ignored my request to keep my location private."

"Not exactly. I remembered Eric had a place in Tahoe from some conversation we'd had a while back. I took a gamble and worked the young lady at Eric's office for the exact address. I told her I was triple checking I had the right house number and zip in Tahoe to give to the florist. She sang like a canary."

Her mouth twisted. "I don't remember any flowers."

He opened his arms in a *hey, you got me there* gesture. A moment later, his playful demeanor vanished, and his eyes turned hard. "I have to tell you, I never for one minute thought you'd be fooling around on me. Now I know how awful you must've felt when you walked in on me."

Not that bad, actually. That had been her first clue.

239

"I did not fool around on you—but I'm sorry this hurts you. You should've listened, and not come looking for me." She rose from the couch.

"Where are you going?" Roger asked.

"To get my phone, and check out your story." She headed for the stairs, ignoring Roger's grumbled, "Nice to know you have such faith in me."

Chapter Thirty-Three

Candace ended her call with Jenna and started down the hall for Logan's room. Roger's story had panned out.

She knocked lightly at Logan's closed bedroom door, frowning. She wasn't used to barriers between them.

He pulled the door open and let his gaze drift over the white sundress she'd taken a minute to slip into. "You look…nice." His lips curled into an almost sneer.

She glanced down at herself, self-conscious. She couldn't fathom why he'd take issue with the fact she'd gotten out of her swimsuit. He'd changed into one of his signature outfits—a pair of well-worn jeans and a t-shirt that read, *I Shoot People For Food*. He'd managed a shower, as well, and the entire room smelled of shampoo, freshly laundered clothes, and hot male temper.

He dropped onto the edge of the bed and slapped his hands onto his knees. His damp black hair curled over one brow as he all but glared at her, making her want to twist her fingers into the silky mass and give a good yank.

Instead she cleared her throat. "Hi," she said, feeling off balance, then frowned a little because she hated the feeling.

"Hi," he answered without inflection. "So, what

did you figure out with me out of the room?"

Her mouth fell open as realization slammed into her. He wasn't angry. She'd hurt his feelings. She eased onto the bed beside him and gazed into his turquoise eyes. "Logan, you know I wasn't hiding anything from you or giving you the brush-off when I asked you to give us a minute. I just thought—"

"What? That three's a crowd? That you and your ex—he is your ex, right? It occurred to me I never did ask—would have a better reunion with me out of the way?"

Fighting tears for reasons she didn't even understand, she stared at her hands balled into fists on her lap. "I-I just wanted to calm things down. But, yes, of course he's my ex."

Logan said nothing.

She squared her shoulders and tried for a cheerful smile. "You'll be relieved to know Rog got Eric's lakehouse address from Jenna."

"What does that prove, other than Eric needs to rethink his office staff?"

She couldn't help defending Jenna. "It was a perfectly reasonable mistake on Jenna's part. She had no reason to think I wouldn't have been the one to inform my fiancé of my whereabouts." She laughed without humor. "No, that honor goes to my mother."

Logan blinked in surprise. "Whoa."

"Exactly. The way Roger worded his question to Jenna made it seem like she was just confirming he had the right address."

"Great. She's not an idiot. That still doesn't prove Roger isn't the one threatening you."

"Of course it does."

"How, exactly?" He cocked his head to the side and crossed his arms over his chest.

She narrowed her eyes at him. He could be quite obstinate when he chose to be. "Whoever sent me those emails sounded deranged—not like a person who would call my agent to sweet talk his administrator into giving him the right address for him to send flowers."

"That. Makes. No. Sense," he said, enunciating each word.

It made perfect sense to her. "First of all, I never believed Roger would resort to violence."

"Like me?" He arched a brow.

"That isn't what I meant, Logan. I meant, he doesn't want to hurt me. He wants—" She broke off, searching for the right words.

Logan sighed, and his angry veneer seemed to crack—slightly. One corner of his mouth crooked upward, though she could see he was fighting the urge to smile. "You."

She cocked her head. "Come again?"

"He wants you," Logan said softly. "But what if he figures out he can't have you?"

"Not if, *when*. He'll have to deal with it."

Logan's eyes softened, and he raised a hand to cup her cheek. His heavy lidded gaze fell to her mouth. "Candace?" he asked in a husky voice.

"Yes?"

"I…" He stared hard at her mouth.

She had no idea what he wanted to say, but she knew she wanted him to kiss her. She leaned forward.

He cursed softly, and leaned back. "No," he said, as if to himself. His hand dropped to fist at his side, and his eyes, when they met hers, were hard. "That guy is nuts, and I want him out of here."

She was starting to get annoyed. "Logan, why won't you listen to me? I'm telling you Roger wouldn't hurt me."

"How do you know?"

"I just do. I just…I know him. I'm asking you to trust me."

"I do trust you. It's him I want to break in half."

She threw her hands in the air and rose abruptly. "And you wondered why I wanted to talk to him alone."

"No. On that note, I'm clear as a bell."

"What is that supposed to mean?" she asked, rounding on him.

He shrugged. "You want some time to catch up." His eyes held a boatload of reproach.

"Not to catch up. Just to let him down easy."

Logan laughed. "Like he did you? Are you sure that's what you want? To let him go?"

"Logan, you know I didn't invite him—"

He cut her off with a slash of his hand and a sharply uttered, "That's a relief."

She frowned. It was her turn to cross her arms over her chest. "Sarcasm is the lowest form of humor."

"Thanks for the lesson, professor. I'll keep it in mind for the future, in the event I run into someone who might give a damn."

His words stung more than she wanted him to know. She raised her chin a notch and forced her hands to lay loose at her sides.

"Look, regardless of how he found you, I'm not going to leave the two of you alone. Not unless he can offer concrete proof he's not your cyber-stalker."

"The only way to get that proof is for me to talk to him," she said.

"Fine. Go on down and talk to your heart's content. But after your nice tête-à-tête, he's outta here. Unless you were planning on inviting him to join us. Or maybe he'll prove himself innocent of all wrongdoing and you'll ask me to leave." Logan stood and reached the door in one stride.

"Where are you going?" she asked, unable to mask the frantic edge to her tone.

He froze, his hand on the doorknob. "Don't worry, Candace. I'm not going to crash your private party. As it happens I have a few calls to make, and need some privacy of my own." He turned to look over his shoulder. He gave her a smile that didn't come close to reaching his eyes. "You see? You can have all the time you need with—" He broke off, baring his white teeth, "Rog."

Candace opened her mouth to tell him how off base he was. She wasn't worried about him going downstairs to where Roger waited, she was still reeling from his comment about leaving the house altogether. About leaving her. She didn't want Roger here, didn't want Logan gone, didn't't want any of this.

But Logan didn't give her the chance. In the blink of an eye, he disappeared in the direction of the stairs.

Her pride wouldn't allow her to run after him. When she re-entered the living room, she found it empty. Logan looked as if he was stalled on his way to the back door. He didn't look at her. Didn't acknowledge her in anyway.

He stood still, his gaze fastened on the front door.

A feeling of doom swamping her, Candace shifted

her gaze to the front door, as well.

It swung open, and Roger stepped into the foyer. He flashed her a chagrined smile.

Going on autopilot, she gave a tentative smile in return. She couldn't deny feeling relieved on Logan's behalf. The fact Roger was up and about added weight to the possibility he might not press assault charges. He couldn't be hurting too badly—he had enough steam in him to go outside and get his luggage.

Her eyes widened. His luggage? Her gaze swung to Logan.

"Are you kidding me?" Logan asked, incredulous. "Candace, did you forget to mention something to me a few minutes ago?"

She shook her head. "No."

"I'm standing right here. I can hear you," Roger said.

Logan aimed one flattened palm at Roger, and locked eyes with Candace. His voice went dangerously soft. "Are we in agreement here?"

In other words, was she going to tell Roger to buzz off? Well, of course she was. And if Logan would've given her a minute upstairs, she'd have told him she was planning to ask him to leave immediately. When this was all over, she and Logan would have a talk about the merits of good communication. For now, though, she answered with a clear, "Yes."

Logan gave one jerky nod. His chest rose and fell as he released a heavy sigh. "I'll be outside if you need me." He narrowed his gaze on Roger. "*Right* outside." He turned on his heel and stalked the rest of the way to the back door. Before he went out, he paused, hand on the door knob, and said, "Just so you know—if you hurt one hair on her head, I'll make sure it's the last thing you do."

Roger rolled his eyes. "Enough with the ridiculous threats and accusations."

Logan stepped onto the back porch.

"Wait," Roger called.

Logan glanced over his shoulder, one dark brow arched in impatience.

"I think at this point I'm entitled to an introduction."

"You're not entitled to—"

"Logan?" Candace broke in. When he looked her way, she pleaded with him with her eyes. His expression softened slightly.

"Roger, meet Logan Shaw. Logan, Roger Graham." Candace felt like an idiot. But the sooner she got this situation under control, the sooner Roger would be gone.

Roger snapped his fingers. "That's why you look familiar. You're *Logan Shaw*. As in the playboy artist that's always in the gossip magazines." Roger's head bobbed in a knowing nod.

Logan's mouth twisted sardonically. "Artist? No one's accused me of being one of those in a long time."

Roger's eyes flicked over Logan, top to bottom, and back again as if considering him for purchase at auction. Then with a derisive snort, he practically strutted toward the couch.

Candace glared at Roger's retreating backside, then turned an apologetic eye on Logan.

But he wasn't paying either of them any mind. He closed the back door without bothering to slam it—or spare her a second glance. Candace followed his progress across the patio, to the iron gate. He went through it, closed it behind him. She rose up on tiptoe, keeping him in sight as he wound down the path to the lakeshore.

Roger's harsh laughter shattered her focus. "Oh, Candy. You kill me." He wiped his eyes. "You finally decide to let your guard down and you choose someone like *him?*"

She glowered at him and shook her head. "I won't discuss Logan with you."

"You walked in on me in bed with another woman and didn't get the stricken look I saw on your face when Mr. Gigolo walked out of here just now. Sorry, babe." He came toward her, taking both her hands in his. "But you do realize you're nothing more to this guy than miss right-now? Unlike me, he's not planning on settling down with you. Guys like him never do."

"Who says I want anything beyond this?" With effort she got one of her hands free to gesture broadly. She immediately regretted her outburst. She didn't want to discuss her current romance with Roger. It was none of his business. She drew herself up. "Let's talk about something relevant. Like what you're doing here, and when you're leaving."

His mouth firmed. "I'm here to try to talk some sense into you about us. Or I was. Now I don't know what I want." He put his hands on his hips. "God, I could use a drink."

That she could understand. "How about a beer?"

"Love one."

She led the way into the kitchen and gestured for him to sit at the island. How odd to see Roger where she'd grown accustomed to seeing Logan. Unbidden,

Roger's words echoed in her brain, chilling her from the inside out. *He isn't going to settle down. Guys like him never do.*

She pushed the words from her mind and busied herself getting a frosted mug from the freezer.

"So tell me. What's with your boyfriend's insistence I'm here to do you physical harm?"

"He's concerned because I've gotten some disturbing hate mail, and you know what they say about the most likely suspect." She popped the top off the bottle of beer.

Roger filled in the blank. "A husband or lover?"

She nodded, pouring beer into Roger's glass. "Or ex-lover." She set the glass and bottle on the counter in front of him.

"Thanks." Roger frowned. "I sympathize with his concern. At least he has that going for him. But you didn't get any hate mail from me." He raised the glass of beer, angling it at her before saying, "I love you, remember?" As if to punctuate his words, he took a long drag from the glass. "Candace, I'm not in this for the short haul, to get what I want and take off for parts unknown when it suits me."

A not so subtle reference to Logan again, of course.

This time, Candace refused to take the bait. "Roger, it's over between us. It has been since before I caught you, if we're being honest with each other. You and I both know it."

"That's crazy talk."

"You shouldn't have come all this way. You realize, of course, you can't stay here. You know that, right?"

"Why not? Because he says so?"

"Because we're through."

"You keep saying that. But could you just hear me out? I have come an awful long way to sing up to your window," he said with his signature charming grin. Then he winced as if the movement hurt. "I quit with the ice too soon, I think."

She walked around the counter and propped a hip on the stool beside him. "So talk."

He leaned back and gave her a thorough, once over. "You look…better than ever."

She realized she couldn't say the same. His normally golden complexion had a lackluster cast she didn't think had anything to do with the blow Logan had landed on him, and he was thin to the point of gaunt. He'd clearly lost weight since their break-up.

"I came here today for a couple reasons. I suppose I needed to see for myself you were all right, after what I put you through. I screwed up, Candace. I'm still dealing with the fallout."

"We both made mistakes. Some of them more blatant than others."

"Mistakes can be fixed. Even," he threw a glare toward the general vicinity of the back yard, "temporary lapses in judgment." Shifting his focus back to her, he gave her a pleading look. "Candace, I can forgive you if you can try to do the same. I came all this way to say we owe it to ourselves to give it a shot. We need to give our love a chance to heal."

Her eyes misted over. Because she now realized she'd never loved him the way she should. Regardless of what he'd done, she hated to see him hurt. "I'm sorry, Roger. It just isn't there for me."

His brows beetled and his tone turned sour. "It's

him isn't it? Do you love him?"

"No, I…of course not. Of course I don't." She shook her head. Stunned laughter bubbled out of her.

"I have to tell you I hope you're telling the truth, and you're not getting serious with Shaw. A guy like that would break your heart. He's a total womanizer, and probably couldn't offer you more than right now if his life depended on it. I still can't believe you left me to come shack up with another man."

"Not that it's any of your business, but this *thing* with Logan is—"

"Casual?" he filled in hopefully.

"Yes. No." She covered her eyes with her hands and drew in a sharp breath. "What I mean is, I'm not going to discuss this with *you,* except to say it's *new.* Nothing was going on between us until recently. I never lied to you, Roger. Please believe me when I tell you, Logan is not the reason we have no future."

She took several fortifying breaths. Beat back the panic threatening to overwhelm her. She wasn't in love with Logan. Roger had it all wrong.

"Fool that I am, I believe you. I blew it with that stupid, meaningless fling."

"We both screwed up. You cheated, and there's no excuse for that in my book. But, I've also realized your complaints were justified. I had been short-changing you." She placed both hands over one of his. "You deserve better from the woman you eventually marry."

He took another drink of his beer. Set down the mug with a decisive clink. "My flight home's not till next week. Are you going to kick me out on my ear, or can I at least spend the night? We could grab an early dinner and discuss the house."

"Discuss your plans for moving, you mean?" she asked pointedly, although no way was she letting him stay.

He smiled. "And I can figure out where I'm staying out the week."

"Sorry, Rog," came a deep voice from just beyond the archway dividing the living room from the kitchen.

Candace's stomach dropped. When had Logan come in? How long had he been standing there? Had he been purposefully stealth, or had she been too immersed in her conversation with Roger to notice his approach? Bottom line, what had Logan overheard?

"Looks like your flight's been rebooked," Logan said.

"Huh?" Roger uttered, confused.

"They have a seat with your name on it on the eight p.m. flight out of Reno. As in eight tonight. We'll need to get moving to make it." Logan slapped his hand twice on the archway frame and disappeared into the living room. "Going to pack—back in a sec," he called.

Candace looked at Roger, who was staring at her.

"Does he have that kind of clout? He can get my flight changed?" Roger asked.

"Apparently." But she wasn't concerned about Roger's flight, today, next week, or next year. Logan had just told them *he* was going up to pack. Logan was leaving?

Chapter Thirty-Four

Logan trotted down the stairs, his hastily packed duffel gripped tightly in one hand. He wasn't running away, he told himself. Wasn't punishing Candace. He was just keeping her safe. Somebody had to. She obviously wasn't planning on doing so.

In the living room the jerk sat on the couch staring at Candace, who perched, ramrod straight, on the edge of one of the armchairs.

His chest tightened at the sight of her, all tanned, and blonde, and so damned pretty in her white sundress. Had she put it on for *him?* For good-ole-*Rog?* Logan wondered for the twentieth time, then hated himself for the jealousy eating up his insides.

"What's this about a flight?" Roger demanded of Logan the minute his feet hit the landing. "You don't have the authority to change my flight plans."

Candace merely eyed his bag, looking sad. Was she upset because Roger was leaving? Because he'd punched *Rog?* Or maybe, just maybe, she didn't want Logan going anywhere. Too bad he didn't have a choice in the matter. Not if he was going to do this right.

Maybe she looks sad because you're acting like an ass, a voice inside him prodded. He ignored the voice.

He shifted his bag to the other arm. "I didn't bother with your existing reservation. I believe in the KISS principle—keep it simple stupid? First, I figured by your luggage you'd planned an extensive stay. Not gonna happen. So I booked you on an earlier flight myself. And because I'm such a nice guy, I thought I'd deliver you to the airport, too. Curbside service." He gave Roger a feral smile.

Roger frowned. "I don't see how you managed it. There's the cost for one thing—"

"Don't worry about it, Rog." He couldn't seem to stop using that godforsaken nickname Candace had uttered so offhandedly. Candace was playing with her hair, and studiously avoiding looking at him. He turned his attention back to Roger. "It's all taken care of. Ticket, tax, and transportation."

"Candace, is this really what you want? You haven't even had time to process the fact I'm here." Roger took one of her hands in his.

Logan didn't wait for her to respond. "The car's right outside. Now be a good boy, grab your bags, go outside, and put them in the trunk. I left it open for you."

"I haven't decided if I'm leaving town, Shaw, much less if I'm getting into any enclosed space with you." He turned back to Candace, traced a finger over the back of her hand.

Candace jerked her hand away, but not quickly enough for Logan's liking. He was ready to rip the guy's arm out of its socket.

"Candace? This is the kind of man you want to spend your time with? *Really*? I'm beginning to wonder how safe you are here with *him*," Roger said.

Candace opened her mouth to speak, but Logan cut her off. "You don't want to say anything else like that.

You want to do as your told."

"Or what?" Roger rose.

Or I'm going to tear you limb for limb, Logan wanted to say. Candace was finally looking at him; she had the most disappointed, heart achingly somber expression in her baby blues. God, didn't she know he was just trying to keep her safe? Didn't she understand she was in danger with this lunatic within a hundred miles of her? Did she expect Logan to just stand aside and let the bastard hurt her—maybe even kill her?

He forced himself to speak coolly. "Either get in my car, or I'm calling the police, and telling them how you broke in here. Then I'm going to show them the emails from you, threatening Candace. And you can spend the next few nights in jail, instead of safe and sound in *Orlando.*"

Roger's nostrils flared with impotent anger. He turned his back on Logan and stood facing Candace. "Are you sure you don't want me to stay?"

"I'm sure," she said in a rush, then sent Logan a look he couldn't interpret.

Roger nodded. "Can you at least let me kiss you goodbye?"

Logan rolled his eyes. Holy God, he wanted to beat this guy into oblivion.

Candace stood. Allowed herself to be enveloped in Roger's arms, and presented her cheek for a kiss.

Logan nearly laughed aloud. Her cheek. That's a girl. *His girl.*

Without another word, Roger strode for the door, grabbed his suitcase, and went outside.

Candace remained where she stood, looking after Roger. In other words, *not* looking at Logan.

Logan stared at her, willing her eyes to meet his.

It seemed like an eternity before her gaze slid to him, and she fixed him with the most blank expression he'd ever seen. "You got your wish. Roger's leaving. And you? I guess you're going somewhere, too?"

"I thought this would be a good time to check on my parents." He didn't mention he'd purchased the commuter flight ticket so he could get through security at the airport, which was the only way he could be sure Roger got on *his* flight out of town.

"How long will you be gone?"

He shrugged. He was planning on coming home first thing in the morning. But it would sure be nice if she said something to the effect of wanting him to come back.

She nodded. "I see. Well, then. Have a good trip." She started for the kitchen, hugging herself.

Jesus H Christ. She wasn't even going to give him a proper goodbye? He didn't even merit the cheek she'd given Roger? Before he could run after her, he strode for the front door. Once there, though, he couldn't quite force himself over the threshold. He raised his voice so she could hear him from the kitchen. "Unless, if you," he swallowed, "maybe you want to join me?"

He'd sprung for two last minute, full fare tickets. Why not three?

Her head appeared in the archway. She gave him a sad little smile. "That's all right. Next time."

He nodded. Frowned. "I'll call from the airport, then."

"Safe flight," she whispered, and ducked back into the kitchen.

Before he could do something stupid like tell

her...tell her...*God*, he didn't even know what he wanted to tell her. He didn't know what he was feeling. Just that he was angry and he didn't know why. He was leaving, and it appeared she didn't give a damn. And the kicker of it was, he didn't want to leave her, *period*. He *wanted* to grab her in his arms and never let her go. And, oh yeah, just looking at her right now hurt like Hell.

So yeah. He didn't want to tell her all that. Instead, he gritted his teeth, tightened his grip on his bag, and walked out the door.

Then slammed it.

****

Feeling morose, Candace trudged up the stairs to their room. She looked out her sliding glass door at the sparkling lake. At the crystalline pool. At her empty float, bouncing against the skimmer flap. The sun shone bright in a sky perfectly dotted with fluffy white clouds. Nothing much had changed. Not really. But the thought of returning to the pool where just a few hours ago she'd been so utterly content, now made her skin crawl.

She eyed her bed. She could lie down and cry. But there'd be time enough for that later when she lay awake all night, missing Logan.

Maybe a long run would help her get a handle on the emotions swirling inside her. She changed into exercise clothes, and headed out. No music. No headset. No phone. Just her and her thoughts.

What had changed inside her in the span of a day? Why had she let Logan leave without a fight? Without a word from her to indicate she didn't want to be here without him?

She ran and ran and ran, concentrating on her

breath and her footfalls.

And then it came to her. The moment things inside her had shifted. Everything had changed the moment Roger mentioned the word *love. He'd accused her of being in love with Logan. And he'd been right.*

She loved Logan. She'd ruined everything.

At the start of this whole thing, Candace had imagined herself delving into her first meaningless sexual fling. A summertime romance at the most. But now, just shy of a month in, she realized she hadn't stuck to her guns. She'd fooled around, and fallen in love.

She was in love. Her pace got faster. A smile spread over her face. She rounded the bend for home.

She'd never really been in love before. That was why she hadn't recognized the signs.

She'd just about concluded she had some missing circuits or something. A woman unable to form the most important bond of all. A woman unable to love. But she'd been wrong. She'd merely been waiting her whole life for him. For Logan. To make her laugh, and listen to her dreams. To make her scream with lust, and share her deepest, darkest memories. To sleep with, and wake with. To grow old with.

So she'd let him go today, because…because she was scared. Scared to find out she was in this all alone.

But that was ridiculous. Of course he loved her. Even a fool could see he did. She just had to give him a chance to realize it for himself.

Why else would he treat her so tenderly, and spoil her rotten, and run her ex out of town, risking jail time in the process? She laughed aloud. The man loved her.

As soon as she got back to the lakehouse she'd call

him. Not to tell him she loved him. No, he might need some more time to figure that out for himself. But she wanted to tell him to get his butt home. Or maybe she'd go to his parent's house in San Fran after all. Whatever. She just wanted to hear his voice.

She wished desperately she hadn't let him leave like that. Without kissing him. Without thanking him for being her knight in shining armor.

Why had she left her phone behind, again? She almost laughed aloud.

One long stretch of road to go.

Several hundred feet ahead of her another runner appeared, emerging from a dirt road that led to nowhere, if she remembered correctly, and the last before the turn off to Eric's long graveled drive. A woman runner. Candace smiled. She loved to see other people enjoying the outdoors, using their God-given bodies to the fullest.

The woman had an interesting gait, she noticed— and winced as the runner mis-stepped and took a tumble onto the shoulder of the road. The poor woman stayed down, and appeared to be cradling her knee. She must be really hurt.

Candace hastened her pace, stopped when she neared the injured runner. "I saw you fall. Are you all right?"

The attractive brunette smiled up at her, looking chagrined. "I'll survive. Mind giving me a hand up?"

Candace took her hand and tugged her to her feet. Dirt and gravel were stuck to the woman's knee and shin, but no blood, and no obvious swelling. "How bad is it?"

The woman wrinkled her nose. "I don't think I can

finish my run. Another four miles or so to go, I think."

Candace eyed her fanny pack. "Oh, dear. Did you bring a phone?"

"Nope. I don't suppose you have one I can borrow?"

"Not with me. You're in luck, however. My place, or rather, my friend's house is just up the road. Can you walk?"

"I think so."

"I can't offer you a ride, since I have no vehicle. But I can let you use my phone and give you a safe place to wait."

The woman blinked. "No car?"

"Afraid not." Candace started walking; the woman hobbled along at her side.

"Wow. How do you and your husband get to town for groceries and things?"

"My...friend who's staying with me has a car. He's not here right now, though. He just left, maybe an hour ago. Sorry. By the way, my name's Candace." She offered her hand.

"My name's JC. Nice to meet you, Candace. I'll definitely take you up on your offer of help. Honestly, I don't know what I'd have done if you hadn't happened along when you did."

Chapter Thirty-Five

"I think she's in love with you, you know. I hope you know what you're doing," Roger said, after a long, much needed stretch of silence between the two men. At least Logan no longer wanted to toss the guy out onto the asphalt, double back, and roll over him.

They crossed under the sign welcoming them to Reno International Airport.

"She loves you, and you're gonna break her heart."

Logan meant not to respond. But he heard himself saying, "I don't know why you would think that. I distinctly heard her tell you she was not in love with me."

Roger swiveled in the soft leather seat, to stare blatantly at Logan.

Logan ignored him. For about five seconds. "What?" he asked through gritted teeth.

Roger barked out a laugh, and faced forward.

Logan slid the man a sideways glance. Roger wore an ear to ear grin.

"What's so funny?"

"You. Don't get me wrong. I can't stand you." Roger began ticking off his fingers. "One, you're sleeping with my fi-*ex*-fiancée; two, you accosted me; three, accused me of unspeakable things, and somehow managed to run me out of town." He lifted one shoulder in a shrug. "Looks like she got under your skin, same as

261

mine."

"Don't compare us," Logan growled. He pulled into the short-term parking space and put his car in Park.

"Oh, darn. We're here." Roger unbuckled his seat belt.

They got out of the car and retrieved their bags in stony silence. The smell of burnt rubber and jet fuel permeated the underground parking area. A sick sense of loss filled Logan's belly. He didn't want to be here. Didn't want to fly away from Candace.

Candace, whom he'd distinctly heard tell her ex-lover she "of course" did not love Logan. Logan and she were...what had she said—casual? No, that had been Roger's word. *New*. That's what she'd summed them up as.

Not that he'd been eavesdropping. He'd come in quietly, wanting to assure himself Roger wasn't strangling her, and give himself an edge to intervene if he was. It had only been an accident he'd heard her breezy response to Roger's assertion she loved Logan.

"So..." Logan began when they were nearly to the automatic sliding doors leading to the terminal. "Why do you think she loves me?"

Roger threw his head back and howled with laughter. Then winced. "Ouch," he said, and gingerly touched his nose.

Logan arched a brow. "Nose hurt?

****

Candace filled two glasses with filtered water from the refrigerator, and handed one to JC who was sitting at the kitchen island, injured leg propped on a stool. "You can use the house phone if it's a local number.

Otherwise I'll get my cell phone from upstairs."

JC took a long swallow from her glass, then grimaced at Candace. "I probably should've mentioned a couple things. Number one: all my phone numbers are stored in my cell phone. I don't know any of them by heart. And two: my fiancé isn't home at the moment. I'm afraid you're stuck with me for a little bit."

Candace blinked. What was she supposed to do with this woman? She needed to call Logan. Needed to smooth things over with him, to let him know she wanted him here, now. She couldn't very well have a heart to heart with a complete stranger milling around. "What about when your fiancé gets back? How will you call him if you don't know his number?"

"I might be able to remember it. Maybe when I try the numbers."

"I'll get my phone." Candace bolted for the stairs.

She found it on her nightstand. She reached for it with a curious mixture of dread and hope thrumming through her veins. Two missed calls. Her heart swelled then sank when she saw neither caller had been Logan. Eric had called. Twice.

A text message came through before she could check her voicemail.

From Logan.

Hi gorgeous. At airport. Just making sure our friend gets on his flight, then I'll call you. Will have about ten minutes to talk before my flight. Please answer.

A huge grin spread over her face. Holding the phone to her chest, she skipped out of the room.

She discovered JC in the living room sitting on the couch, rather than in the kitchen where she'd left her.

Pretty presumptuous for a total stranger.

She eyed her phone just to make sure she hadn't somehow missed Logan's call on her trek downstairs. She still needed to check Eric's voicemail, too.

"So, Candace. You said this place belongs to a friend? Is he staying here with you and your other male friend, or are the two of you staying here alone?"

Candace tried to make sense of JC's question. "What do you mean?"

"You are staying here with a male friend, right? But not the owner of the house."

"True," Candace answered slowly. She held out the phone to JC. "I brought my phone if you want to try your fiancé. I'm expecting a call, though, so, if it rings…"

"You want me to answer. Got it. Thanks." She took the phone and smiled up at Candace. "I brought your water." She gestured to a glass atop a coaster on the coffee table. "How far did you run just now? You should hydrate."

"I don't know. Five miles? How about you?" Candace picked up her water. She took a long sip, and wandered to the floor to ceiling single paned glass partition, her eyes on the sparkling lake. JC was weird, she decided. She hoped the woman would remember her fiancé's phone number, or she'd have to push the idea of calling a cab sooner than later.

All in all? Between Roger and JC's coming, and Logan's leaving, this had been a crap day in paradise.

"Looks like your friend, Eric, really wants to hear from you. He just texted you." She paused to read the test. *"Please call me, I'm worried."*

That did it. "If you can't come up with the number,

we can always call you a cab." Candace took another sip of her water and turned to face JC, who was studying her intently. "I never asked. Do you live around here, or are you visiting, too?"

"I'm here visiting my fiancé. I've only recently arrived. It was...I planned the trip as a sort of a surprise for him." JC smiled beatifically.

Candace thought of Roger, and inwardly remarked on the irony. "You're staying in North Tahoe, then? Can't be too far from here since you were running on the main drag. Um...did you try your fiancé?"

"Mm." JC got up off the couch and wandered toward the mantel. She no longer appeared to be limping.

It occurred to Candace to suggest she continue on her run if she felt recuperated. She didn't mean to be uncharitable, but the woman had read her text for crying out loud. JC had a few things to learn about the do's and don'ts of accepting help from a stranger.

Like the way she was making herself at home in Eric's house, strolling around like she owned the place.

"This is a beautiful view. My fiancé would probably love it. He's a professional photographer. Actually we both are. It's one of the things we have in common."

A photographer? The hair on the back of Candace's neck stirred. "Oh?"

"What do you do, Candace? Oh, let me guess." JC studied Candace with narrowed eyes, as if she could see into Candace's mind.

This woman was beyond weird. Logan had sure picked a great day to disappear. Candace's phone made a chiming sound, indicating another text had come in.

Probably Eric again. "Would you mind handing me my phone?" Candace reached out.

JC had it gripped in one of her hands. "Author," she announced triumphantly. Either she hadn't heard Candace's request, or she chose to ignore it.

Candace opened her mouth to ask for her phone again and it began to ring. It sounded strange. Like it was playing in a tunnel.

JC glanced at the screen.

"Please hand me my phone," Candace demanded—or meant to. Her tongue felt thick, and her voice sounded very strange. Almost like it did when she was a child and spoke directly into a fan.

JC took a step back, and simultaneously tucked Candace's phone behind her back. "Nope, Candace, I don't think so."

The phone stopped ringing.

This was utterly ridiculous. Candace took a step toward JC. The water glass dropped out of her hand and rolled on the carpet. She stared at it in confusion. Shook her head.

"I'm impressed, if I do say so myself. That stuff really hit you fast. I wonder if it's because you just had a nice long run?"

Candace's legs buckled. She tried—God she tried to keep herself from tumbling, but her legs just gave way. Her palms slid against the glass, barely slowing her fall, and she landed hard on her knees, although, funny enough, it didn't hurt as badly as it should.

JC smiled a Cheshire grin. *Two* JC's grinning according to Candace's vision.

"You're taking all the fun out of this. You didn't even ask how I know what you do."

J.C., the room, everything around her swam in and out of focus.

"I recognize you from your photos. From the website promoting your books. The website that credited *my fiancé as the photographer*."

Candace swayed on her knees. Tried desperately to grasp the woman's words, and couldn't. Hell, staying conscious was damned tough.

"You thought...clever, I'm sure. Sneaking...with Logan. Keeping him away... Probably thought you'd get...scot-free, too... Nothing, no one...keep Logan and me apart. We...made for each other."

A wave of nausea hit Candace and she crumpled to the floor. Couldn't open her eyes. Couldn't follow the woman. So tired. Just needed to lie on the cool tile. Rest her cheek on the tile. Rest.

****

The gate agent typed at her keyboard and still managed to fix Logan with an evil eye. "Sir? Are you planning to board? Maybe you heard me announce that was the *final boarding call* for the flight to San Francisco?"

Logan nodded. He glanced at his cell phone screen, hoping beyond hope he'd somehow missed Candace's call in the last thirty seconds.

No missed calls. No texts. He lifted his pointer finger, gesturing to the agent to wait and moved to the thick glass window overlooking the tarmac. Maybe he had no service.

And maybe he was the tooth fairy.

He'd called Candace three times. Previous to that, he texted her, and specifically asked her to answer the phone when he called because of the limited window of time he had to talk. When she didn't respond to the text, he assumed it was because he told her he would call shortly. But now she wasn't answering his calls.

Evidently had no intention of doing so.

Evidently had her pert little nose out of joint over his giving her ex the boot.

Or maybe she was pissed because he'd acted like a Neanderthal.

If she'd just answer the phone, he'd let her rip him up one side and down the other.

"Sir?" the agent prodded, somehow infusing the one-syllable word with both impatience and finality. Board now or never.

Logan jammed his cell phone into his duffel and approached the boarding door.

Chapter Thirty-Six

Candace was dreaming.

In her dream, she was lying on her side in a dark cave. No light source anywhere. No way to tell which way to get out. Her throat burned. Her knees throbbed. Her head pounded. Hard to breathe. Had to get out. But which way to go?

She could follow the noise. The strange chatter she couldn't quite make out. No. That seemed wrong somehow. Dangerous.

She would grope her way out of the cave. Slide along the stone walls till she found an exit.

But her hands wouldn't cooperate. She strained against—against what? Bindings. Her wrists were bound—behind her. And her ankles?

Oh, God. This wasn't a dream.

Where was she? What had happened?

With effort, she opened her eyes a crack. A rolling wave of nausea slammed through her, bringing with it fragmented memories.

JC. She'd invited the woman into Eric's house to help her, and consequently been drugged. That much was as obvious as the binds securing her limbs. Candace flexed against them, just enough to test them. Tape, probably. Around her wrists, ankles and *knees*? Clearly JC didn't want Candace getting away. But why? Why had JC singled her out?

The woman was clearly unhinged. Even now, from the sound of things, JC was pacing the room, muttering to herself.

Candace struggled to discern the words.

"…had it all worked out…wrecked everything…have to think."

Candace couldn't differentiate between what was real and what was nothing more than a fabrication made by the quicksand in her mind. She had to *wake up*. She inhaled, long and deep. Kept doing it until her mind steadied a bit.

"No car…*haha*…no *car*. Great. Now what am I going to do with you?" JC shrilled. Her pacing picked up speed, and from the sound of the rantings, she was fast working herself into a lather.

Candace needed to get her bearings. She risked opening her eyes.

She was facing the floor to ceiling window in the living room. So JC hadn't removed her from the house. That was good. Plus whatever knocked her out was starting to wear off.

A mixed blessing. The more she came to, the more she hurt. Everywhere. Her head ached, and her eyes burned like she'd rolled them in glue and sand. The dryness in her throat suggested she'd swallowed some, too. Shoulders, knees, ankles all throbbed with competing pulses of fire and needles. Her fall—she'd landed on her knees—and her bindings all played a part in the symphony of pain resounding throughout her body.

Enough with the self-pity. She could lie here, or act. Since lying here wasn't accomplishing anything other than putting her limbs to sleep, that ruled out the passive approach. Perhaps she could talk some sense into JC.

She straightened as much as possible and rolled onto her back, smashing her hands beneath her, then heaved over onto her other side. She sucked in a breath as the shift unleashed a flurry of pins and needles along both legs.

JC stopped pacing, put her hands on her hips, and gazed at Candace in disgust. "Great. Now you're awake. The drug worked fast on you—faster than I expected. And now you're awake. Nothing's going right."

Candace took a chance, voicing the question to which she'd already guessed the answer. "Was it you?"

JC smiled with satisfaction. "You mean, was it me who sent you the lovely emails? Just wanted to get a little of my own back. You can't believe how much work it took me to pinpoint those mountain views, then work out where you were staying, but I didn't slave for years in research departments of magazines for nothing."

"But...why?" God, her throat hurt. But her voice was sounding more like her own.

JC's face morphed into a mask of fury. "Why? Logan, that's why. He's *mine.*"

Candace's mind went to one of the first messages she'd received from her then unknown harasser. Something about taking what didn't belong to her. Aha. Not what, but *who*.

Everything clicked into place. JC's supposed fiancé was a photographer. She'd also mentioned she and her intended had a love of photography in common, and hadn't Logan mentioned the woman who'd pursued him to the point of running him out of town had delved in photography?

Oh, God. It all made perfect, sick sense. None of it had had to do with her career, or anyone's obsession with her; it had been about Logan all along.

JC narrowed her eyes at Candace, and aimed an accusatory finger. "Logan's leaving today seemed perfectly timed. I had options. Plan A: I could put you in the garage in a running car, and wait for Logan to come back." JC's face screwed up in rage. "But you don't have a car."

She'd actually formulated a plan to kill her?

JC resumed her pacing, wringing her hands with each step. "That ruled out plan B, too: put you in the driver's seat and roll you down the hill to your death."

Not one plan, but two. Both featuring Candace committing suicide. As if.

"No car, and now you're awake. And you're probably going to fight me when I do figure out what to do with you. I almost hope you do," JC hissed between her teeth.

Candace worked her mouth until she produced a drop of saliva to moisten her throat. "Wh-why kill me?" she forced out.

JC stepped to within an inch of Candace's head. Squatting, she grabbed a fistful of hair, and glared into her eyes. "Did you just ask why? Why do you think? You don't just go around stealing other people's fiancés to play house with. Yes, little miss Jezebel. I know what you've been up to here. Trying to seduce Logan away from me. You lured him here, and worked your wiles on him. If it hadn't been for you, we'd be fine by now. He'd have called. Invited me here to stay." JC's eyes welled with tears, as if she truly believed what she was saying. "But no. You had to butt into the picture." Abruptly, the direction of her gaze darted to an area beyond Candace.

She half-dropped half-flung Candace's head, and Candace just managed to stiffen her neck before her skull dropped like a bowling ball onto the tile. Small favors.

JC was on her feet, laughing aloud and doing a little jig in place.

Couldn't possibly be a good sign.

"I've got it. The pool. I'll drag you out there and dump you in." She gave Candace a mighty shove, rolling Candace onto her stomach.

A second later, her collar tightened around her neck as JC grabbed a handful of shirt and tugged. Candace dug her feet into the travertine and prepared to fight for her life.

Abruptly, JC released her. "But wait. If I do that, he'll find you. Tied up at the bottom of the pool."

"Why don't you just untie me, JC? We can talk this through," Candace suggested hoarsely.

"Shut up!" JC screamed. She hauled back and delivered a kick to Candace's ribs.

Candace saw stars. She gritted her teeth against the pain and struggled to follow JC's frantic chatter.

"The lake. It'll have to be the lake. This is going to take all night. And you're not as light as you look."

JC's footsteps receded. What now? One thing was certain: She wasn't going to lay here and wait to be dragged to her death. Candace heaved herself onto her side again, and raised her voice to be heard in the other room. "JC, you know you can't get away with this.

And…and Logan's not going to be happy when he finds out what you did."

"Shut up shut up shut up!" JC barreled back toward Candace.

Candace pinched her eyes closed and stiffened. Here came another kick. But instead of a shoe to the ribs, something whistled through the air. It landed on her, covering her body. She opened her eyes and stared into the fleece throw from the couch.

"Where's that tape? I'm going to tape your mouth shut first, *then* wrap you up like a burrito."

The tip of JC's running shoe appeared in Candace's line of sight as she kicked the blanket off Candace's head. JC wore a big grin as she waggled the roll of duct tape in triumph.

The woman was truly deranged.

Candace's phone rang, distracting JC from her mission.

"Again?" JC sounded irritated. She stalked toward the sound.

Sensing time was running out, Candace struggled against the tape bindings. No use. They only seemed to grow tighter.

Across the room JC released a guttural scream that caused gooseflesh to spread all over Candace's body. A small object—Candace's cell phone?—sailed over Candace's head. A nanosecond later it crashed into the glass wall with awesome force. From the sound, it landed in splinters on the floor.

JC's breath was ragged, almost coming in sobs. When she finally spoke, she delivered her statement in the most deadly calm voice Candace had ever heard. "I guess he won't be calling you again. Ever again." She started back toward Candace.

If Candace didn't do something now, JC would drag her down to the lake, and submerge her.

She wouldn't let that happen. Wouldn't let JC use her to hurt Logan, and she damn sure wasn't going easily to her own execution. Hell no. She sucked in a deep breath. Tensed her body. Waited.

A beat later, JC stood over her. Bent forward.

Candace bucked herself onto her shoulders, and swung her legs up with all her might. Instinct had her bending her knees, and releasing all her body's power into JC's midsection.

JC screamed as her body jackknifed in on itself, then flew backwards.

Candace collapsed onto the hard tile, her skin registering a few fresh scrapes, just as a loud crash came from across the room. JC connecting with the coffee table? God, she hoped so.

Okay, Candy, she told herself, *get up.*

Chapter Thirty-Seven

Logan rode through the gathering dusk in complete silence, save the humming din of the air conditioner blowing in the car. He didn't turn on music or sports or the news. Didn't want anything to distract him from his primary goal: to get back to Candace.

He was a schmuck, plain and simple. No one had been more surprised than him when he found himself turning from the aircraft door, running up the jetway he'd just descended, and snatching his boarding pass out of the agent's hand. "Sorry, change of plans," he called over his shoulder as he hightailed it to short-term parking.

Now here he was. Chasing after a woman like a...well, he didn't want to even think the term *lovesick fool,* because that would be a serious exaggeration. A horny teenager, then. An infatuated youth. Except he wasn't all that young.

So just infatuated and constantly horny, and...something else was going on inside him, too. A cross between an ache and flat out pain, like he'd just slammed his thumb with a hammer. Except instead of his extremities, it hurt in the general vicinity of his heart. The fact was, he was missing the hell out of her. He twisted his hand on the steering wheel and glanced at the glowing dials of his watch. Nearly nine o'clock. A measly few hours.

So he was scurrying back to her, even though she hadn't answered calls, or responded to texts.

His cell buzzed in the console. Logan pressed the Talk button on his steering wheel a second before he noticed the caller was *not* Candace. Damn. He wasn't in the mood to talk to Eric right now. "Logan here."

"Logan—where is Candace? I've been trying to reach her for hours."

Join the club. "Maybe she doesn't feel like talking," Logan said, deliberately belligerent.

"That may very well be the case, but when I send her a text saying it's urgent she call me, and *that* after sending multiple texts and voice messages, I expect her to suck it up and call me anyway." Eric paused to huff out a breath. "She's never left me hanging like this. Ever. Which is why I'm calling you. Because, frankly, I'm damn worried. Now, tell me she's with you and her phone got dropped in the drink."

Eric's palpable concern reached across the phone line to turn Logan's flesh instantly clammy, despite the cool, dry air filling the car. "No, she's not with me. What do you mean you left several messages?"

"Exactly what it sounds like. I came into the office to find Jenna crying hysterically at her desk. When I finally got something out of her, she told me about how she gave Romeo my Tahoe address, and how he showed up there unannounced. I guess Candace called Jenna to check his story."

"Exactly right."

"Naturally, I called Candace to see how she was handling the situation, and the rest you know."

"You can relax about Roger. I took care of him."

There was a lengthy pause. "How exactly?"

"I booked him a flight, then took him to the airport and waited at the gate for him to board. Then I waited a little longer for the flight to take off. He's gone. Now I'm heading back to the house."

"That's good then," Eric said, relief evident in his tone. "You're in communication with her, at least."

Another pause.

"Logan?"

"Not exactly. Actually, not at all. I've been texting and calling her, too. She hasn't answered. Not a text, not a message, nothing."

Another pregnant pause.

"She's probably fine." Eric's dubious tone belied his words.

"Right." Logan was suddenly more sure than he could bear: she was *not* fine. His hands thrummed from the death grip on his steering wheel. He mashed the accelerator, even though he'd already been going eighty. If a cop tried to pull him over now, he'd damn well have to catch him.

"Tell me, Logan, did Roger admit to being the one behind the threatening emails?"

Logan's jaw ached from the force of his molars grinding themselves into dust. "No. He denied any wrongdoing, or knowledge of any such thing. *Adamantly.* Candace backed him all the way, too. She insisted he'd never hurt her. But I didn't listen," he said, his voice growing soft with self-disgust and recrimination. "I decided I would take care of it. Take care of her. I swooped in and got rid of the bad guy," he said with a humorless laugh.

"Logan, we don't know she's in trouble," Eric said.

"Don't we?" Logan spat, simultaneously punching

his steering wheel. "Goddammit. *Damn* it." In about two seconds his head was going to explode. He was a first class asshole. He'd been so sure the person threatening her had been Roger. But now he was just as sure he'd majorly miscalculated. He hadn't been open to listening, and she'd been right all along. Some deranged fan out there wanted to hurt Candace, and he'd left her wide open for her stalker to swoop in. If anything happened to her…

He couldn't think about that now. He just needed to get to her. "Eric, I've got to go."

"I don't need to ask you to call me as soon as you find her, right?"

"Right," Logan said.

"Think there's any stock in me calling the authorities?"

Logan thought for a moment. Registered the sick certainty in his gut. "Do it."

****

Through the trees lining the drive, the outside lights shone. But the lights were as expected. They were set on a timer. That told him exactly nothing.

Logan eased off the main drag and onto the winding gravel road leading to Eric's house. He switched off his headlights and laid off the gas pedal as he rounded the final curve. A second sense told him not to alert anyone to his presence.

He slowed the car, easing it onto the shoulder of the road several yards from the house lot, put the car in park, and shut off the ignition. He tossed the keys onto the passenger seat and set the interior lights to the Off position before cracking his door open. Nothing but crickets and the gentle breeze through the thicket of leaves reached his ears.

He slid out of the car, left the door slightly ajar to avoid the telltale thunk of a car door closing and started toward the house.

No lights on upstairs. But at least one light burned in the living room. Except Candace never lingered in the living room, unless they were together. Maybe she wasn't home. Maybe she'd fooled them all by going out for the night and had forgotten her phone. Except she didn't know anyone around here.

He did a quick scan of the grounds.

The garage door was open. That was unusual. Logan jogged over, a small burst of hope filling him, then fizzling out when he saw the scooter still parked where it had been when he left.

He squinted at the house. Moved toward it with as much stealth as he could muster. Schooled his breath. Tried to prepare himself for…whatever he needed to do to keep her safe. He took the front stoop in two strides. Reached out. Grasped the doorknob. The metal was cold in his grasp. He held his breath and tried the handle. It turned. Unlocked.

He pushed open the door and stepped into the alcove.

"L-Logan?" Candace said his name as if she didn't really believe he was there.

Holy shit. In two seconds flat he registered about a million details. Where she stood, wobbling at the side of the couch all one-limbed like an inchworm or a mermaid. She was dressed for running and her hair was half in and half out of a ponytail. And she was wrapped in duct tape.

He reached her in two strides, grabbing her into his

arms. "Baby doll, what the hell hap—" The words died in his throat as he took in the other woman lying in a heap on the floor in front of the couch, on what used to be Eric's coffee table.

She was, apparently, just coming to.

Julie Braun blinked up at him. "Logan, is it really you?" She sounded glad to see him.

"I'll deal with you in a minute. Don't so much as move." Turning from her in disgust, he scooped Candace into his arms and carried her into the kitchen. He needed scissors. Needed to get this damned tape off her. Check her for injuries. She was shaking like a leaf.

"I thought you weren't coming back," she said in a small, tinny voice. "I thought—"

"Shh," he said against the top of her head, pressing a kiss into her hair.

Using one arm to hold her, he rummaged in the knife drawer with his free hand till he found a pair. He had so many questions. So many. But first he had to get her free. "Are you hurt?" He took her into the dining room where he could prop her in a seat to work on her bindings while also keeping an eye on Julie.

"I don't think so." She gazed at him with wide-set, trusting eyes. Like he deserved that. He'd gotten her into this mess.

He had to look away. Or he might quit what he was doing and use the scissors to kill that woman, moaning and crying like a fool in the other room. He set his jaw and cut through the layers of tape, first freeing her wrists, then her legs.

"This is going to hurt a little," he said as he peeled the adhesive from her skin.

She gritted her teeth, but otherwise didn't

complain. When he grasped her side to get a better grip on her, she sucked in a breath.

"What is it?" He jerked his hands back.

"A bruise, I think. It's nothing," she said, though she had instinctively covered the area with her now freed hands.

Moving slowly, so as not to frighten her, or maybe because he was afraid what he'd find, he peeled her hands back, then lifted the edge of her shirt. An ugly black and blue bruise marred the skin covering her lower rib cage. A low, guttural curse emerged from deep in his throat.

Candace laid a hand on his forearm. "Logan. It's all right. I'm all right."

He glanced up sharply, locking eyes with her. Saw compassion there—for *him.* "Candace." He tried to speak, but couldn't seem to force any words over the lump in his throat.

She cupped her palm over his cheek, attempting to soothe him. It only made the fire burning inside him more violent.

A knock sounded at the door. "Tahoe police. Open up."

Logan closed his eyes, and pulled himself together with the force of his will, shoving the emotional storm currently taking ownership of him into the darkest corners of his mind. "I'm going to get the door," he told her in a voice that sounded surprisingly normal, "then I'm calling Eric. Don't move."

Chapter Thirty-Eight

Candace sat beside Logan at the dining room table massaging the herb scented balm the paramedic had given her into her sticky, raw wrists. Across the table sat the two police officers who'd arrived on the scene, one of them taking notes, the other asking questions of Logan.

Candace stifled a yawn so he wouldn't catch her and order her upstairs. The cops had been here going on two hours, and not that she wasn't grateful for their presence, but she was ready for them to wrap it up. It gave her the creeps knowing JC—or Julie, or whatever she called herself—was just outside. The police had her in custody, strapped onto a gurney, loaded in the ambulance in the driveway. She needed medical treatment prior to her incarceration—evidently smashing into the coffee table hadn't agreed with her.

As comforting as the thought of JC locked behind bars was, knowing she was still in the driveway was too close for Candace's comfort.

She pushed thoughts of JC aside and tuned in as Logan responded to the police about how he knew JC, aka Julie, and how he figured into this scenario.

"Julie was the stalker from the magazine where I work—worked." He tunneled his fingers through his already disheveled hair. "I can give you the contact information of my editor if you want more details.

Anyway, the point is, I haven't seen her for months, certainly haven't contacted her, and never expected her to follow me here." His gaze slid to Candace. The second their eyes met, he looked away, as if that small connection cost him.

His forearm rested on the back of her chair, and his fingertips grazed her nape. She laid a hand on his thigh under the table. Gave a little squeeze.

He didn't look at her, but he dropped his free hand under the table to cover hers.

It occurred to her he'd had some part of him touching her from the moment he arrived. His hand on her thigh. His arm around her waist. His hand on her nape. For the first time in hours, she allowed herself a small smile.

The officer in charge of questioning gave the notetaker a nod. The notetaker snapped his pen closed, and straightened his papers on the clipboard.

"That's it?" Logan rose from his chair and simultaneously pulled Candace's seat back.

As the four of them made their way to the front door, one of the police handed Logan a business card. "Here's our information, and your case number. Feel free to call if you think of anything else you want to add, or if you have any concerns. Otherwise, someone'll be in touch."

A few minutes, that seemed like an eternity, later, Candace and Logan stood on the front stoop and watched the flashing lights of the patrol car and ambulance disappear from view.

In unspoken agreement, they went inside.

They got as far as the foyer before Logan froze, hands on his hips, head hung low. He stared down at her, a miserable expression on his face. His mouth worked, as if he wanted to say something to her, but couldn't force out the words.

Candace couldn't wait another second. She flung herself into his chest, catching him slightly off guard. He stumbled backward, but managed to steady himself as his arms banded around her.

"Candace," he breathed into her hair. "I'm so sorry. I never should have left you alone."

"I'm just glad you came back."

"I couldn't stay away. I can't believe it. Julie. Here. All my fault of course."

She took a shuddering breath and rubbed the tip of her nose on the warm, stubbled skin of his neck. "You couldn't know she'd trace the photos from my publisher's website back here."

"I should never have approved the use of my name on the site. If Jenna hadn't credited me as the photographer, Julie's search would never have turned me up."

"Logan, it's not your fault she's deranged."

As she spoke, Logan scooped her into his arms and moved toward the stairwell. "She's clever. I'll give her that." He started up the stairs.

She giggled. "You can put me down, you know."

He merely tightened his grip. "No. No, I can't do that," he said, his voice thick with emotion.

"Logan?" Candace used her fingers to tilt his face in her direction.

He paused on the stairs when their eyes met. Never had she seen such a tortured expression on another human's face. She opened her mouth to speak, but he shook his head, silencing her.

He carried her to her room. Didn't touch the lights, just walked through the moonlit room, to the bed. He laid her down as if he thought any sudden move might cause her to break.

At first he made no move to join her. Just stared down at her, that same tortured expression darkening his eyes.

She wanted to tell him how much she loved him right then and there. Wanted to drag him down to lie on top of her. But instinct bade her wait.

For several moments he did nothing but draw in raspy lungfuls of air. Then he propped one knee on the bed and leaned over her. He cupped her face with palms warm and slightly damp. Whispered her name.

Her heart responded to the need she felt pouring out of him, filling her chest with a heavy, sweet ache. An ache that turned into something hot and urgent and greedy for him, low in her belly with each murmured endearment from his lips.

Still, she lay quiet. Let him touch her. Let him tug the useless ponytail holder from her hair, and tunnel his fingertips close to her scalp. Let his face draw close to hers.

So close. So close she could feel his hot breath against her cheeks.

Then closer. Till finally he pressed his lips to hers, and she realized he was shaking. Everywhere. Tiny tremors transmitted themselves to her wherever their flesh met. His lips to her lips. His fingertips to her cheeks.

Moving slowly, almost as if she could gentle him, she parted her lips under his, tasting his tongue, tasting him. Pulling the molten emotion seething within him into her. Hot, weak, needy, exultant.

A low, urgent, moan purred out of her. At his answering groan, Candace gave up the fight.

She arched upward closing the distance between them. She tangled her legs with his, pulling him onto the bed, joining his hips with hers. At the same time she grasped the hem of his shirt, jerking it up with one hand, while her other hand roamed over his fevered flesh.

When the shirt got caught at his shoulders, Logan snatched the material from her hand and ripped it over his head in one move. Then his hands got busy on her clothes, tugging down her running shorts, her nylon-tee up.

No words, just the gasping of air, the sounds of mouths tasting skin, the soft thump as Logan scooped her up and tumbled backward so she lay on top of him. He feasted on her mouth, the rough stubble of his beard scraping her cheeks, while his hands searched every inch of her flesh as if to ascertain she was solid and real and his.

Candace's hands were just as greedy, coursing over his sculpted chest, diving into his hair, skimming down his rock-hard abdomen to open the fly of his jeans and then sliding over the bulge in his briefs.

He gave a little whimper when she lingered there. "Can't...wait," he whispered hoarsely. He groped for the nightstand, and yanked open the top drawer. She heard him rustling through the contents till he found the small foil packet.

He tore into it with his teeth, while his free hand reached between them to shove at his jeans and briefs, freeing his hot erection to press into her belly.

Wet and needy and panting, she stared into his passion drugged eyes and, unwilling to wait one second longer, snatched the condom from the wrapper he was wrestling with. She wedged her hands between the slick area where their bodies met, and rolled the condom onto him. She'd barely gotten it in place and he was inside her, thrusting. Hard. Deep. Agonizingly slow at first, and then building tempo.

Again and again he drove himself into her, filling her, claiming her in the oldest, most primitive way known to man. She welcomed his thrusts, arching back, pressing her sex down onto him. Her nails bit into his chest as she threw her head back and allowed the delicious thick heat of him to tighten the coil of need inside her. Tighter and tighter he wound her till she thought she might explode from the pleasure of it. She was a simmering volcano, ready to erupt.

"Sweet Jesus," he whispered hoarsely as he pumped his hips into her. "I can't...I need...Candace."

The raw emotion in his voice unleashed the exquisite release in her. It built on itself like a boulder rolling downhill picking up speed. She gasped out his name, again and again, heard his own guttural murmurings of need and wonder, each unintelligible whispered word intensifying her climax. And then she heard her name torn from his lips as he convulsed beneath her in an answering climax that seemed to reach from his soul to hers.

Then they were still, Candace sprawled atop Logan. Both of them misted with sweat. The button of his fly dug into her hip, but it hurt so good. Slow, fat tears leaked from her eyes even as her heart rejoiced. God, she loved this man.

"Did I hurt you, baby?" He wiped a tear from the corner of her eye with the pad of his thumb.

She shook her head, and he didn't ask any more questions. Just rolled to his side, taking her with him in his arms. He petted her, running his large hands over her hair, down her back, curving over her hips as if he still needed assurance she was there, beside him.

I love you. She ached to say the words. Her throat literally contracted, making it hard to swallow. But she told herself the words could wait. For tonight, this was more than enough.

****

Candace woke before Logan. She slipped out of the bed, grabbed a swimsuit and tiptoed from the room.

She needed to think. No iPod, no computer, nothing to distract her from her thoughts. In the hall, she put on her suit then trotted down the stairs headed for the pool. The sun was barely up as she submerged into the chilly water and shocked herself into full wakefulness. She swam. Long, sure strokes.

With every breath, she felt herself coming into a deeper awareness of the situation, right now, in this moment. Of the choice she no longer had to make—but had made.

It felt so good. So right. For the first time in her life, she was madly, deeply, passionately, in love. Maybe it had started as a meaningless sexual fling, but no more. Logan had become as necessary to her as air.

And he loved her, too. Why else had he gone crazy with worry when Roger arrived yesterday? And why had he come back, instead of taking off to his parents like he planned? He'd said he *couldn't* stay away.

Then last night. He'd made love to her as if his life

depended on it.

They loved each other. That was a good thing. A great thing. So why were her insides tied in knots?

Her mind went silent. She reached the deep end wall, did an underwater flip and shoved off, emerging from the water to draw a breath and begin her strokes anew.

It was the memory of Logan's face last night, of the change in him that was getting to her. The tortured expression darkening his eyes every time he looked at her. The bleakness and self-recrimination he hadn't even tried to hide when he realized it was his past and not hers, that had threatened Candace. She'd sensed a part of him shutting down. Wanting to push her away.

Thank God his fear hadn't won out. In the end he turned to her, not from her. But she'd seen the struggle all over him. She doubted very much the war within him had ended. Which begged the question—the most important question of her life. Which part of Logan would win?

If he walked away…

Her heart seized, stealing her breath and she slowed her strokes, swam to the shallow end, and stood, pushing through the water on rubbery legs toward the steps.

Eric had once told her she was Logan's weakness. Well, his theory was about to be put to the test, because their fairytale time here had run out.

Chapter Thirty-Nine

Candace stepped into the house and found Logan waiting for her. He was showered and shaved, and looking good enough to eat in a white linen shirt with the sleeves rolled to his elbows and worn jeans. He had a cup of black coffee in one hand and a folded *New York Times* in the other. "You didn't wake me."

"I thought you needed your rest," she said.

At his confused look she gave him a wink. "*After* everyone left?"

"Ah," he said, one corner of his mouth hitching up. "How are you feeling, sweetheart?"

"I have a couple bruises, and I feel like an idiot for inviting a lunatic into the house, but I'll live."

"Hey, she's crazy all right, like a fox, and she had a pretty decent plan for getting an invite. I'd say you fared all right, though." He propped a hip on the arm of the leather couch, his gaze traveling over her with lazy thoroughness.

Right. But, do you love me? a part of her wanted to scream. Instead, she said, "Coffee smells good. Think I'll grab one, and run up to shower."

"I'll bring it up," he set his coffee and paper aside, "for a price."

She arched a questioning brow.

"Give me a kiss, baby. I missed you." He pulled her into his arms.

"I'm gonna get you all wet," she protested.

He gave a husky chuckle and nibbled her neck. "I got scared when you weren't in the room. Broke out in a cold sweat wondering if someone had snatched you away." He was going for a teasing tone and not quite pulling it off.

Yep. The man definitely loved her.

"You can't get rid of me that easily." She tilted her head back to meet his eyes. "By the way, I don't think I ever thanked you properly for rescuing me."

He broke eye contact. "Right. I rescued you. Was that after I ran your not-so-guilty ex out of Dodge, and left you vulnerable and on your own?" He released her to cross his arms over his chest, and tapped a finger on his chin. "Oh. No. It must have been when I came in and found you standing over Julie, after you'd knocked the breath out of her." He gave her a sardonic smile. "Sweetheart, I'd say you pretty well rescued yourself."

She cupped his cheek with her palm. "I couldn't have managed without you, Logan."

He shook his head. "I keep thinking it never would've happened if I'd had her locked up when I found her standing over me in my bed several months ago. I can't believe how stupid I was. I never once thought the person harassing you might be her."

She thought a moment. "Me neither. Poor Roger."

His brows furrowed. "I wouldn't go that far."

Her heart flooded with sweet, aching love she knew must be written all over her face.

Logan smoothed her damp hair over her head, a serious expression darkening his eyes. "On the ride back here from the airport, when I talked to Eric and found out he hadn't been able to reach you either, I knew something was wrong. I was so afraid I wouldn't get here in time. I've only had that breath-knocked-out-of-me feeling one other time in my life."

When he heard about Luke, she guessed. "I'm sorry I put you through it."

He pulled her to stand between his legs and wrapped his arms around her. "Sweetheart. I'm sorry."

"You have nothing to be sorry for. You came back." She rubbed her nose on his warm neck. "What made you so sure I was in danger?"

"Eric. You. I don't know. I just knew."

"Ok, Monsieur Seer. Care to tell me what's in my immediate future?"

He crooked a finger under her chin to tilt her head back, and gave her a slow smile.

She giggled and shoved away from him. "Nope. Coffee and a shower."

A while later, she stood in her bathroom drying her hair.

Logan poked his head in the open door and motioned for her to shut off the hair dryer. "I got a message I need to check my PO box, and I thought you might want to get out of the house for a while, so I'm taking you to lunch."

"You don't have to do that. But I do need to mail something."

He shook his head and flashed her a grin. "And you need to eat."

"Give me ten?"

Candace dressed with care in her pink striped gingham wrap dress and a pair of strappy sandals. She applied a little makeup and dabbed on her favorite perfume. She needed as much self-confidence as she could muster this afternoon. Because she was about to take a wild leap of faith. She was ready, too. The question burning up her stomach lining was whether or not Logan was ready to leap with her.

Logan was waiting for her downstairs. When he saw her his eyes widened with alarm. "Candace, whoa. Go back upstairs and change into a sack or something."

"Excuse me?" she said with a laugh.

"You're too pretty to leave the house. At least go outside and smear some dirt on your face," he said, one corner of his mouth curving upward.

"Come on, joker, I'm hungry." She took his hand and dragged him toward the door.

"I am too," he said with a suggestive leer.

"You are insatiable."

"Must be something in the water." He reached past her to open the front door, and put his other hand on the small of her back to guide her with gentle pressure.

"Uh-huh."

"Spoilsport." He hit the unlock on his remote.

He took her to a small restaurant on the North shore. They got a table on the outdoor deck overlooking the lake. The sun was shining, occasionally hiding between puffy white clouds. A soft lake breeze blew through often enough to keep temperatures comfortable without stealing the umbrella from above their table.

After the iced-teas arrived and they placed their meal orders, Logan fixed Candace with a measured gaze. "You seem pensive. Are you sure you're all right?"

"Fine. Really."

He gave a slight shrug. "You went swimming

without me this morning. You didn't have much to say in the car. You're not looking at me." He drummed his fingers on the table and searched her eyes. "I know a lot has happened in the last twenty-four hours. We haven't really talked about the whole Roger debacle. Are you upset with me for kicking him out of town?"

"What? No. You went slightly above and beyond, but no. I'm glad he left."

Logan nodded slowly, his gaze never leaving hers. "Did he say something to upset you? Something about me?"

In an instant, Roger's words came back. *You realize he isn't going to offer you anything beyond now? Guys like that never do.* "What do you mean?" she hedged, sipping her tea.

"Now you're being evasive," he said with a smile that didn't quite meet his eyes. "He...I got the feeling he didn't have too high an opinion of me."

She snorted softly. "Did you expect him to sing your praises?"

One corner of his mouth curved in wry acknowledgment. "What I'm getting at is, how did you feel about what he said?"

"Logan, I don't need someone to tell me who you are. I know who you are. And I'm exactly where I want to be."

His eyes narrowed as if he didn't exactly know how to take her words. "Did you get any funny feelings when you saw him? I mean, before he showed up, we never got around to discussing exactly what your status is."

She stared at him, cocking her head.

He shifted in his seat as if he'd grown suddenly

uncomfortable, then pressed on. "Is he definitely in your past?"

"It's over between us, Logan. Surely you know that?"

"I thought I did." He raked a hand through his hair, looking everywhere but at her. "Sorry. Don't mean to act like a…like I'm, you know…"

She grinned. She did know. Still, she wanted to hear him to say it.

The waiter arrived with the food. Logan clapped his hands once, rubbing his palms together like he couldn't wait to eat.

Candace's gaze never left his face.

He picked up a fork and toyed with his quesadillas. "You're going to make me say it, aren't you?"

She smiled sweetly, and smoothed her napkin on her lap.

"I was jealous, okay? Undeniably, horribly, disgustingly jealous. You never told me he was so damned good looking either. It would've helped if he'd been short. Or bald. Or cross-eyed or something."

Candace's shoulders shook in silent mirth.

Finally his gaze locked with hers. "I love it when I make you smile," he said in a husky voice.

"I love it when you make me smile, too." *And I love you.* "So, what comes to your PO box? Work stuff? Personal mail?" She picked up her fork and dug into her salmon salad.

"Everything gets forwarded here for now, till I go back to New York or decide on a new permanent address. But there is one package in particular I'm having sent straight to our door."

"What's that?"

"I sent those digital images to a buddy of mine to develop in his lab." He slopped a dollop of sour cream on his tortilla and took a big bite.

"What images? Oh, no. The pictures of me—in my nightie? To one of your friends?"

"You'd rather the local junior photo dude develop them and make copies to give all his friends?"

"Now that you put it that way." She shuddered. "Remind me never to let you take pictures of me again."

"Darlin, don't say that. Don't even think it." He gave her a sexy grin and leaned in, rubbing his thumb over her bottom lip. Then he gave her a slow, bone-melting kiss. He smiled at her dazed expression, then sat back and picked up his silverware. "As far as the PO box goes, however, there is supposed to be something important waiting for me, at least according to an email I received."

"What's that?" She dabbed her napkin on the corner of her mouth.

"Remember I told you I'd been looking into snapping photos over the pond?"

She nodded slowly, her stomach folding in on itself with dread.

"I wrote to Getty Photos expressing interest in their organization. Getty's an exclusive photojournalist group with access to some of the most restricted areas on the globe. A few days ago I got an email from their offices saying they'd sent me a certified letter."

She forced a light smile. "Think they might offer you a position?"

"Maybe." He shrugged. Ate more of his quesadilla.

"That's great, Logan."

"We'll see. Speaking of the post office you said you had something to mail."

"My book. I'm sending the hard copy and a thumb drive to Eric's office. It's time to let go of my baby."

Logan blinked a few times. "Really."

"Yes."

He looked down. Unfolded then refolded his napkin.

She took a breath and forged ahead. "I'm thinking it's about time to reenter the real world, and return Eric's house." She forced a chuckle as the small amount of lunch she'd eaten threatened to come back up.

Logan eyed his plate like it would run away if he took his focus off of it. "Ready to run home to Florida, are you? I suppose being mugged in paradise—twice— would put a damper on things."

She wondered if he could see her heart trying to beat its way out of her chest. "It's not that. I'm just, ready as I'll ever be." She set her fork and knife on her plate, and gave up trying to smile, since she feared it was coming across as little more than a grimace. She gazed intently at Logan's profile and waited.

He said nothing.

The waiter asked if they needed anything else.

A few minutes later they pulled out of the parking lot and took the short drive to the post office. They split apart to take care of their individual tasks, then reconvened at the double glass doors.

"Did you get the letter?" Candace tried unsuccessfully to quell the butterflies in her belly.

Chapter Forty

Logan held up an envelope marked Certified mail. "Are you going to open it?"

"After we get home. You ready?"

"Yes."

In between shifting gears, Logan reached across the console and took her hand.

Candace smiled, and put on her best carefree mask, even though she felt her dreams of once in a lifetime love melting away like an elaborate sand castle at high tide. Everyone knew castles made of sand never lasted. Eric had warned her to not get too attached. In his own way, so had Logan. Even Roger had known what was in store for her.

She was a first class fool.

She had to stop thinking, or risk blubbering like an idiot in the front seat of Logan's car.

She wanted nothing more than to get back to the house, but when they arrived, she didn't know what to do with herself.

Logan had carried the mail into the kitchen. Should she trail after him? Leave him to read in private?

She opted for the latter. She didn't think she could keep a straight face much longer anyway. "I'm going up and change into a swim suit," she called from the base of the stairs.

She trudged to her room. Was this it? Was it really

the end for them? She could hardly make herself believe it.

The definitive answer came a half hour later when she went downstairs to find Logan waiting, his eyes brilliant with excitement.

"Getty wants to take a look at my portfolio and discuss the opportunities in person. A rep is in San Fran for the next couple of weeks. Candace, did you hear me? They're in California *now*."

"That's great, Logan. When will you meet with them?" She felt numb. Like she'd suddenly turned to plastic.

"I phoned their corporate office. I've got a meeting scheduled morning after next. I figured I'd drive in to San Fran tomorrow and stay at my folks, then get up bright and early for my meeting."

"Tomorrow. That's...wow. I'm happy for you, Logan." She sank down on an armchair, mostly because she didn't trust her legs to hold her up any longer.

Logan squatted beside her and the subtle scent of his aftershave, so masculine and sexy, cut into her senses like a knife. He cupped her knee. "Why don't you come with me? You can meet my parents. I'll show you around San Francisco. We can stay an extra day or two. It'll be fun."

Fun? When her heart felt like it was holding itself together with chewing gum and silly string? "I don't think so, Logan."

He gave her a strained look. "Is it the idea of staying with my folks? Don't worry about it, babe. I should have mentioned I'll book us a room at the Ritz. No sweat."

"No, it's not that. I've got to...pack. And get the

house ready."

"Graciella will do the serious cleaning, as always. You don't need to—"

She put out her palm to stop him. "I don't think it's a good idea. I don't see any point in my meeting your parents. Do you?" She held her breath.

A muscle ticked in his jaw. "You know I can't leave you here after—"

Her heart sank even further. So that was why he'd invited her. "Logan, I'm a grown woman. And besides, the danger's passed. JC's in custody."

He tunneled a hand through his thick, ink-black hair and stood, glowering down at her. "Candace, you're not being fair and I don't think you're looking at this from the right perspective. This is important to me." He huffed out a breath. "It'll only be for a few days. Three days, max."

"No one's asking you not to go, Logan."

His turquoise gaze pierced her like blue steel.

She tilted her head and smiled. "I'm happy for you. What you've always wanted is right at your fingertips. Of course you have to go. I want you to." *Liar, liar.*

****

At seven o'clock the next morning Logan drove down Highway 89 feeling cranky and anxious, as if he'd had one too many cups of coffee on a hangover. He ought to be on top of the world. He ought to be excited about his future prospects. Why wasn't he?

He wished like hell Candace had come with him. If she were here he could talk to her and she'd help him figure out what was eating him. But she hadn't wanted to come. And he damn sure wouldn't beg.

She had no way of knowing it was the first time in

his life he'd ever asked a woman to meet his parents. Well, second if he counted the fact he'd asked her to meet them just two days ago.

Both times she'd turned him down flat. No hesitation.

Dammit. Nothing had gone right since Roger showed up. His presence had cast a shadow over everything like a putrid black stain.

He glanced at his Breitling. Seven-ten. Too early to call Sleeping Beauty. He smiled picturing Candace as he'd left her. Naked. Tangled in the sheets.

When they'd made love last night, she'd been amazing. God, she'd driven him crazy, like always. But something had been different about her. Almost like she was sending him off to war or something. But he was only leaving for a couple days.

He drove for a while in brooding silence. When he saw the sign announcing he'd hit San Francisco city limits he got the first niggling of what was troubling him. His uneasiness had started with that conversation. The one at the restaurant he tried to pretend hadn't happened. When she'd told him it was time to go home—and he said nothing.

Nothing.

It had been on the tip of his tongue to say "What? Not yet? Let's stay a little longer." *Like forever.* But that would've been ridiculous, since they couldn't stay at Eric's indefinitely, and at some point he'd need to get back to work.

Not that he really *needed* to work. He'd made good money over the years and had been wise enough to hire an investment genius who turned his nest egg into a pot of gold. But in another sense, the part of him that craved meaning did need to work. Needed his life to count for something.

And therein lay the crux of the issue.

His life had meaning. Satisfaction, fulfillment, dreams. Ever since he met her. Candace had gotten inside him, pulled out everything that was good and real, parts of him he didn't even know existed, and brought it all into the light of day.

If she left, the sunshine would disappear, too.

He needed her.

No, he *loved* her. Dammit, he'd known for a while. Why had it taken so long to admit the truth to himself?

He jerked the wheel and skidded to a halt on the shoulder of the road. An angry motorist laid on his horn and blew past. Logan waved in apology and scrolled through his phone contacts to her information. He pressed Send and promptly got Candace's voicemail.

Why did that woman have a cell phone? It wasn't even on half the time. He left a message for her to call when she woke, and eased back onto the highway. In a half hour he'd be at his parents'. Candace would get his message and call back, and he'd tell her how he felt.

He laughed aloud. His chest felt light, like a weight had been lifted. Just like that. God, he couldn't wait. He was going to tell a woman for the first time he loved her. Over the phone, no less. He laughed again and drove on.

Chapter Forty-One

Something was wrong.

Hell, everything was wrong.

He couldn't reach Candace. In a span of less than twenty-four hours he'd called her ten times and left as many messages.

She texted. Said not to worry, everything was fine, but she didn't want to talk. She said—what was it? He re-read the text for what seemed like the thousandth time.

Can't talk now. Lots of things on my mind. Need to think. Have a great interview and see you soon. And then, *Logan, please stop calling. I'm fine. Enjoy your time with your parents and focus on your big day.*

Oh sure. He'd surely have a *great* meeting with Getty, with visions of Candace lying on the bathroom floor, having slipped on the travertine running through his brain. He checked his cell one more time for missed calls. From the corner of his eye he saw his mother's alert gaze.

"Logan, you must be expecting an important call."

"Sort of." His parents had been thrilled when he told them over dinner last night how he'd opted against going to Afghanistan. He hadn't explained why. Maybe he was being superstitious, but he didn't feel right telling them he'd found Miss Right when he hadn't even told *her* yet.

Nor had he told them about the whole Julie debacle. He'd had to excuse himself when he called the police department in Tahoe to verify Julie hadn't been released from jail. She hadn't.

He needed to hear Candace's voice. Needed to tell her how badly he missed her. How he couldn't stand being without her for one day, much less be separated by hundreds or thousands of miles.

History was repeating itself. No. *He* was repeating himself, making the same damned mistake he made once before. He couldn't live with making it again.

Luke had asked Logan to go with him. He'd said no. Blamed it on work.

Now Candace had asked. Not in so many words, but only a fool would miss the signs. All he'd had to do was open his dumb mouth. Tell her he wanted to be with her. That they could work out the logistics, but as long as they were together everything else would fall into place.

"Mom, I won't be staying for breakfast. I left something important back in Tahoe and I have to go get it."

****

Two hours and thirty-five minutes later, he pulled into the drive. He didn't bother with the garage, but parked beside the front doors.

He jogged up the stoop, glancing down at the package leaning against the door. He scooped it up and tucked it under his arm, and twisted the doorknob. Locked.

He inserted the house key with his shaking hands. Witch. She'd done something to him. Cast a spell or something. He felt himself smile at the thought. He wanted to be angry with her. But he couldn't seem to hang on to the emotion.

He stepped over the threshold and yelled for her. "Candace? I'm home. Baby girl, have you got some explaining to do."

The house was eerily quiet.

It was nine a.m. She hadn't brewed coffee yet or he'd smell it. Which meant she was still in bed. He grinned and headed to the stairs, taking them two at a time. Maybe she was in the shower.

Or taking a run. God, he hoped not. He didn't want to wait one more minute to kiss her lips. He frowned when he reached the hallway and saw both bedroom doors hanging wide open.

"Candace?"

He walked toward the room he'd begun to think of as *theirs*, his heart pounding like he was watching a horror flick unfold. Jesus. He broke out in a cold sweat before he reached the end of the hall. He stepped over the threshold and tried to process what his eyes were seeing.

A fully made, unslept-in, bed.

In two strides he crossed to the closet. Except for the hangers, empty. Had she gone on a trip? That fast? He'd said three days max. It had only been one. Barely.

He looked around the room, absent of every single trace of her. Even the bathroom had been stripped clean. He left the room in a daze and moved down the hall to the room he'd stayed in prior to Candace. The folded sheet of stationery placed on the center of his pillow drew his eyes like a beacon.

"Dammit, Candace. You could've had the decency to leave it on the right bed," he growled, snatching up the sheet.

Dear Logan,

I hope you find everything you're looking for with Getty, or whoever you decide to work with. I fully support your decision to pursue your career dreams and understand you can never be satisfied with the life you've led up to now—

"You got that right," he muttered.

and that you feel drawn to answer the call leading you to distant lands. I truly treasured—

Past tense.

the time we spent together, Logan, and will always remember you fondly. You touched my life and changed me in ways you can never know.

I hope you will indulge my selfish wish to leave without saying a proper goodbye. But I truly thought it would be easier for everyone involved if we parted this way, with you on your way to bigger and better things, and no muss, no fuss, between us holding you back.

Yours,
Candace

A goddamned Dear John letter. She hadn't even bothered with the word love.

Logan crumpled the letter into a ball in his fist, uncrumpled it, read it again, balled it up even tighter and threw it against the wall. In a pain-filled fog, he remembered the package still tucked under his arm. He grabbed it with one hand and studied it dispassionately. Fed Ex. He ripped the perforated edge to open the cardboard envelope and dumped the contents onto the bed.

Candace's pictures.

He laughed softly, fanning out the glossy photos.

Candace smiled up at him, playful, sexy, innocent. Too beautiful for words.

And gone.

Chapter Forty-Two

Candace sat in her sunroom, stone faced, staring out at the garden.

She'd gotten great news today. Her spring release, the second novel in a series of three, had made it to number five on the *New York Times* best-seller list, and to number four on *USA Today*'s list. Eric had emailed her a link to her favorite romance writer's blog where a shining review of that book, plus its prequel, had been posted.

Eric was thrilled.

Too bad she didn't feel anything.

Maybe she had the flu.

Yeah, right. Maybe I've had the flu since I got home two weeks ago.

She looked down at herself in disgust. Noon and still in her robe. She really needed to get a grip. She forced herself off her favorite seat, the cheerful brocade sofa she had re-covered specifically for this room, and glared up at the sunny sky outside. She wished it would rain so she could have an excuse to stay in bed. Good ole sunny Florida.

Candace dragged herself through the living room and bedroom into the bathroom and turned the shower on full blast. While she waited for the water to heat, she wrapped herself in a towel and crossed back to the nightstand, just to satisfy her curiosity. She picked up her cell. One missed call and a voicemail from Eric several hours old.

Nothing from Logan. Not since she'd chickened out and ran. Ten calls and ten messages asking her to call him. And then nothing for two weeks.

What did she expect? Hadn't she wanted a clean break? Hadn't she cut him loose to fly unfettered into his bright exciting new future?

Fifteen minutes later she felt somewhat better. At least her hair was washed and her legs were shaved. Prior to today she hadn't shaved in a week.

Wrapped in a towel, she padded across the room to the closet. A tear leaked from the corner of her eye. She angrily dashed it aside, sick of crying. She would get dressed and then…what? She threw on a pair of white denim capris and a bright pink tank hoping the colors would cheer her up, then twisted her hair into a knot at her nape.

On the nightstand, her cell phone buzzed.

She sighed and shuffled over, flicking the phone around to read the screen. While she showered, there was another missed call and voicemail from Eric. She'd better check messages. Just because she was feeling sorry for herself was no reason to neglect her friend, or her agent. She hit the voicemail button and held her phone to her ear.

"Candace, call me. I need to ask your permission about something, and I need to ask you ASAP."

She frowned. The message was at least an hour old. She should've checked it earlier. He sounded unusually stressed.

She listened to Eric's next message. *"Candace, I'm sorry. I couldn't reach you, and so did what I thought was best."*

Her brows furrowed. What in the world? She pressed the button to return Eric's call. The ring sounded in her ear just as the doorbell rang. She ended the call. Probably the UPS guy or the postman, and everyone knew it was better to just get the package the first time.

"Coming." She pulled open the front door.

And promptly got swept off her feet and carried into the house by a six foot two GQ super model she'd thought she'd never see again. He kicked the door shut and set her down. "Candace," Logan said before taking her mouth in a hard possessive kiss, "Don't ever," another kiss, "ever," another kiss, "do this to me again." His palms cupped her face, and his mouth sealed over hers.

She kissed him back for everything she was worth, plastering herself to him—and then reality crashed in. She slithered out of his arms and stumbled backward till she contacted a piece of living room furniture.

"Logan?" She blinked a couple times trying to get her bearings.

He stood, one hand on his hip, breathing hard. His eyes narrowed on her face. "Glad you remembered."

"I didn't know you were planning a visit to Florida."

He looked as if he had no idea how to respond to such an inane comment. Finally he shook his head and stepped past her.

She twisted around to keep him in view. The sight of his well-worn, bum-hugging jeans, and his broad muscular back covered in a vintage cotton tee made her mouth water. She probably resembled a lost puppy right about now. Luckily Logan wasn't looking at her.

"Nice. The décor suits you." He wandered toward the soft leather, yellow couch and fingered the chenille throw draped over the back. He circled the couch and perused her personal book collection displayed on an antiqued black bookshelf. After a minute he continued toward the back of the house and stood staring out the bay window at the concrete fountain bubbling peacefully in the center of the yard.

She ached to go to him, to wrap her arms around him and never let him go. Instead she balled her hands into fists at her sides and waited to hear what he'd come to say.

"I drove back the very next morning and you were gone. You must've had a good laugh, planning your escape while I was thinking only as far as San Fran, stupid man that I am."

The frost in his voice reached inside her, chilling her to the bone. She hugged herself. "I thought it would be better that way."

He rounded on her. He looked haggard and tense— like he'd lost weight and hadn't slept in a year. "Better for whom?"

She flinched at the hurt and accusation in his eyes. But he wasn't blameless. She raised her chin a notch. "You never made any bones about the fact you weren't looking for anything permanent. And then you got the opportunity you'd been hoping for with that international photography organization and I knew you had to take it. And okay, I didn't want to stick around to hear you tell me about how…" her eyes welled with more hated tears, but she didn't even bother to brush them away, just let them roll down her cheeks,

"...excited you were to be going to Afghanistan or Serbia or wherever."

Logan reached her in two strides, and pulled her into his arms. "You little idiot," he said into her hair.

The floodgates opened and all the things she'd imagined herself saying to him in Tahoe but hadn't came spilling out. "It wasn't as if I didn't broach the subject. I told you it was time for us to quit the fairytale and rejoin our real lives. And what did you say to that? Nothing."

"I know, baby. I know."

"You do?" She pulled back to search his eyes.

He ran the pads of his thumbs over her cheeks, wiping away her tears. "I knew something was wrong when I left for San Francisco. The whole drive to my folks I stewed over this really bad feeling I couldn't name. When it finally came to me, I saw it'd been right in front of me all along. Something's changed in me, Candace. Ever since I met you. I hadn't even gotten off the interstate when it hit me. I don't need to keep looking for...whatever I thought I'd been missing."

She shook her head doubtfully. "Logan."

"Hear me out." He unknotted her still-damp hair and twisted it around his wrist. Their eyes locked. His jaw ticked but he didn't speak for a long moment. When he finally did, his voice was low and husky. "God, you're pretty. And you smell so good. Your whole house smells like you." He held her hair to his nose and breathed deeply. After a minute he grinned at her with his eyes. "Where was I?"

She smiled tremulously. "I think you were about to tell me why you're here."

"Right. For as long as—no." He swallowed. "Ever

since Luke died, I've been floundering. And maybe that would've been my fate forever if my own poor choices and that nitwit of a girl hadn't chased me out of my comfort zone at the magazine.

"Then I met you. Candace, you showed me how black and white my life's been, by filling it with color and…and *you*. You opened my eyes to all the possibilities around me and inside me, and right in front of me."

She started speak and he laid his fingers over her mouth.

"And I'm not talking about the possibility of heading off to photograph people killing each other over what's essentially manmade conflict that will never end." He cupped her nape. "You reminded me of what's good in life and you gave me peace—something I hadn't had for a long time. A peace that got dimmer and dimmer the further I got from you.

"I know I should've said something. I should've told you how I feel, but I guess old habits die hard. I got scared." He paused to gaze into her eyes. "But not so scared I didn't figure it out. I canceled my meeting with Getty and hightailed it back to you to tell you, but you'd already gone."

The love in his eyes made it that much harder to say what she knew she must. "Logan, don't you see? You can't give up your dreams for me. If you did that, you'd only end up hating me in the end."

He shook his head and grinned, surprisingly unmoved by her unselfish pronouncement. "Darlin' there's dreams and then there's dreams. And what I thought I wanted, what I'm leaving in my dust isn't a sacrifice. It's a choice. The best choice of my life."

"I don't understand."

He blew air out of his cheeks. "Sweetheart, I've just flown all night from Reno to New York to barrage a very good friend with threats, bribes, and pleas, and then flew here—all without sleeping. Do you think we could sit down?"

Her eyes widened. "All that? In one day? Sure. Please. Can I offer you something to eat?"

He gave her a lazy grin. "Later." He pulled her by the wrist to the couch.

Her lips curved upward.

"Now listen carefully, because I need you to understand what I'm going to say."

"I'm all ears."

"For years I thought I needed to do something risky, push the envelope both physically and mentally, in order to feel. In order to justify being alive. I'd done it for so long I didn't realize I'd outgrown the fix."

"But, what about your career? Are you going back to the magazine, then?"

"Nope. I considered it. When and if this latest development gets settled, I could slip back into my niche and get back to taking the assignments of my choosing." He gave her an arch look. "I don't know if you realize it, but *Rolling Stone* covers a lot of current events."

"I realize it. I didn't think you recognized the fact."

"Huh." He gave her a sexy grin. "God, I want to kiss you. Everywhere."

She laid her palm against his chest. "Finish what you were saying."

"In a nutshell? I'm ready to get back to my artist roots."

Her mouth opened. "Really? Like what you and Luke planned?"

He smiled tenderly. "I love how you aren't afraid to mention Luke's name. And how you always listen to me. Yes. Like that. And I've discovered a passion for a new style I hadn't considered before."

"How exciting, Logan. What is it?"

"Funny you should ask," he said, rising. "Stay right there. I want to show you something." He strode to her door and only then did she realize he'd left a giant manila envelope lying on the foyer table. The sort of envelope that would hold an x-ray or something.

He approached slowly, unwinding the threaded coil sealing the contents inside. "I used to love black and whites, and playing with light and shapes. Then I got interested in portraits. Now I've developed a taste for using both black and white and color, and blending shape, light, and...the beauty of the human element." He pulled out a glossy photo and held it in front of her. A black and white photo of a starry night. Lightning burning across the sky. And the faintest translucent image of...her face, peeking out from behind her curtains in her room at Tahoe, floating in the silver lined clouds. "I particularly love your angel's smile."

"That's me," she said in awe.

"That's right." He looked at the print and asked softly, "Do you like it?"

"I love it."

"My agent loves it, too. He thinks he can get a gallery in the City to exhibit my first series."

"You never mentioned an agent."

"No? Maybe you've heard of him? Eric Palmer? I signed with him this morning. It was part of our agreement."

"What do you mean by that?"

"In exchange for him giving me your address, I agreed to sign with him exclusively and to let him walk out of his office alive." He smiled at her sweetly.

Her shoulders trembled with silent giggles.

"Now that that's out of the way, I have something to ask you."

Chapter Forty-Three

Candace gazed at Logan, afraid to believe in the love she saw reflected in his eyes, yet unable to squelch the hope bubbling inside her. "What do you want to know?"

He let out a shaky laugh. "I'm doing this backward again. Wait. Let me start again."

"Okay."

"I love you."

She stared at him through eyes that could not seem to stop leaking tears.

"Okay." He drew out the K and raised his brows. "Not exactly the response I was hoping for."

Her face cracked with a wobbly, face-splitting grin.

"I suppose it was too much to hope you'd make this easy for me, since you haven't made anything easy so far. Except making me want you. You handled that like a pro. And making me love you."

"Oh, Logan." She launched herself onto him. "Logan, I missed you so much." She pressed kisses over his cheeks and down his neck. She got a little over excited and gave in to the urge to nip his skin.

"Hey. Ow!" He yanked her up his chest till her face was even with his. "Come here," he growled, falling backward onto the cushions with her in his arms, his long legs bent over the side.

Their lips collided in a long, wet, hungry kiss, and

Candace gave her hands free rein to roam his arms, his chest, his hips, his....

"Whoa." Logan grabbed her wrists.

"What?" She'd only managed to undo the button of his jeans when he'd nabbed her.

"Not so fast." He gave her a sexy wink. "I'm not that kind of boy."

"Are you sure?" she breathed and wriggled her fingers over the pronounced bulge at his zipper.

He closed his eyes and drew in a sharp breath. "I'm sure. I'm looking for a commitment before I go there. Think you can risk it?"

"Definitely." She propped her chin on his chest and gazed at his face, willing him to open his eyes.

He did. His expression sobered and a red stain slowly darkened his cheeks. "Candace. I need to hear you say the words. If...that is, if you feel half of what I do." He hesitated. "What I'm asking is—"

"I love you, Logan," she cut in, jackknifing upright, her bent legs bracketing his hips.

He gazed up at her with hope-filled, brilliant turquoise eyes. She cupped his face with her palms. A shudder went through him and she had to fight the compulsion to melt onto him. But she needed to say this—for both their sakes.

"I love you more than I've ever loved another human being in my life. More than I knew I could. This last week has been the worst, most tortuous week of my life.

"In Tahoe I decided I was ready to take a leap— just like Bliss and Invincible Lion did when they went up against Chief No-Name." His chest vibrated with silent laughter and she smiled, down at him through misty eyes.

"But when I realized you weren't there—metaphorically speaking—I ran. I thought I could stuff the genie back in the bottle. But I was way off there. I'd taken the leap the moment I let you steal into my heart, by listening to me when I talked, caring for me better than me when I got those threatening emails, cooking for me, and a thousand other ways. You made me love you just by being you. You thrill me, soothe me, and fulfill all my innermost, secret desires. And I can't believe you're really here." She fell into him, coiling her arms around his neck.

"You love me," he whispered reverently against her cheek. "Sweetheart, I've been going crazy without you. Promise you'll never do that to me again."

"I promise," she whispered.

"Promise you'll love me and stay with me forever?"

She hoisted herself up onto her forearms, resting her weight on his chest and gazing deeply into his eyes. "I'll take the leap if you will."

"Babycakes, I'm already over the cliff, waiting to catch you."

She gave him a brilliant, triumphant smile. "See? I told you Lover's Leap had a happy ending."

"You did." Grabbing the front of her tank, he tugged her down till her face met his and pressed a hard, possessive kiss on her lips. A moment later, he scooped Candace into his arms and rose off the couch. "Ready, Miss Bliss?"

"What do you have in mind, Mr. Irresistible, oops I mean Invincible Lion?"

He flashed her his glamorous smile. "Mr.

Irresistible works fine if we're talking about you and me. But to answer your question." He crossed the living room, then interrupted himself to ask, "Is this the way?"

She nodded, knowing without needing to ask where he was headed.

"First, I'm going to make love to you. Slow, torturous, love that'll have you begging me to end your suffering."

"Mmm," she murmured, biting her lower lip.

"Then I'm gonna disconnect the phones, shut the blinds, fold you in my arms and sleep." He gave her a tender smile. "I haven't slept a wink since you left me."

A word from the author...

Writing romance is my passion, and I feel truly blessed to know exactly what I was born to do. I write both contemporary and historical romance novels, both series length and long, but the theme remains ever the same: Love heals.

Lover's Leap is my first baby to be published. While still a work in progress, *Lover's Leap* placed as a finalist in the Spacecoast Romance Writers' Launching A Star contest.

I welcome visitors to my website and blog located at http://www.kimberlykeyes.net. I love hearing from readers and hope you'll visit often to keep abreast of my upcoming releases. Better yet, subscribe! Happy reading, fellow romance junkies.